OTHER PEOPLE, OTHER PLACES

A COLLECTION OF SHORT FICTION

by
New York Times Bestselling Author

Joe Hilley

Dunlavy + Gray
HOUSTON

Dunlavy + Gray ©2021 by Joe Hilley

Library of Congress Control Number: 2021911364
ISBN: 978-1-7364105-4-7
E-Book ISBN: 978-1-7364105-5-4

This book is a work of fiction. Names, characters, businesses, organizations, places, events, and incidents either are the product of the author's imagination or are used fictitiously. Any resemblance to actual persons—living or dead—events, or locales are entirely coincidental.

Cover design and typesetting by Fitz & Hill Creative Studio.

Table of Contents

Ludlum

A Novella

CHAPTER 1

In winter, everything seemed worse. It looked worse and smelled worse and felt worse. The cold slid down the mountains. Settled in the valleys and hollows, thick and heavy. Trapping the dust and stench beneath its weight, as though it intended never to leave. The trees, leafless and gray and hard. Clattering in the wind. Drifts of snow, dirty and stained, huddled in the shade. Bare spots in the yard, with little tufts of grass, brown and limp from the frost, the ice, the snow.

And everywhere there was coal dust. It drifted through the air, gathered on the sidewalks and roadways and roof tops, then turned to a gritty grime when the snow thawed, or the rain came. Sprayed and splashed onto the fenders and doors of the cars and trucks, covering them in a filthy gray film that dried and stayed and, like the cold, seemed destined always to remain. To cast the whole town in an eternal, depressing pall. The town of Ludlum. A coal town in a remote corner of Virginia.

Once it had been a booming place with theaters and bands and plays and a high school that won state championships. Football, of course, but basketball, too. And even the girls excelled, though fewer took notice and most seemed only to endure them, even the fathers. But not the mothers. They understood.

Ludlum was a mining town. A working town. Born of the dirt and the men who dug the riches from it. Soft coal. Black coal. Bituminous coal. Dusty, dirty, grimy coal. Laden with that viscous, oily substance. Shovel it out. Haul it off. Black on the streets and trees and houses and on the miners' faces. Money in the miners' pockets.

Now, the boon was coming to an end. Had come to an end. Only thing left was the working out of the end. The final resolve. Mines and miners, done-in by cheap natural gas and by an economy no longer focused on steel and iron and steam. By changing sentiment and worry over the climate. By government regulation and fear. Finally. At last. For the environment. But mostly done-in by the gas.

With the mines closed and closing, jobs were lost. Revenue shrank. The streets became as quiet and desolate as the shafts that led to the veins and seams that made it all possible. Every day another store was emptied, its windows and doors boarded up, its signs left to dangle and squeak in the breeze.

Every day another truck loaded with family possessions headed out of town, the family following behind in the car or the pickup, on their way north to Blacksburg or Roanoke. South to Kingsport or Johnson City. And east as far as Asheville. Anywhere the miners could find a job—any job—to pay for groceries, a place to stay, clothes for the children. A night out, once in a while. And maybe another state championship. Especially for the boys.

But not for Rita Fletcher. For her there was no leaving. No going. No moving on. For her there was only remaining. Enduring, bearing, suffering the constancy of it all. With no abatement, no cessation, no letup, no relief in sight. Every day. Every night. The humiliating, grinding pain. Emotional pain. Cognitive pain. Physical pain. Hollow and aching. Dreams dashed. Joy trampled. Dignity beaten, pounded, siphoned, starved. Until all that remained of life, of her, was as bare and hard and gray as the trees that clattered in the wind.

That day, Rita stood in the kitchen and stared at the back yard through the window above the sink, watching as the sun sank slowly over the mountain. Settling lower and lower, the two-bedroom house becoming darker and danker. Its sparsely furnished rooms sadder and sadder by the moment. And the cold seeped through the walls and into her bones. Billy Ray would be home soon, and that would be the worst time of all.

Billy Ray was a miner. He used to be a miner. Used to work in the mines from daylight to dark. Dark to daylight. Busy all the time. Money was good. Times were good. Always harsh and verbally cruel, but the money made him tolerable. Mollified the demons. Rounded the corners of his temperament. Smoothed off the edges. The rough places. Especially on weekends, and after a beer or two or three.

Then the mine closed and Billy Ray went in with Harry. A friend. Harry Jackson. On a still. Making moonshine. To bide the time. To make ends meet. They sold a lot of it, but they drank a lot of it, too. And most nights Billy Ray came home drunk, if he came home at all. The backside of a mollifying intoxication. The black side. That unleashed the demons and turned his harsh personality mean, cruel, sadistic.

As she stared out the window she thought of these things, and more. Their first kiss. The first time he touched her. She touched him. The warmth of their nakedness. Being wanted. Being needed. The hope it gave her. A false hope. Dissipated by desire. Only desire. Desire but nothing more. Even after the hope was gone, the memory of it gave her hope, but nothing more. And then only filled her with sadness. Aching sadness. Hollow sadness.

But that day, looking out the kitchen window, she felt something different. Deeper. Darker. Resolute. It had been building for a while. Unnoticed at first. Then ignored. Yet, it grew and expanded. Until it could no longer be avoided. And that day, the thing that had been building inside finally pushed through to the surface. Sadness gave way to anger. Desperation blossomed into resolve. To make a difference. Take charge. Regain control. Reclaim hope. True hope. Of something different.

While she still was looking out the window, Timmy came from the hallway into the kitchen. His sudden appearance startled her, and she turned to face him. He seemed not to notice. "I'm going over to Paul's house," he said as only a fourteen-year-old could say it.

"Now?" she asked.

"Yeah." By then, he was at the back door and he paused to look at her. "Why not?"

"It's getting late. Your father will be home soon."

Timmy seemed unfazed. "I won't be gone long." He didn't wait for a reply but pulled open the door and stepped outside.

The door banged shut behind him and Rita turned back to the window. Watching as he crossed the yard. A jaunty gait. An untroubled gait. The way it was supposed to be. The way it almost never was.

When Timmy was out of sight, Rita began preparing dinner. It wasn't much. Dried beans, cornbread, boiled turnips. In a little while, though, she heard a noise from outside and looked out the window to see Billy Ray coming from the woods into the back yard. Staggering. Drunk. A glass jar in one hand. Clear liquid inside. No label. Sloshing on his hand. His shirt. Down the front of his pants.

"Damn," she whispered.

Despite her earlier resolve to make things different, fear shot through her like a bolt of electricity. Tingling up her spine. Reality. Desperation. Panic. Or was it adrenaline?

As she adjusted the flame beneath the bean pot, she heard the thump of his feet on the back porch. Then the door opened. Billy Ray appeared. "Rita!" He shouted, even though he could see her standing just a few feet away. His voice was loud and belligerent. And Rita knew—it was that time again. When the beating started.

Billy Ray staggered across the kitchen and grabbed her by the wrist. Clamped down on it. Squeezed it hard. "You're hurting me," she complained.

"That's the way you like it, ain't it?" He sneered. Leered. Swayed from one side to the other.

"No," she protested. "I don't." Her voice had a plaintive tone. As if pleading. Begging. She didn't like the sound of it.

"Not what I hear. I hear you like it rough." Spittle flew in droplets from his mouth as he spoke. "Well, I'm gonna give it to you rough." He stepped forward, pressing his weight against her. His chest against hers. Crotch against her thigh. Forcing her backward across the room. She banged into the kitchen table, striking it with her hip. Bounced off the counter. Hit a chair with her knee. Brushed her shoulder against the door facing. Then stumbled into the hall. Still his body pressed against her. His breath. Hot. Stale. Sickly sweet.

Billy Ray forced her up the hall to the bedroom. Pushed her onto the bed. Straddled one leg. His other between hers to hold her in place while he loosened the buckle on his belt. Pulled it through the loops. The leather making a flapping noise against the fabric of his pants.

"I'm gonna teach you how to please a man." His words were slurred, and he fumbled with his hands as he doubled the belt, then raised his arm to strike her. She knew what would happen next and already could feel the sting of the strap against her arms. Her thighs. Her buttocks.

But before Billy Ray could bring his arm forward. Before he could swing the belt like a whip. Before the biting pain of its sting. Rita rolled on her side. Reached for the nightstand. Groped for it. Struggled for it. Snatched open the drawer.

Billy Ray's hand clamped around her throat. His eyes were wide with rage. "What are you doing? I'm giving you what you want. The way they say you like it."

The drawer was open, and Rita reached inside. Her fingers dangled over the edge. Reaching. Stretching. Until finally she felt the grip of the pistol. She coaxed it into the palm of her hand and brought it around. Pointed the barrel in his direction. Hands shaking. Mind resolved.

Billy Ray's eyes opened even wider, then a grin spread across his face. "You ain't gonna shoot me." He leaned forward, pressing the muzzle of the gun against him with his weight. "I'm gonna shoot you. I'm gonna take that thing away from you and shove it up your—"

BAM! BAM! BAM!

Three shots rang out. With each one, a red blotch appeared on Billy Ray's shirt. First on the left. Then on the right. And as he leaned backward, a third squarely in the center of his chest. Blood filled the air behind him with a fine mist. Sprayed onto the ceiling. The wall. The light fixture above them.

For a moment, Billy Ray sat motionless, his weight pressing down against her leg. His eyes fixed on a point. On no point. On nothing at all. Then he slowly fell forward, collapsing toward her. Rita avoided him. Mostly. And he landed face down on the bed beside her. Their legs still were entwined though, and she pushed him off. Frantically. Desperately. Moving his body aside.

When she was free of him, she went to the bathroom and in the mirror saw there was blood on her face. Her arms. Her hands. She washed it away with soap. Water. A washcloth. Then walked back to the bedroom door. The smell of gunpowder hung in the air. Billy Ray lay motionless on the bed.

Suddenly, the back door opened. Rita jumped at the sound of it and listened as footsteps came toward her. Oh, no. Timmy. He can't see this. He mustn't see this. The footsteps were closer. Heavier. And as she realized their heaviness, she was terrified. Those weren't Timmy's footsteps. They were from an adult. But who?

Resolved to a fate of misery at being discovered, Rita turned toward the door to face her accuser. To face the truth of what she'd done. The reality of it. And she saw Linda, her neighbor.

Linda paused at the doorway and stared a moment at the bed, then looked over at Rita and their eyes met. "You alright?"

Rita nodded in reply.

"I heard the shots," Linda continued. "Knew something happened. Thought it was you who would be dead. Glad it's not."

Rita trembled. "What do we do?"

Linda entered the bedroom and began pulling the sheets and bedspread loose from the foot of the bed. She gestured with a nod. "Get that other end." When Rita didn't move, Linda pointed. "Come on," she urged. "Get that end."

Rita pulled the covers loose from the head of the bed and together they rolled Billy Ray inside them, wrapping him tightly in a bundle. When that was done, they slid him to the floor and dragged, carried, tugged him through the house to the kitchen.

At the back door, Linda asked, "Where's Timmy?"

"He went to Paul's house."

"Good. I'll get the truck."

"Shouldn't we call the police or the sheriff or somebody?"

"Hell, no." Linda grinned. "We ain't calling nobody. I been prayin' for this day for a long time." She yanked open the back door. "Wait here." Then she went outside.

Rita took a seat at the kitchen table and waited. And worried. Deep, troubled worry. About what she'd done. Who she was. What she might become. About Timmy and how he would react to his father's absence. Not knowing. Never knowing. Loss. Abandonment. It would be better than the abuse she was certain would come. Had seen it growing in Billy Ray's eyes already, every time the boy spoke. And there was more to come, surely. Now that he was that age. Something to say about everything. Opinionated. Mouthy. A teenager. Sort of. And if he ever found out it was her? What then? What would he say? Do? Think? Feel?

A few minutes later, Linda returned with a pickup truck. She parked it near the porch and came inside the kitchen. "Let's get him loaded," she said.

With Linda at one end and Rita at the other they drug, slid, carried Billy Ray's body to the truck. Struggled. Strained. Groaned. And succeeded in getting him into the back. Linda slammed the tailgate closed, then started around to the driver's door. She gestured to the opposite side. "Get in."

Rita hesitated. Timmy would be back soon. Wonder where she was. What happened. Why she was gone. Might get worried. "Where are we going?" she asked, stalling for time.

Linda was insistent. "Get in. We can talk on the way."

Rita glanced toward the house. The back door was unlocked. Timmy could get inside. He knew how to find something to eat from the refrigerator. Knew enough to check the beans. The beans. The pot. The stove. They would be alright. She had no choice. She got in the cab on the passenger side.

Linda drove them from the house through town and out to Damper's Hollow, one mountain over from Ludlum. Rita avoided eye contact. Looked out the window the whole way. But when they reached the Hollow she said, "This is Smith Town."

"Yeah," Linda said. "This is Smith Town." That was the name locals gave it. Smith Town. Where the Smith family had lived for generations.

"Won't they see us?"

"It won't matter."

"Why not?"

"Ain't nobody gonna see anything," Linda said. "And even if they do, ain't nobody gonna tell nobody what it was they saw."

For the first time in the truck, Rita looked across the seat at her. "You sure about that?"

"Positive."

"How can you be?"

Linda grinned. "I'm a Smith."

Rita frowned. "I thought you was a Taylor."

"That's Johnny's name. Homer Smith is my daddy." Linda said that last part proudly. Homer Smith was the patriarch of the Smiths and ruler, despot, king of Damper's Hollow.

They followed the road all the way to the end of the hollow. Where the blacktop came to an end and the mountain rose almost straight up. They turned onto a two-rut trail and followed it along the base of the mountain. Mountain to the left, a garden to the right. Untended since summer. Corn stalks flapping in the breeze. A row of crumpled tomato vines turned brown and wrinkled by the frost, the snow, the cold.

Eventually, the trail came to an end and Linda brought the truck to a stop. "Come on," she said as she flung open the door. "Let's get him out."

She lowered the tailgate and they each took hold of Billy Ray's shoulders. One on one side. Other on the other. Gave the bundle a tug. Slid him from the truck to the ground, then drug him over a clump of bushes and rolled him to a spot where he would be out of sight.

Rita looked over at Linda and asked, "What now?"

"Now, we go home," Linda said.

"That's it?"

"Yep."

"We're just leaving him there?"

"Yep." By then, Linda had the driver's door open and climbed onto the seat of the cab. "Get in," she said, and she slammed the door closed.

Rita walked around to the passenger door and got in, but she was worried. And she stayed worried as Linda backed the truck down the two-rut trail toward the road. When they reached the pavement, she said, "Won't someone find it?"

Linda shrugged. "Like I said, it won't matter."

"'Cause this is Smith Town."

"That's right." Linda grinned again. "This is Smith Town. And besides, the bears and foxes and possums will have him chewed down to the bone in a day or two."

"What about the sheets and the quilt?"

"Nothing we can do about that." Linda looked at her. "You got some more?"

"Yeah." Rita sighed. "I got more."

"Good." Linda pointed the truck down the paved road, and they headed back toward the highway. Somewhere on the way, she reached across the seat and gave Rita a pat on the thigh. "Don't worry," she said. "You done good."

JOE HILLEY

By the time they arrived at Rita's house, darkness had fallen, and the air was noticeably colder. Linda brought the truck to a stop in the driveway. "I don't see that old SUV of yours. You got a way to get around?"

"I'll get it back tomorrow."

"You know where it is?"

"Yeah." Rita looked over at her and smiled. "Thanks."

Linda nodded. "Come find me if you need anything."

Rita got out of the truck. Linda backed it to the street and drove away. Before she was gone, though, Rita crossed the yard to the house.

Timmy was in the kitchen, eating leftover ham from the refrigerator. Rita grabbed him with both arms and hugged him close. Timmy looked up at her. "What's the matter?"

"Nothing."

"Something smells funny."

"I...I was trying something new today."

"What is it?" Timmy sounded eager. "I'm hungry."

"It didn't work out." She checked the pot on the stove and noted the flame was out. "Thanks for turning off the beans."

"Where did you go?"

"Linda needed me."

"Oh."

She turned the flame on beneath the pot. "The beans are almost done. Eat some more ham."

"Yes, ma'am."

Rita noticed drag marks on the floor. Smears of blood. An image of Billy Ray, wrapped in the sheets and quilt, flashed through her mind. Then she remembered the bed. She left the beans to heat on the stove and walked down the hall to the bedroom. Closed the door. Stared at the blood stain on the mattress. Not too large. Would be dry soon. Might be dry now. She didn't want to touch it. But she couldn't leave it in the open. With the blood stain showing. And she couldn't cover it. If it was wet, the blood would only soak through.

With herculean effort, she slid the mattress off the frame. Pushed it. Shoved it. Pulled it toward the closet side of the bed. Until it tipped over and one end rested on the floor. Then she lifted it up, spun it around, and let it fall back over with the bottom side up.

Fresh sheets from a shelf in the closet. Another handmade quilt, too. Smoothed in place. Flat. Wrinkle free. The pillows were fine. No blood on them. She changed the pillowcases anyway. She stood back, hands on hips, taking a moment to admire her work. Checked for leaks. Was it dripping on the floor?

She noticed the nightstand. The drawer was closed. She opened it and found the pistol lying inside. Didn't remember putting it there. Checked the cylinder. It held five bullets. Three had been used. The dimple from the pin on the hammer was clearly visible. Two were left. She removed the spent bullets. Placed them in the drawer. Found three new bullets lying loose and used them to reload the pistol, then snapped the cylinder closed and returned it to the drawer.

The beans would be hot. Timmy was hungry. She needed to feed him. That was her obligation. He wasn't supposed to cook for himself. Everyone wanted their sons to cook. Admired them for learning to do it. For mastering the art. Of chicken. Potatoes. Bread. Especially cornbread. Biscuits for some. But no mother felt right about leaving a child to fend for himself. Not when it came to food. She needed to get to the kitchen. Do her duty.

As she turned to leave the room, Rita noticed blood on the wall. Looked up. Saw the fine mist of red spray on the ceiling. Oh no. The beans would have to wait. She stepped quickly to the bathroom, took a rag and a bottle of cleaner from beneath the sink.

Timmy called from the kitchen. "Are the beans done yet?"

"I think so," she replied. "Just a minute." She set the cleaner and the rag on the nightstand, then came from the room and pulled the door closed behind her.

When she reached the kitchen she said, "There's some potato salad on the bottom shelf from last night. Not much. Get it out."

Timmy opened the refrigerator and took out a bowl. "Is Dad coming home tonight?"

Rita turned her back to him and stirred the beans. "I don't

know," she answered. "Never can tell with him. Did you need him for something?"

"No," he replied. "Just wondering."

She gave the beans one more stir, then nodded toward the cabinet. "Get us some bowls."

Timmy took down the bowls and set them by the stove. Took out plates for the potato salad, too. Rita spooned the bowls full of beans, dropped in a piece of cornbread, and set them on the table. "Spoons and napkins," she said. He did as she said and then took a seat across from her. They ate in silence.

When they finished, Rita put Timmy to work cleaning the kitchen. She went to clean the bedroom. Sprayed the wall with cleaner and wiped it. Stood on the bed and wiped the ceiling, then the light fixture. It didn't take long.

After returning the spray bottle to its place beneath the sink in the bathroom, and after rinsing the rag, she came to the kitchen. The dishes were washed and dried and put away. Rita checked the temperature of the beans in the pot, set them on a cold burner, and placed a lid over the plate with the cornbread.

Timmy was seated at the table. She turned to him. "Do you have homework?"

"Yes, ma'am."

"What is it?"

"Math."

Rita smiled. She had been good at math in school. To the ninth grade. Her dad died. She dropped out. Two years after that, she married Billy Ray. But still enjoyed thinking about math. "Get your book. I'll help you."

"Where's Dad?"

"You asked me that before."

"I know. But where is he?"

"I don't know."

"He didn't come home last night, either."

"Well. I wouldn't worry about him." She tousled his hair the way mothers do. "Get your math book."

That night, after Timmy was in bed, Rita sat at the kitchen table and thought about what to do. She was worried about the police. But not worried about the sheriff. Or Harry. Billy Ray always said Harry paid the sheriff to look the other way. Harry wouldn't report anything and even if someone did, the sheriff would be careful not to find too much. But she was Billy Ray's wife, and her husband was missing. Shouldn't she report it? Shouldn't she make a show of looking for him? Wouldn't they expect it?

No. Not yet. Not now. Not with Billy Ray. It was too early. Too soon. He'd been gone three or four days at a time before. Several times. Shouldn't get worried until the fourth or fifth day. Maybe the sixth. But she should get the house in shape, clean it up, make sure the blood was wiped away. Thoroughly. The floors swept and mopped. No trace. No fragment. No sliver.

An hour or so later, when the beans were cooled enough to place them in the refrigerator, Rita put them away, turned out the light in the kitchen, and went to bed. The house was dark. The room was dark. She lay in the darkness. Stared up at the ceiling. Thought about the shooting. The look on Billy Ray's face when the first bullet hit him. The gasp at the second. The light going out in his eyes with the third. A smile came to her at the thought of it. The memory of it. The son of a bitch had it coming. She rolled on her side and went to sleep.

CHAPTER 2

The next day, after Timmy had eaten breakfast, gathered his books, and boarded the school bus, Rita mopped the floors. Began with the bedroom first, then down the hall. The bathroom. Timmy's bedroom. The kitchen. Living room. Cleaned the door facings. All of them. To be sure. To be certain. Wiped down the baseboards, too. The walls in the hall. Their bedroom. All the way around this time. And the ceiling, again. And the light fixture.

Wiped the pistol and each of the bullets in the cylinder. Inside the cylinder. The hammer. The pin on the end of the hammer. Collected the spent brass from the drawer. Wiped them down, dropped them in her pocket. Couldn't leave that lying around.

With the house cleaned, Rita ate something for lunch. Beans, cold from the refrigerator. A piece of bread to go with them.

When she finished eating, she took the spare car key from a hook where it hung at the end of a cabinet by the door. Placed the key in the pocket of her coat. It tinkled against the spent brass she'd collected from the nightstand in the bedroom. Left the house through the kitchen door. Didn't bother to lock it.

She walked across the back yard to the woods and continued down a well-worn path. The path, wide and obvious, led to the Fancher homeplace. There was a road on the other side. Dirt road. Farm road. Used to be. Grown up now. Less recognizable than the path.

After Fancher died, the house sat empty. Children lived in Mobile or Pascagoula or somewhere down there. On the coast. Gulf Coast. Where it never snowed. Almost never. And never smelled like coal dust. Or bitumen. Certainly.

As the years went by, and with no one there, the house showed signs of neglect. A tree fell against one end. The roof caved in. Trees growing through the middle of it now. Weeds. Bushes. But you could see an outline of the house if you knew where to look. What to look for. How to sort it from the gray, leafless winter. Or the rich green of spring. Rita knew. But she didn't bother to look. Didn't want to look. She had a purpose. Head down. Concentrating on the path. On her thoughts. On what she would say when she got there. To the place. To Harry. To the still where they made the moonshine that had brought out the demons in Billy Ray.

Beyond the Fancher house, the path was not so obvious. Not a path at all but a trail. Like the trail of a rabbit or fox that led deep into the woods. Trees towered above. Old growth now. Ancient. Untouched by anyone. Limbs forming a canopy overhead. Sunlight filtered through the limbs. Bare of leaves like all the others. Thick enough, though.

In a little while, Rita smelled smoke. Wood smoke. Hardwood. Oak. Hickory. Slow burning. Hot burning. She paid closer attention. Cast a wary eye. Left and right. Slowed her pace. Deliberate. Intentional. Watching. Watching. Always. Constant. Alert. Knew what to look for.

A few minutes later, she saw it. The thin silvery strand. A tripwire stretched between the trees. Taut. Unmoving. But shimming in the light, for those who knew what to look for. At either end, a shotgun duct taped to a board. The board nailed to a tree with nails thicker than her thumb. Farther on, another one. Then a spot where the leaves were disturbed. Beneath it, a pit. A hole. A deep hole. Too deep to climb out of. Lightly covered with branches and leaves. Not strong enough to hold anything. A mantrap, but they sometimes caught a deer.

Rita knew to watch for them. Knew where most of them were placed. How to pick her way past them without getting caught. She'd been there before. Two or three times. With Billy Ray. He showed her the pattern. Shotgun, shotgun, mantrap.

Past the traps, the woods opened a little and a clearing appeared. She paused before reaching it. Positioned herself behind an oak with a thick trunk. Maybe three feet wide. Watched. Three stills working. Sickly sweet scent in the air. Four men tending the fires and kettles. Steel drums to one side. Shotguns propped against them. A pickup truck was parked a few yards away, next to an older SUV. Billy Ray's. Hers, now.

Rita watched for a moment, then stepped into the clearing. Strode toward the men. Leaves rustled. A twig cracked. They heard her coming and turned to see. Eyes wide. Alert. Two of them reached for the shotguns. Harry, a tall man, broad shoulders, blue jeans and a waistcoat, held up his hand in a gesture for them to stop. "Leave her alone," he said. His voice was firm, but not overly so. A stern expression. "Harry ain't here."

She would not be deterred. "I come for the car."

"We need it."

"Billy Ray ain't been home for two days. I got things to do. I'm taking the car." She continued past him. Opened the driver's door of the SUV. Looked back at Harry. "I need his half of the money, too."

Harry avoided her. Glanced down at the ground. "Well…We ain't got paid yet."

She glared at him. "Don't lie to me, Harry."

"I ain't—"

"You ain't never delivered an ounce of nothing that you didn't get paid for. On delivery. Bring me Billy Ray's half of the money, Harry. Bring it to the house. I need it today." Rita climbed into the SUV. Put her hand in her pocket for the spare key. Felt the spent brass from the pistol against her fingertips. Found the key. Started the engine. Drove away.

A trail led through the woods toward a dirt road. Before she reached the road, Rita lowered the window, took the spent brass from her pocket, and tossed it out. One at a time. All three of them. Scattered separately. Where no one would find them. And even if they did, it wouldn't mean anything to anyone. Nothing about her.

Nothing against her.

When she came to the dirt road, Rita turned left and in a little while came to a paved highway. She turned left again and drove toward town. Still unsure what to do next. Whether to report Billy Ray missing or not.

Harry would ask around, eventually. Might have already, but probably not yet. Though he might now that she had appeared and took the SUV. Bobby Joe—Billy Ray's brother—would come looking for him in a day or two. Ask about him. Ask around. Check the usual places.

And Thelma, Billy Ray's sister, would get worried. They talked regularly. Thelma talked a lot. About everything. She would talk about Billy Ray being gone. Make wild accusations. Probably against her. Thelma never liked her.

But none of them would say anything to the sheriff. Or to the police chief in Ludlum. Doing that would draw attention. To Harry. To the stills. The moonshine. The clubs they sold it to. And if the sheriff got paid not to know about it, like Billy Ray said, wouldn't nobody do nothing to upset that arrangement.

Ludlum police might be a problem, though. The chief knew what Billy Ray was like. Rita reported him once. Maybe twice. That time with the beer bottle, for sure. But maybe the one with the ropes and the leather strap, too. Chief tried to do a good job. If he heard Billy Ray was missing. When he heard Billy Ray was missing. He would come around. Ask questions. Lots of questions. Probably none of them difficult, though. He wasn't like that.

She held the steering wheel with her right hand. Reached over with the left and pushed up the sleeve of her dress. Glanced at her arm to check. The bruises were still there. Dark blue, turning purple, a tinge of yellow around the edge. From earlier in the week. If she was going to report Billy Ray missing. Officially report him. File a notice and all that. She needed to do it quick. Before the bruises faded. That way, if they asked questions. Hard questions. Difficult questions. Questions she couldn't answer. She could put them off with the beatings. The rage. The temper. The bruises. Nobody could doubt the bruises. Especially the ones on her back.

When she arrived at home, Rita parked the SUV at the end of the driveway, where it always was parked, then opened the glove compartment. She was curious. Wondering. Might be something in there she needed to know about. No telling who had been in it last.

The door of the glove compartment fell open and inside she found a pistol lying atop an envelope. A dirty envelope. Smudged. Stained. Wrinkled. But thick. Bulging. Full. She took it out and saw it was stuffed with cash. Hundreds. Twenties. Not many tens. No ones. She wondered if Harry knew it was there. "I'm not telling him," she said to herself. She put the envelope in the pocket of her dress. The pistol in the pocket of her coat. Came from the SUV, slammed the door shut, and walked toward the house.

After only a step or two she noticed a bundle of something on the back porch. Instinctively slipped her hand in the pocket of her jacket. Curled her fingers around the grip of the pistol. Didn't think to check if it was loaded. Surely no one would put a pistol in a vehicle without loading it. Especially with all that money. And them being in the liquor business like that.

She approached the porch slowly. Carefully. Cautiously. And when she got right up to it, she saw the bundle was the sheets and quilt they used the day before to haul Billy Ray's body from the house. Washed and folded. Stacked neatly in place. A laundry service couldn't have done any better. She leaned over. Put her nose against the one on top. Sniffed. It was fresh and clean and smelled like Damper's Hollow. Washed by hand. Hung up to dry outside on a clothesline. Rita slipped one arm beneath the stack. Bundled them up against her chest. Turned with them toward the steps.

As she lifted her foot to start up, fear seized her. Stabbed her straight through the chest. And she froze in place. Right where she was. Her left foot still in the air. Held in place by the horror. The realization. The awful awareness. Someone knew. Someone saw them. Found the body. Knew it was Billy Ray. Knew where he was. How he got there.

What would she do? Where could she go? Who could she tell?

The whole thing was unraveling. Coming apart of its own weight. Had to stop it. Had to put it back. The time. The place. The moment. Had to get it back. Put the pistol back in the drawer. She could grab Billy Ray. Pull him close. Make it worth his time. Make him forget about the belt in his hand. If she could just go back.

The police would come. Soon. With questions. Serious questions. Hard questions. Difficult questions. One right after the other. Rapid-fire. Who? When? Where? Why? Her heart pounded. Veins in her neck throbbed. She took a deep breath.

They would not come. No one was coming. Not the sheriff. He was paid for. And if she showed the bruises, not the police chief either. He might come once, but not a second time. No one was coming.

After another breath she was calm enough to remember she was going inside. On her way with the sheets and quilt. She couldn't stay out there by the steps. By the porch. Not like that. One foot in the air. Mouth open. Eyes wide. Someone might think she was having a problem. Stop to help. Rush over. Ask questions. Troubling questions. Questions she might feel compelled to answer. To her detriment.

She glanced down to place her foot on the next step, then saw a carton of eggs and a slab of salt-cured pork lying by the porch post. Near where the blankets and sheets had been left. A sign. It came to her at once. A sign. They meant no harm. Whoever brought the quilt and sheets was a friend. They meant no harm. Damper's Hollow. Smith Town. The Smiths. Linda was a Smith. They would never tell.

A sense of relief swept over her and she continued on her way inside the house. Took the quilt and sheets to the bedroom and laid them on the bed, then returned to the porch for the eggs and pork. Placed them in the refrigerator. Took a seat at the kitchen table and counted the money from the envelope she'd taken from the SUV. It was about five thousand dollars. About. Some of the bills clung together. She did her best to keep the count straight.

She threw away the envelope, then took the pistol to the bedroom and placed it in the drawer of the nightstand. Put the money in a suitcase that sat on the shelf in the closet. Stacked the sheets and quilt beside it, then thought about it and took one of the pistols from the nightstand, put it in the suitcase, too. Went to the bathroom. Washed her hands. Dried them on a towel.

She thought about the eggs and pork. Came back to the kitchen. Fried an egg and warmed a piece of the pork with it. As she placed it on a plate, the back door opened, and Linda appeared. Smiling. Grinning. Always with a grin. "I see you found the sheets and quilt," she said.

"Yes," Rita replied. "That was you?"

"I thought you wanted them back."

"Not if it meant—"

"Daddy sent you the eggs. Uncle Jim sent the pork."

Rita set the plate on the table and gestured to it. "You want this? I can fry more."

Linda shook her head. "I ate already." She took a seat. "They found the body," she continued.

Rita glanced at her. "They?"

"Don't worry about it. Daddy has a backhoe."

"You told him what happened?"

"Didn't say a word. Didn't have to. He was waiting for something to happen to Billy Ray. Half the county's been waiting for it. Other half's been planning it." She giggled.

Rita nodded. "What did they do with the body?"

Linda grinned even wider, if that was possible. "Billy Ray's down so deep, ain't nobody ever gonna find him now."

Later that afternoon, when Linda was gone but before the school bus arrived to bring Timmy home, Rita heard a vehicle in the driveway. Not Linda's truck. Something else. She looked out a window in the living room and saw Harry's pickup. It came to a stop near the SUV and Harry got out, then disappeared around the corner of the house. Rita met him on the back porch.

Harry glanced around warily, as if checking, then took a wad of cash from his pocket. While he was doing that, two men who came with him, opened the rear door of Rita's SUV and removed a couple of cardboard boxes. Rita wasn't sure how many, but she could see they were filled with glass jars. The jars were filled with clear liquid. Moonshine. She hadn't noticed them before. Harry saw the look in her eyes. "We were loading up for a run when you arrived." He pressed the wad of cash into the palm of her hand. "This squares me with Billy Ray through last night." He turned to leave.

Rita, still on the porch, said, "Make sure you keep track of what you sell. He'll want to know when he gets back."

Harry gave her a knowing smile. An amused smile. A smile that said too much. Then he tipped his cap as he continued toward the truck. Rita noticed the look on his face. In his eyes. But she wasn't worried. Not about Harry. Not about the men who were with him, either. It felt good not to worry.

By Friday, no one from Billy Ray's family had been by to ask about him. They wouldn't wait much longer. Billy Ray usually saw one or the other of them every week. Rita considered her options once more. She could wait until they came to her house looking for him, or she could go to them. Better to do what she would have done if this had happened a different way, rather than shy away from them because she knew the truth. But what would she have done? If he had simply disappeared.

After thinking about the situation, she decided it was better to go to them. She'd done that before. When he hadn't come home. So, she began rehearsing the story. That was easy enough. He left on Monday, which he did. She should say that. Omit the days in between until now. Forget about them. They don't matter. No need to fill them in with made-up stuff she'd have to remember later. He left the house on Monday morning, about the time Timmy left for school. Drove off in the SUV. Said he was going to work. Haven't seen him since. Harry hasn't seen him, either. That's the story. Stick to it.

CHAPTER 3

On Saturday morning, Timmy went over to Paul's house. Rita watched out the kitchen window as he made his way across the yard. It wasn't far. If she walked up to the corner, she could see him all the way to Paul's yard. But she didn't. She let him go on his own.

Wonder what they do over there? Is it a bad situation for him? Drinking? Cussing? Pictures of naked women? Whatever it was, it couldn't be worse than what he encountered at home. The tension. The shouting. The fighting. With her and Billy Ray.

Half an hour later, Rita drove to Bobby Joe's house. He lived on the west side of town. Didn't take long. He was in the yard, working on his truck, when she arrived. Hood up. Bent over a fender. He glanced at her as she got out. A look of concern. "Something wrong?" he asked.

"I ain't seen Billy Ray all week. Any idea where he is?"

"No." Bobby Joe shook his. "What about Harry? He ain't seen him?"

"Not since Monday. At least, that's what he said earlier in the week."

"You talked to him? To Harry?"

"Yeah," she said.

"Hmm. Not really like Billy Ray to be gone this long, is it?"

"Not really. I mean, he might be gone a day or two. Maybe three. But not like this."

"And the last time you saw him was Monday?"

"Monday morning," she said.

"When did you talk to Harry?"

"Wednesday. I think. The week has been a blur. Taking care of Timmy. Worrying about Billy Ray."

"And you went out to…the place?" Everyone knew what Harry and Billy Ray were doing but nobody wanted to talk about it. Might cause trouble.

"I had to do something." Rita tried her best to sound desperate without going too far. "He'd been gone two days by then. Timmy was asking about him. So, I went to find him. Figured he was out there in the woods. Laying out with the others. Drunk or something."

"But he wasn't."

"No."

"And Harry didn't know where he was?"

Why was he going back through everything she'd already said? Was he suspicious? Did he not believe her? Had she been unconvincing? Or was it Billy Joe being Billy Joe, thinking while he talked, talking while he thought? "No," she said. "He didn't. Said he didn't." She put too much emphasis on it. She knew it as soon as she said it.

Billy Joe frowned. "You think Harry was lying?"

"No. Not at all. I believed him."

Bobby Joe gestured to the SUV. "Where'd you find that?"

"Out there. At…the place."

"He didn't take it with him?"

"It was out there," she said. Damn, Billy Joe. You think he could take it with him, and me have it, at the same time? She avoided the urge to snap. "Harry and them was using it," she added.

"I don't know." He picked up a rag from the fender and wiped his hands. "I'll ask around. See what I can find. But we don't run with the same crowd, you know. Not sure what good it will do, but I'll ask."

"Anything would be helpful at this point."

"Okay." He nodded. "Okay. But don't make too much of a fuss about this just yet. Billy Ray has a way of turning up." That was Bobby Joe code for 'try not to get hysterical.' He didn't think much of women. Except when he was hungry. Or wanted sex. Or needed something else. Sex and supper, mostly.

The next day was Sunday. Rita took Timmy with her and they rode out to see Thelma, Billy Ray's sister. She lived on a patch-farm south of town. The area didn't really have a name. Nothing distinctive. No Smiths. No Youngs. No Whites. A few Holcombs, but not enough to name the place for them.

Thelma's house was the old kind. Wood siding on the outside. Plaster walls on the inside. Nothing in between. Built before electricity and indoor plumbing. Before screens on the windows, too. All of that was added later. Water, electricity, screens. But still no heater. No air conditioner. Had a wood stove in the kitchen. An old one. Pot belly stoves in the bedrooms. They were old, too.

Timmy went outside with Thelma's daughter. They were about the same age. Rita and Thelma sat in the kitchen. It was warm in there. And smelled like fried bacon, stale cigarette smoke, and onions. People around there ate onions in everything.

"Bobby Lee says you been looking for Toot." That was Thelma's name for Billy Ray.

Rita did her best to seem hopeful. "Have you seen him?"

"Not in a while. Me and him don't see much of each other anymore. Not like we used to. How long's he been gone?"

"Left the house on Monday, ain't seen him since."

Thelma frowned. "And you're just now looking for him?"

"I talked to Harry on Wednesday. And I talked to Bobby Lee yesterday. I thought you and Billy Ray got along. Did something happen that he stopped coming to see you?"

Thelma had a wry expression. "I broke up with Carl and started seeing Butch. Billy Ray didn't like it."

"Who's Butch?"

"Butch Allgood. A guy I met at the club." Thelma was a waitress at a club in town. "Billy Ray and Butch ain't never liked each other." The Allgoods were trouble. Every one of them. Nothing but trouble and everybody knew it. Thelma looked over at Rita. "You say you talked to Harry?"

"Yes."

"And he ain't seen Billy Ray?"

Rita shook her head. "Not since Monday afternoon."

"A week ago."

"Yes."

They continued to talk while Thelma prepared lunch. She seemed unconcerned about Billy Ray. That was not what Rita expected. Maybe the new boyfriend. Maybe what Billy Ray said about him. Maybe something else. But it was different with her. It wasn't like how she thought it would be and she wondered if that was good. Or bad.

The next day, Monday, Rita sent Timmy off to school as usual. When he was gone, she drifted to the kitchen and sat at the table. Stared blankly. Thought about making another pot of coffee. What she really wanted was a nap. Lie on the sofa. With the room dark and nothing to disturb her. But she forced herself to stay awake. Made coffee instead. Stood at the sink while it percolated in the coffee pot.

Through the window she saw a bundle of turnip greens on the back porch and went out to get them. A carton of eggs sat beside it. Linda must have left them. She brought the eggs into the house and put them on the counter, then went back outside to wash the greens. Couldn't leave them out there long. They'd start to wilt, and she didn't like them that way.

An hour later. A galvanized washtub on the porch. Another on the ground. A water hose running in it. Slowly, to keep clean water flowing. Greens with turnips attached lay in the tub on the ground. She methodically broke off the tubers, washed the dirt from them. Dropped the leaves back in the tub. Set the tubers aside on the porch.

When the tubers were detached and washed, she turned her attention to the greens. Dousing them by the handful in the water, shaking them out, dropping them in the second tub that sat on the porch beside the pile of turnips.

Before she finished, a police car appeared on the driveway. A black and white with the City of Ludlum logo on the door. She caught sight of it from the corner of her eye as it came to a stop behind the SUV. The driver's door opened, and Luke Wilson stepped out.

Luke was the chief of police for Ludlum. About Rita's age. Nice chest. Big arms. Narrow waist. Once commanded a substantial force. A dozen officers or more. With the mines closed and closing, city revenue wasn't like before. Everything got cut. Slashed. Reduced. The police department had been reduced to the chief, one patrolman, and one auxiliary who filled in between shifts and nights during the week as part-time help. Some of the time. Not always. The city didn't always have the money for it.

By then, Luke was at the back porch. "Mrs. Fletcher." He said it as a form of greeting. She looked over at him. He was pleasing to look at. "Chief." She wanted to smile. Wanted to look him over real good. Take in the details of how his arms bulged against the sleeves of his shirt. Imagine what was behind the buttons down the front. But she resisted and turned back to the greens.

Luke continued. "I understand Billy Ray's been gone a while."

"He ain't been here since last Monday." Rita continued with her work. "Who told you he was gone?"

"Bobby Joe came by to see me yesterday. Said you were looking for Billy Ray. I said I would check on you."

She gave him a quick, tight smile. "I'm fine."

"And Timmy?"

"He's fine, too."

"But you haven't seen Billy Ray at all since Monday?"

"No." She shook her head. Grabbed another handful of greens from the tub. Shook them off.

"When's the last time you saw him?"

"Like I said, he was here Monday morning. I ain't seen him since then." These men. They asked the same question two or three times. Same answer. Then the same question all over again. First Bobby Joe. Now Luke.

"So, it's been almost exactly a week," he said.

"Yeah."

"And you didn't think you should have reported that to us?"

She looked at him now, full on. Her eyes on his. Not wandering. "You know Billy Ray. It ain't nothing for him to be gone two or three days at a stretch, and he's been gone longer than that before."

"You don't seem too worried."

"To be honest, I'm relieved."

"Relieved?" Luke appeared puzzled. He sounded puzzled too.

"Yeah."

"Why's that? He's your husband. And he's gone. And you're relieved?" The puzzled look was replaced by a pained expression.

Rita stood up straight. Shook the water from her hands. "Because as long as he's gone, I don't get no more of these." She lifted the sleeve of her dress to reveal a faded, round bruise on her upper arm. A bruise about the size of a man's fist. Luke winced. She lifted the other sleeve and showed him one on that side, too. Before he could say anything, she put her back to him and pointed behind her neck. "Unzip my dress and you can see some more on my back." Luke hesitated. "Go on," she urged. "Ain't nobody here but us. Unzip my dress and see for yourself."

Luke hooked a finger in the collar of her dress and pulled the fabric back so he could see the skin of her back. Then leaned forward for a close look. Large, deep bruises, blue and black and yellow around the edges covered her back from her shoulders to the top of her bra strap.

"Damn," he whispered as he let go of the dress.

Rita straightened her clothes and turned to face him. "I say a good sight more than 'damn' when he's beating on me." She wanted to say more right then but thought better of it.

Luke had a troubled, uncomfortable, awkward frown. He took a step back. Folded his hands together and rested them at his waist. Assumed a reverent stance. "I understand he works with Harry Jackson."

They exchanged looks that said they both knew what that meant. Rita nodded. "Sometimes." She didn't think she was supposed to concede the point. Couldn't acknowledge the relationship. The still. The moonshine. The place. Payments to the sheriff. Looking the other way. All of that had to remain a secret. Untouched. Unspoken.

"And Harry hasn't seen him?"

"Saw him Monday. Last Monday." Suddenly she wasn't sure. She hoped that was right. Harry must have been out there on Monday. The day Billy Ray came home drunk. Wasn't he? And why the uncertainty now? The story was simple. Stick to it.

Luke seemed to consider her answer, then said, "Anybody after him?"

"After him?"

"Out to get him."

She frowned. "Luke, this is Billy Ray we're talking about. People all over these parts got something against him."

Luke smiled. "I mean, anyone in particular. Over something recent."

"Not that I know of."

"Hadn't had trouble with anyone? A fight or something?"

"Nothing out of the ordinary. That I know of."

Luke shifted positions and shrugged his shoulders in an exaggerated manner. As if adjusting them against the fit of his uniform. "This is a difficult question to ask but I think I have to ask it."

"Go ahead and ask me."

"Does Billy Ray have a girlfriend?"

"Luke, Billy Ray Fletcher would have sex with anyone who gave him the chance, but he wasn't the girlfriend type. Not someone steady."

Luke nodded. Stroked his chin as if thinking. Adjusted his gun belt at his waist. Had a contemplative expression. Then said, "Okay. We'll keep an eye out for him. Ask around at the clubs and joints. Maybe drive by a few times at night just to make sure you're safe."

"I'm sure we would appreciate that," Rita said. He could stop if he wanted to. Come in and sit with her a while. Stay longer, if Timmy wasn't around.

"Just doing our job," Luke said. "Let us know if you need anything." He tipped his hat, then turned away and walked to his car. Rita avoided the urge to watch and went back to washing greens.

She heard the car as it backed down the driveway, reached the road out front, and drove away.

When the tubers and greens were clean, Rita carried them inside. The tubers by the armful, using the fabric of her dress to hold them. The greens in the tub. She set the tub on the floor by the table, then began slicing the tubers into a pot to boil. While she worked, she thought again about her situation.

She had two thousand dollars from Harry. She knew he was shorting her. Billy Ray said he always did. But there was nothing she could do about it. With the cash from the envelope that she found in the glovebox, she had seven thousand, total. That gave her options. A few options. Not unlimited. But more than nothing.

The house was a rental, but it didn't belong to the mining company. Wasn't tied up in the mine closings. The layoffs. None of that. She could pay the rent and they could stay in it as long as they wanted. As long as the money held out. Or she and Timmy could leave. Go to Blacksburg or Asheville. Like everyone else. Start over. Or Knoxville. She'd always wanted to see Knoxville.

If they left town now, with Billy Ray missing and fresh on everyone's mind, they would wonder why. If they stayed, she would have to endure questions. Lots of questions. Repeated questions. Detailed questions. Picky questions. And snide comments. Some would wonder why she didn't report him gone before Luke came around but that wouldn't be enough to cause a problem. She'd already headed off any trouble with Luke when she showed him the bruises. Luke liked her. She smiled at the thought of it. Knew it from the way he looked at her that time in church. A long time ago. Before Billy Ray. Before Timmy come along. If she'd known how things were going to turn out, she might have paid him more attention back then. Maybe.

By the time the turnip tubers were sliced into chunks she had decided they better stay in Ludlum. In the house. Use the money to keep going while she found a job. Any job. A job that paid enough for them to live on. Not sure what that might be. Most of the miners couldn't find one like that. Not in Ludlum. Or maybe they could find one but wouldn't take it. Too much pride. Too worried about how it looked if they were stocking shelves at the store. Not much happening around there. A little though. Some of it unsavory. Not all of it. Might get a job at a restaurant. Or looking after some old person. Lots of old people in the county. Some of them with money. Not a lot of money. But enough.

The next day, about midmorning, there was a knock at the door. Rita looked through the window in the door and saw David Adair on the front stoop. She wished it had been Luke, the police chief, but Adair was the owner of the house. She had no choice but to let him inside.

"I heard Billy Ray is missing," Adair said.

She pushed the door closed behind him. "We ain't seen you in six months."

"Well, everything's been good for the last six months," he said. "Now I hear this about Billy Ray. Wanted to check with you. You know. Stay on top of things. Stay ahead of trouble."

"You think there's trouble?"

"Just showing some concern, Rita. That's all. I'm not looking for an argument."

"Am I supposed to think you're concerned about him? Or me?"

Adair grinned. Shook his head. "I'm not worried about Billy Ray. And I'm sure not worried about you. Just concerned about the rent."

"I might have known."

"That's my end of the deal. Your end is living here. My end is getting paid for it."

"Well, we ain't never missed a month yet."

He grinned. "I'd be willing to help, if you need it."

She knew what he meant. "We're good," she replied.

"Well, just keep it in mind. If Billy Ray doesn't come back and you need to work something out. I'm sure we can reach an accommodation."

"What makes you think he might not come back?"

"You know, just a hunch."

"When Billy Ray comes back and hears about you proposition-ing me like that, he'll kill you."

"Hey." Adair held up his hands in mock protest. "Who's prop-ositioning anyone about anything? I'm just offering to help you out if you need it."

She gave him a skeptical look. "We both know what you're talking about."

He grinned. "Well, might never come to that."

"Might?"

"I think he'll wander home before long. Some people think Billy Ray isn't ever coming back. But I think he'll turn up."

"People are saying he's dead?"

"Some are. Others think he might have just left."

Rita gave him a look. "Some of them are saying they think some-thing happened to him?"

"Some of them."

"And what do they think happened?"

"The usual things."

"They think I killed him?"

"Some."

"You?"

He shook his head. "Not me."

"Luke?"

"I don't think so."

"Then who?"

"Just people, Rita. It's just talk."

"They're talking."

"Rumor has it, Billy Ray was beating the hell out of you. Just about every night. People are thinking you got enough of it and gave him what he deserved."

Rita realized at once that Luke had been talking. About the bruises on her arms. The bruises on her back. Anger, raw and hot, spewed out of her mouth. "Is that what you want to do? Beat the hell out of me? Jump me. Pound me like an animal?"

"No." Adair had a boyish grin. Almost embarrassed. "I just want to have sex with you."

"I'll try to remember to forget you said that when Billy Ray gets back." She opened the door and pointed for him to leave.

Adair stepped in that direction but paused. "Well," he said. "Let me know if you need an...arrangement on the rent." She hit him with her fist in the center of his back. He laughed as he stepped outside. She slammed the door closed behind him.

After Adair was gone, Rita collapsed on the sofa. Lay on her back. Stared up at the ceiling. And thought about their conversation. About Adair. The house. The rent. The proposition. And about Luke.

She was certain Luke had talked to Adair. Told him about their conversation. Wondered who else he had been talking to. About Billy Ray. About her. She had seen them together in the past, Luke and Adair. And she wondered if she should do anything about it. Talk to someone. Complain to someone. Why was the police chief discussing his cases with the likes of Adair? Finally, she decided to let it go for now. No point in calling attention to herself. Not yet.

And she remembered the first time Billy Ray didn't come home. She had been worried. Then jealous. Accused him of seeing an old girlfriend. They fought for three days about it. Later, after he was gone like that a couple of more times, she came to accept it as part of the rhythm of his life, even when he worked in the coal mine. By the time the mine closed and he went in with Harry on the still, it was Billy Ray. The way he was. His life. His routine. He'd lay out like that two or three nights a week. Never in a row. Usually. But sometimes. By then, though, she didn't mind if he did. It was quiet and peaceful with him gone. No shouting. No fighting. No beating. All she had to do was brace for the time when he returned because he usually came home drunk. That was part of his habit, too.

CHAPTER 4

On Wednesday afternoon. After lunch. The week after Billy Ray died. Rita went to the Ludlum police department. The building. Cinder block. One story. Painted white. Next to the jail. A police car was parked near the door. She knew Luke was there.

Went inside. Found him in his office. Seated at his desk. He glanced up as she appeared. His eyes alert. "Rita, is everything okay?" He stood.

"Billy Ray still ain't come home," she said. "I've talked to everyone I know to talk to. Nobody's seen him or heard from him since Monday, a week ago. I guess we should file a missing person report."

"I already did that," Luke replied.

"Oh." She hadn't expected that. "I thought I was the one who had to do it."

"After talking to you I had a bad feeling about the whole thing," Luke explained. "So, I opened a case. We've been asking around about who might have seen him. Trying to piece together a timeline."

He gestured to a chair. She took a seat across the desk from him. Did her best to look forlorn. "Find out anything?"

Luke sat in his chair. Took a file from a desk drawer. Laid it open on the desktop. Glanced through notes while he talked. "Last Sunday. Ten days ago. He was at a gas station on the highway over in Clear Creek. And that night he was seen at a club in Norton. But ain't nobody seen him to identify him since then."

Rita frowned. "What do you mean to identify him? Has someone seen something or said something?"

"Several people said they saw someone on Monday they thought was him, but they weren't sure."

"Anybody around here seen him?" She wanted to know the details. What to expect.

"We talked to your neighbors," Luke said. "Linda Taylor and Mrs. Lancaster."

A bolt of energy shot through her at the mention of Linda's name, but it passed quickly. "What did they say?"

"Linda said she saw Billy Ray Saturday morning. He left from your house in the SUV. That's the last time she'd seen anything of him. Mrs. Lancaster, the lady on the other side of you. She said she hasn't seen or heard either of you in more than a week. Sees Timmy getting off the bus in the afternoons. She sits by the front window to have coffee about that time. But didn't remember seeing you or Billy Ray in a week or two." Luke leaned back in his chair. "So, it doesn't look like any of them has really seen him since Sunday night. Are you sure he doesn't have a girlfriend somewhere?"

Rita shrugged. "I don't know. Not one I know about. Did you talk to anyone else?" Surely, he talked to Harry. Didn't he?

Luke turned a page in the file. "We talked to Billy Ray's brother and sister, but they didn't know anything. Said you'd been out there to see them. Looking for Billy Ray. But that was the first they heard about him being gone and neither of them had seen him since the middle of the week before."

"And Harry Jackson?" He still hadn't said anything about Harry. She had to ask about Harry. "Did you talk to him?"

"Harry said he hasn't seen Billy Ray since Sunday night. The same night he was seen in that club over at Norton."

Rita knew that was a lie. Had to be. But she knew better than to challenge what Harry said to the police. "So," she said slowly. "Billy Ray was with Harry Sunday night and that's the last time anyone has seen him?"

"Looks like it. Except for you."

Fear ran through every cell. Fiber. Being. Then she remembered. "Right," she said. "He was at the house Monday morning."

"So, you're the last person to see him alive."

It was obvious Luke hadn't pieced together all that he knew. She told him Billy Ray left the house that morning. True enough. But he went to the still and Harry was there. She knew he was from the mash they were cooking the day she went to get the car. It didn't get like that without a couple of days to work off. Harry lied. Luke would have realized it if he had talked to Harry at the still. But he couldn't. Harry would never let that happen.

"Well." Rita stood. "I appreciate you asking around and looking for him. What should I do next?"

"Just wait." Luke stood and came from behind the desk. "We'll keep searching for him. And if you have a photo of him, that might be helpful. We've been using a mugshot from when he was arrested before, but something more recent might be better."

"I'll see what I can find. We ain't too big on pictures." Billy Ray didn't like having his picture made. And didn't like her having hers made either. Afraid someone would notice the bruises. The look in her eye.

"I understand," Luke said.

They walked together from the office to the exit, then she paused. "But what about after that?"

He had a quizzical expression. "What do you mean?"

"What do people do in situations like this? When somebody goes missing and they ain't never found?"

"Right." He seemed to realize what she was asking. "After seven years, you can ask the court for an order declaring him legally dead. But don't worry about that right now. Most of the time, these cases get resolved in a few days."

She grimaced. "It's been ten days."

"There's still time." He placed his hand on her shoulder, lightly. A shock like electricity ran through her body. "Don't give up yet."

Rita came from the police building to the SUV. Thought about where things stood. She was certain Harry didn't tell Luke every-thing. Told him hardly anything. Almost nothing at all. And she wanted to know what he said. Exactly. Precisely. To keep her story straight. But she couldn't return to the still to talk to him. Luke might follow. Might see. Might be watching her. And anyway, if she talked to Harry, he might ask about the money from the glove compartment of the SUV. Better to leave Harry alone. At least for now. Let things take their course. Trust that she'd be able to feel her way along. Muddle through. Probably better to let the story unfold rough. Unfinished. Disjointed. Unpolished. Rather than trying to remember things exactly the same way every time.

After talking to Luke, Rita knew more about what the police knew. More about what Harry might say if questioned. And she knew what they were thinking. Looking. Wondering. Why hadn't she sounded an alarm earlier? She'd answered that. What was life like for her at home? She'd answered that, too. The only thing she hadn't done was question people around town. She could do that. Talk to people. Make it look like follow up. Like she'd talked to the police and wanted to hear for herself. A wife, doing all she could to find her missing husband. It couldn't hurt to be seen like that.

From the police building, Rita rode around town, stopping at all of the clubs and bars she knew Billy Ray frequented. It was strange. Surreal. Asking for him like she would if she didn't know what happened. Like she would if she didn't know he was dead. Like she would if things were different, and she hadn't killed him.

Of course, no one knew where he was. She knew that before she asked the first question. But she learned what they knew, and no one knew anything more than Luke had already discovered. Which wasn't much.

It was late in the afternoon when Rita arrived back at home. Later than she wanted. Later than she'd planned. Timmy was in the kitchen, eating beans from a bowl. Cold from the refrigerator. "Where have you been?" he asked.

"Looking for your father."

He stared at her a moment, as if what she'd said was wrong. Out of place. Unnecessary. As if she already knew the answer. As if they both knew. Rita was unsettled by his look. "What?"

"You know where he is," Timmy said.

The statement hit her a ton. "What do you mean?"

He gave her that look again. "You know," he repeated.

"I know what?" Timmy didn't respond immediately. Rita took him by the shoulders. "I know what, Timmy?"

His gaze dropped to the floor. He was suddenly nervous. Unsettled. Self-conscious. Lowered his voice. Whispered, "I saw you and Miss Linda."

Panic seized her. She felt flush. As if the sea-level inside her body had shifted. In a bad way. "You saw me and Linda?"

"Yes, ma'am."

"What did you see?" Again, he didn't respond immediately. She pulled him close. Softened her voice. "What did you see, Timmy? Tell me what happened."

"I did like you said and didn't stay at Paul's house very long. When I got back, I heard you and Dad shouting and fighting. Then I heard gunshots and I looked through the bedroom window and he was lying on the bed. You pushed him away and stood up." He looked up at her. "You had a pistol in your hand."

She squeezed him tighter against her. "And then what did you do?"

He turned his head to one side, still pressed against her. "I went to the garage and hid."

"Were you scared?"

"No. But I didn't know what else to do."

"Did you see anything else?"

"I saw y'all carry Daddy from the house."

She winced. "Oh, Timmy," she gasped.

"He was rolled up in the quilt that was on the bed. I couldn't see him very good, but I saw the top of his head. And his boots."

She continued to hold him against herself. Unflinching. "Have you told anyone?"

"No, ma'am."

"Not even Paul?"

"No."

"Or your Uncle Bobby Joe?"

"No, ma'am."

"Or Aunt Thelma?"

"I ain't told nobody."

Tears came to Rita. "He hit me," she said.

"I know. He was hitting you that day, too."

"You saw it?"

"I heard it."

"He was hitting me. And he was about to do something worse to me."

"Yes, ma'am. I know that's how you got all those bruises."

"You know about the bruises?" She had been careful to keep them covered. She thought.

"And about when you broke your arm. Both of them. And the stitches on your forehead from that bottle he swung at you."

"Oh, Timmy." Rita sobbed. "I tried to keep it from you. All of it. I tried to protect you from it. From him."

"He never hit me."

"I know. But I didn't want you to see the things he did to me, either."

They stood together a moment longer. Both of them silent. Then Timmy pushed away and dropped onto a chair at the kitchen table. He looked over at her. "So, what do we do now?"

She wiped her eyes with her fingertips. Ran her fingers through her hair to put it in place. Straightened her dress and forced a smile. "Do you have homework?"

"Yes, ma'am."

"What is it?"

"History."

"Good," she said. "I love history. Bring me your book and I'll help you with it."

Johnny Tamburillo

A Short Story

When I was ten years old, we moved to St. Francisville, the parish seat of West Feliciana Parish, about thirty miles north of Baton Rouge. Daddy was a district supervisor for the highway department. We moved a lot. Mama said it was for the best.

Our house was a two-story wooden frame with clapboard siding. It sat on a foundation that made it five steps up from the yard and when I asked why it was so high, Daddy said, "You'll find out when it starts raining."

Sure enough. Not long after we moved there a storm came up from the Gulf and it rained for eight days straight. Water in the yard reached the third step of the porch. A man at the grocery store said it came to the fourth step at his house.

A few days after we arrived, I was in the back yard and noticed the house on the next street behind us was similar to ours. A boy about my age was sitting on the back porch. Feet on the top step. Arms folded across his knees. Head down. From a distance, he seemed to be upset so I walked over to where he was.

"Are you okay?" I asked.

Without looking up, he retorted, "Mind your own fucking business."

The year was 1979. Life was different then and I had never heard that word before, but it sounded interesting and when I got home, I tried it out on my mother. She was busy in the kitchen and when I walked in, she casually asked if I met any of the children in the neighborhood. I said, "Mind your own fucking business."

Before I could move at all, she snatched me up by the back of the shirt, threw me over her knee, and started walloping my backside. When that proved not as painful as she expected, she pulled down my pants and began slapping the flesh of my bare bottom with her hand. That got my attention right away and I began screaming and yelling.

After she calmed down, she explained to me that "fuck" was bad—the word, not the act. Sex, I think, was the only thing that kept my parents together. Daddy used to grab her in his arms and bury his face against her neck. She would start giggling and then they would head off to the bedroom. Just as they closed the door, one of them would say to me, "Don't bother us unless the house is on fire." From the sounds that came through the wall—more giggling, laughing, the rhythmic squeak of the bed—and from the satisfied looks afterward, I knew whatever they did in there must have been fun.

Once, when they were in the bedroom with the door locked and the bed squeaking and banging around, and Mom gasping for breath, the toilet overflowed. It was a problem, but it wasn't fire. So, I ignored it and went outside to play.

Later that night, Dad yelled at me about the mess in bathroom. "Why didn't you tell me the toilet was overflowing?"

"You and Mom were in the bedroom," I replied. "The door was locked, and you said for me not to bother you unless the house was on fire."

His shoulders slumped in a defeated pose. Mama giggled. They both laughed. Dad handed me a mop. "Come on, little man. Help me out in here." He could be really angry sometimes and say terrible things, but when confronted with the truth of a situation, he usually calmed down and did the right thing. Most of the time.

After a week or two, the guy at the house behind us warmed up to me enough to tell me his name was Johnny—Johnny Tamburillo—and he stopped cussing every time he saw me. When he learned I knew something about football, he warmed up even more. And we became really good friends when he found out I had a transistor radio. During football season that year, we sat on his back porch—or under a tree in the yard if his mother had visitors—and listened to the games. His mother had lots of visitors. Usually at night. But sometimes two or three during the day on weekends. In succession. One after the other. Never at the same time. Johnny complained about the noise they made and when I asked what it was, he described noises like the ones Mama and Daddy made when they were in the bedroom with the door locked.

"Fucking," Johnny said. "That's what they're doing."

When I asked what that meant, he laughed at me for not knowing. "I keep asking," I retorted. "But nobody will explain it to me. They just get mad at me for using that word and beat the hell out of me for it, but they never tell me what it means." I didn't cuss much but hanging around Johnny had made it seem necessary, so I tried it out.

With glee, Johnny explained what fuck meant, including the mechanics of it. In great detail. Explicit detail. Unmistakable detail. After hearing that, my life and everything else was never the same again.

A visitor to their house was the reason Johnny had been sitting on the porch that first day when I saw him. When I asked him how long she'd been taking in visitors he said he didn't remember, but that it hadn't always been that way. Mostly since they'd moved to St. Francisville, though she always had a boyfriend. "It's not so bad, really," he said. "We eat better after she started having visitors. She says they're a necessary evil."

After a while, I noticed that I had never seen Johnny's father. He was never around and there was never any mention of him. When I asked about him, Johnny dodged the question. Not understanding why he wouldn't want to talk about him, I persisted and finally Johnny said, "He's in prison at Angola, damn it."

Angola was the state prison. It was located on an old plantation site in a bend of the Mississippi River, northwest of St. Francisville. Everyone knew about Angola. Even kids our age. It was a notorious place.

"What's he in for?" I asked.

"Robbery," Johnny said. "Armed fucking robbery." Johnny really liked that word and he used it all the time. And knowing what it meant, technically speaking, I couldn't figure out if he was using it to mean he approved of something or disapproved it. But I think he would rather have had his father at home with him. Especially if it meant his mother wouldn't need to have visitors. And if he had someone else besides me to listen to the ballgames with him.

One day when we were sitting in the side yard at Johnny's house, thinking about what to do next, a black Cadillac arrived and came to a stop in the driveway. The front door of the house opened and Johnny's mother—her name was Sadie Doucet—came out. She wore a tight red dress with high heeled shoes and when she walked all of the noticeable parts of her body seemed to jiggle beneath the fabric. Having been educated by Johnny about the nature of the relationship between men and women, and after exploring the subject through magazines furnished by older guys at school, I found it difficult to watch her walk and keep my young imagination under control.

As Sadie came towards the car she called over to Johnny. "I'll be late tonight. There's supper in the refrigerator."

The driver was out of the car and opened the rear door for her. With the door open the dome light came on inside and I could see through the front windshield that the car was empty. When she was seated in back, the driver closed the door, came around to the other side, and got in behind the steering wheel.

As they drove away, I looked over at Johnny. "That's a big car."

"Yeah."

"Whose is it?"

"The governor's."

My mouth fell open. "The governor?"

"Yeah."

"Of Louisiana?"

"Yeah, ya' dumbass." His voice was loud and abrasive. "Where'd ya' think? Mississippi?"

"I don't know. But the governor?"

"He sends his driver to get her sometimes."

By then, the car was at the corner. It stopped for traffic, then turned right, and I saw Johnny's mother wave to him through the window. He waved back and the car disappeared down the street.

Johnny and I sat together in the side yard until the sun went down, and we continued sitting there until Mama called me for supper. I asked Johnny if he wanted to come eat with us, but he said his mother had left him something and he would be fine. I went home and while we ate, I told them about Johnny's situation. My parents exchanged furtive glances, the way they did when they thought "something was up." At the time, I had no idea what that meant, but that's how they looked at each other that night.

At school the next day, I learned from Johnny that his mother had not returned home. He spent the night alone and she wasn't there when he woke up. After hearing that, I was surprised he came to school at all. Left to our own devices like that, most of us back then would have declared a free day for ourselves. I think if asked about it the day before, Johnny would have had the same opinion, but having experienced a night by himself, I think he was feeling lonesome and neglected.

That afternoon when I got home, I asked Mama if she had seen Johnny's mother and she gave me a puzzled look. "She wasn't there this morning when he got up?"

"No, ma'am," I replied. "He spent the whole night by himself. Got himself ready for school this morning, too."

I changed clothes and went over to Johnny's house as usual. He was sitting on the back porch like he did when his mother had visitors and I was relieved to see it. "Y'all got visitors?"

Johnny shook his head and when he looked up at me, I saw that he had been crying. "She's still not here," he said.

"Did she come back and go again?"

He shook his head. "She hasn't been back since yesterday afternoon."

We sat on the porch and talked a while. Threw the football and talked about the previous Saturday's game. Threw the ball some more and talked about the game for the coming Saturday. Then I said, "Let's get your clothes."

He had a sullen expression. "Why?"

"You're coming to my house tonight." His expression didn't change but he didn't argue with me either and we packed his clothes in two grocery sacks, then started across the yard.

Mama saw us coming and met us at the back door. She seemed to understand when I told her Johnny was staying with us a while. Daddy didn't argue about it, either. We put his clothes and things in my room, and he slept with me that night.

Johnny's only other relative that he knew about besides his mother was a grandmother who lived in Opelousas. He didn't remember ever seeing her and didn't know how to get in touch with her. Mama tracked her down the next day and talked to her on the phone, but she didn't want him. "Sadie brought this on herself," his grandmother said. "And I don't feel obligated to help her."

"It's not about Sadie," Mama argued. "It's about Johnny. A boy who needs a family to support him."

"Well, I'm sorry but I can't do anything about that. I'm not in a position to look after another kid. I raised mine. Someone else can raise hers."

Mama never told Johnny the details of the conversation. I didn't find out until years later, right before Mama died. We got to talking about things one day and she told me about it. I was glad she never said anything at the time. It was better the way it worked out, with both of them—Mama and Daddy—telling Johnny something different. "We talked to your grandmother and we convinced her that you should stay with us." Johnny liked it that way, too.

At first, Johnny and I stayed together in my room, but a few days later, Mama rearranged the spare bedroom and made it Johnny's room. The day she moved him into it we went over to the house and got the rest of his stuff and a week or two after that, Daddy had everything else in the house put in storage. Johnny's house was a rental. The landlord wanted it back.

When Johnny heard they were cleaning out the house, he was alarmed. "We have to get over there," he insisted.

"Why? Daddy took care of everything. It's safe."

"We gotta get the jars out of the flower bed."

I was puzzled. "What jars?"

"Get a shovel and come on." He was already to the back door, so I jumped up and hurried after him. We found a shovel in the garage and went over to the house.

There were flowerbeds on both ends of the house. We started with the one on the left, opposite the place where we usually sat in the lawn chairs. After a moment to get his bearings, Johnny said, "The first one is right here." He carefully sank the blade of the shovel into the ground and I heard a clink as it struck something. Johnny stooped over and brushed the dirt aside to reveal the metal top of a two-gallon pickle jar. The kind that was made of glass and sat on the counter in a store or gas station. You can still find them like that today in stores on the back roads. Even after all that's happened with viruses and this and that, people buy pickles from them and eat them right there, wrapped in a napkin.

Johnny pulled that first jar out of the ground and before he got the dirt wiped off of it, I could see why he wanted it. The jar was full of cash. Mostly twenties and hundreds. We found two more on that side and three at the opposite end of the house.

"Is that all of them?" I asked.

"Yeah," he said. "All that I know of."

"Anything else hidden in the house?"

"No."

He seemed to be thinking it over, so I said, "Nothing in bedroom?" He shook his head. "Nothing in the living room?" He shook his head. "What about the attic?"

Suddenly his eyes opened wide. "There's a box," he blurted.

"What kind of box?"

"A cardboard box."

We moved the jars to the back porch and set them near the door, then went inside. "Where's the box?" I asked.

"In here." Johnny led the way across the kitchen and down the hall to a closet in the back bedroom. He pointed to an access panel in the ceiling. "It's up there."

"How do we get to it?"

"Boost me up."

I knelt down with one knee out and he used it to climb onto my shoulders. When he was seated and holding on with his feet hooked against my back, I stood and moved directly beneath the access panel. Johnny reached up with both hands but he wasn't high enough to touch it, much less push it out of the way.

"What'll we do now?" I asked.

"Hold still," he said. "And don't move." He braced himself with one hand against the shelf in the closet and the other against the wall on the opposite side, then began climbing around as if trying to untangle his legs from their position against me. The pressure on my shoulders was almost more than I could take, and I wobbled from side to side.

"What are you doing?" I shouted.

"I gotta stand up," he replied.

"Stand up? On what?"

"Your shoulders."

"That'll never work."

"Sure it will. Just hold still."

His knee dug into my shoulder on the right side, then I felt the sole of his shoe on the left and thought I would collapse any second. Somehow, though, he managed to climb onto my shoulders and from there, he succeeded in knocking the panel out of the way. With the passageway open, he hauled himself up to the attic. I collapsed against the wall and slid to a sitting position on the floor. My muscles were exhausted.

Before I was rested, Johnny appeared in the opening. "Take this," he said, and he dropped a small cardboard box through the hole. It fell toward me and I caught it without moving, then put it beside me on the floor.

"Is that it?" I asked.

"Yeah," he replied. "That's it."

I stayed put and closed my eyes as I continued to catch my breath from before. He was impatient. "Are you asleep?"

"No," I replied. "I'm tired."

"From what?"

"From you climbing all over me."

"Well wake up and let me get down. It's hot up here."

I sat there a few more minutes, then stood beneath the access hole and waited while Johnny lowered himself through it. He dangled in the air a moment while his feet found me, then replaced the panel. The soles of his shoes dug into the muscles near my neck.

"How are you gonna get down?" I asked.

"That part's easy," he replied. "Just kneel and I can step off."

I tried to kneel in an orderly, controlled manner but before I was halfway down my knees buckled from the weight and strain. We collapsed onto the floor in a heap and busted out laughing.

When we recovered, we took the box to the back porch and added it to the jars. Johnny waited, guarding the treasure trove, while I ran over to the house for the wheelbarrow. The jars and the box filled it up. Johnny pushed the load across the yard. I carried the shovel.

When Mama saw us with six pickle jars of cash, she was beside herself. "Where did that come from?"

Johnny said, "Mama didn't trust banks."

My mother just shook her head and said, "Bring it inside and let's get those jars cleaned up. We'll have to ask your father what to do with it. He'll know."

After the jars were cleaned, we put them on the dining room table and waited for Daddy to get home. When he saw them, he said we needed to open a bank account. And that's what they did. He and Mama opened an account for Johnny and put all of that money in it. Mr. Destrehan, the bank manager, was amazed at the amount of cash but he took it and didn't ask any questions.

The money stayed in a bank account for a few years, but when we were in the tenth grade, the bank got a new manager. He put some of Johnny's money in a different kind of account that let it make more than simple interest. By the time we graduated, Johnny was the richest kid in the class.

When we turned sixteen, Johnny and I obtained our drivers' licenses and got jobs at the grocery store near where we lived. He was a bag boy. I worked with the stock clerk. After working there a few months, we went in together and bought an old pickup truck. No one ever mentioned using the money in the bank. We paid for it from our jobs. That was a fun truck and I still have it. Drive it all the time and think of the days when we loaded our friends in back and went for a ride around town, singing, and hollering, and laughing.

One day, near the end of our senior year in high school, Johnny drove me to a shack at the river, just down from the ferry crossing. There was a dock behind the shack and two boats were tied up there. Near the end of the dock, a man was sitting on a five-gallon bucket tying hooks on a jug line. Even with his knees folded up like that, I could see he was tall and skinny. He wore a white t-shirt with blue jeans and dirty sneakers. His hair was long and unkempt and poked out from beneath a cap that sat at an angle atop his head.

As the truck came to a stop I said, "Who is that?"

"That's my father," Johnny replied. "You asked about him once. So, there he is." He pulled the handle to open the door. "Come on. I'll introduce you."

We walked down to the dock and Johnny introduced us. His father's name was Michael Tamburillo, but I already knew his friends called him Rufus. He didn't have much to say to me, but he and Johnny talked a while, as if I wasn't there. Then Rufus said, "Come on in here. I got something to show you." Before we could respond, he was up from his place on the five-gallon bucket and started toward the shack. We followed.

The shack was a typical trapper's cabin. Made of cypress lumber, it sat atop concrete piers that were three feet tall. From the look of it, the cabin was old, but the piers on which it sat were of recent vintage. A porch ran across the front and a door on the left opened into a single large room that served as the kitchen, dining room, and bedroom. A bed sat along the back wall. A bathroom was located in the far corner. The place was stuffy and hot and smelled like fried gator meat, which was greasy and rank.

A table occupied the center of the room with a bench down one side and chairs pushed up against the other. To the right of the door was a cabinet with shelves that held a few books on one end and the rest was cluttered with odd bits of junk. Detritus, I learned to call it as an adult.

Rufus walked over to the cabinet and took down a book. He rested the spine of it against the palm of his hand and the pages fell open to an envelope. He removed it and offered it to Johnny. "This come to me while I was at Angola. Right before I got out." Johnny took it from him and held it in his hand, staring at it, not saying a word. "There's a letter in there," Rufus said. "You need to read it."

I glanced over Johnny's shoulder and saw the letter was from Sadie, Johnny's mother. The postmark was a little over twelve months old. And then it hit me. She was alive.

Johnny slid the letter from the envelope and read it, then handed it to me. I glanced at Rufus to be sure it was alright, and he nodded. I started reading.

"Dear Rufus: I am writing you to let you know that I am alive and living in Spokane. If you talk to Johnny, please tell him not to come for me. I don't want him to see me like I am now and I don't want him to get tangled up in my doings. It's a mess up here. And him being here would only make it worse. You should be getting out soon. When you do, please find him and look after him and help him to understand. I love you both. Sadie."

Johnny pulled a chair away from the table and dropped onto it. I sat next to him and re-read the letter, then laid it on the table in front of him. Rufus and I exchanged glances as if checking with each other about what to do next. He frowned and shook his head. I kept quiet. We waited. And while we waited, Rufus lit a cigarette.

Finally, Johnny said, "She's been alive all this time."

Rufus nodded his head slowly. "It would appear to be the case."

"Do you think it's really her? Did she really write that letter?"

"No reason to doubt it."

Johnny glanced over at me. "You think that letter is really from her?"

"I would have no way of knowing for sure. But the letter was addressed to Rufus at Angola. And it references you. If she didn't write it, then whoever sent it would be someone who knew about both of you and knew where he was."

"Lot of people fit that description," Rufus said.

"But not too many who would care to let us know," Johnny replied. "Have you tried to find her?"

Rufus shook his head. "She moved y'all up here to be near the prison, but she only came to see me once or twice. Once she started running with the governor and his crowd, she stopped coming around."

"If one of them was into something," Johnny said, "and she knew about it, they would know you were getting out soon. They might have a reason to keep you from getting involved. And, if you did get involved, they might have put that return address on the letter to send you off to Spokane."

Rufus had a sheepish smile. "Not even sure I know where that is."

"Way out in Washington," I offered. "The state."

"That's a long way away."

"And that's my point," Johnny said. "If somebody knew you were getting out of prison and thought you might be interested in finding her, they might be trying to send you in the wrong direction."

"Way the hell in the wrong direction."

"Yeah."

Rufus looked over at Johnny. "So, where do you think she really is?"

"I have no idea. Did you get any other letters from her at all while you were in there?"

Rufus took a long drag on the cigarette, then slowly let it escape. "There were a few," he said.

"Did you keep them?"

"Yeah."

"Get them." Johnny responded. "Let me see them."

Rufus went over to the shelves where he found the book with the first letter and sorted through the items on the top shelf. A kerosene lamp sat at one end. He took it down and behind it was small cigar box. He brought it to the table and opened it. Inside were three envelopes bound together by a rubber band. He took them from the box and handed them to Johnny. "These are all the letters she sent me."

Johnny removed the rubber band and sorted through them. The first two were postmarked from years before Johnny and I met. He glanced at them without response. But when he came to the third one, he studied it a moment, then looked over at me again. "We were in the sixth grade when you moved here, right?"

"Yes," I replied. "We moved here the summer before the sixth grade."

"And we started sixth grade together that year."

I nodded. "We had Mrs. Lewis."

"Right. And Mama disappeared when we were in the eighth."

"Spring of the eighth," I said. "The school year was almost over."

"So, what year was that?"

I had to think for a minute and count with my fingers to keep it straight. "That was 1982," I said finally. "April or May of '82."

Johnny pointed to the postmark on the third envelope. "This letter was mailed in June of 1983."

I took a close look just to be sure. "So, she sent two letters after we saw her leave with that guy."

Rufus took another drag on his cigarette. "You two talk like a couple of old women."

Johnny ignored the comment and turned the envelope for him to see. "This one came to you after she disappeared. Just like the other one you showed me." He pointed to the postmark. "Only this one was mailed from Memphis. Not Spokane, Washington."

Rufus glanced at it, then back to Johnny. "Don't mean she's there now."

Johnny removed the letter from the envelope and read it, then handed it to me. "Dear Rufus," it began. "I left things in a mess with Johnny, and I'll need you to explain things to him when you get out. Too much partying has brought me to an end, I think. The court up here says I have to do a rehab program. If I complete it and stay clean, they'll drop the charges. I'm going to rehab. We'll see what happens after that. Not many people who get on this stuff ever get off. If I live and things work out, I'll come find both of you. Otherwise, please make sure Johnny stays out of trouble. Sadie."

"She had a drug problem," I noted.

Johnny looked over at Rufus. "What was she doing?"

"Crack cocaine," Rufus said.

"How do you know that?"

Rufus pointed to the other envelopes. "She wrote to me about it." He took an ashtray from the counter by the stove and stubbed out the cigarette in it. "Some of those guys she was seeing used cocaine. She did that for a while, but she needed something more. And she needed something cheaper. That's when she found the crackpipe."

Johnny looked angry. "She was a whore and a drug addict."

Rufus glared at him. "Boy, don't talk about your mama like that. She was just trying to survive and take care of you."

"But she sold herself. And then she ran off."

"She sold herself because that's all she had to sell. And I don't think she meant to run off."

"Then what do you think happened?"

"I think she went out for the evening, got caught up in a party. Before she knew it, days went by. One thing led to another. Then got herself in trouble."

Johnny seemed unconvinced. "Memphis is a long way from St. Francisville."

"Not if the people you're with have their own airplane."

"You think they would have taken her up there and just left her?"

"I think when it came time to leave, they wouldn't go out of their way to find her."

Rufus had a point, and Johnny seemed to sense it might be right. "If that's true, do you think she's still alive?"

"Might be."

"Do you think she's still in Memphis?"

Rufus shrugged. "Maybe. Could be. Especially if she had trouble with the law."

"What do you mean?"

"Once people get in the system, it's difficult to get away from it. Probation. Suspended sentence. It hangs over you. And if you have to report to a probation officer, maybe do random drug tests, it limits how far you can go."

"Memphis isn't that far," I suggested.

"You think she could have gone there on her own?"

"I don't know." I smiled. "But I wasn't thinking about that. I was thinking about us."

"Us?" Johnny frowned. "What about us?

"She might be there, she might not. But there's one way to find out."

A look of realization hit him. "You mean, go up there?"

"Yeah."

Rufus didn't think it was a good idea for us to go to Memphis in search of Sadie, but he understood Johnny's eagerness to find her. She was his mother. If there was a chance she was alive, a son would feel compelled to try. And I think he understood my eagerness to help Johnny do it. But to him, we were mere teenagers, and even to a former inmate—maybe especially to former inmate—the world was a dangerous place. Filled with hardened people intent on imposing their will on others. He wasn't eager for us to venture out into it on our own.

When we got home, Johnny went to his room. I sat on the back porch for a while so he could have some space, then went for a walk around the neighborhood. I thought of it back then as airing out my brain. And I still think of it that way, though I now say, "Just give me a minute."

During supper that evening, Johnny and I told my parents about Johnny's father living in the shack by the river, about visiting with him, and about the things we'd learned from his letters regarding Sadie. They didn't say much in response, so I said, "We want to go to Memphis and see if we could locate her."

Dad, ever the practical one, said, "It's been a long time since she left. I doubt she's even there now."

"But she could be."

"Yes," he conceded. "She could be. But even so, I don't think it's a good idea for two teenagers to go off on a trip like that by themselves."

"We're eighteen, not eight."

He glared at me. "And I'm your father, not your football coach."

"Yes, sir," I said apologetically. The last thing I wanted was an argument with him about who was in charge.

Mom stepped into the conversation, as she often did at tense moments. "Johnny, this has been a big day for you. Seeing your father and learning about your mother."

"Yes, ma'am."

"Been a long time since you've seen him."

"Quite a while."

Dad took a few bites in silence while they talked, and I smiled at him. He smiled back. So, I said, "Could you go with us this weekend?"

He frowned. "To Memphis?"

"Yes."

"No, son. I can't go to Memphis this weekend and neither can you."

"Why not?"

"You both have to work at the store."

Work. That was always a convenient excuse. He worked hard. Devoted himself fully to it. I understood his purpose in life, supporting us and taking care of us. There was honor in it. But sometimes, it seemed like work was an easy way out for him when he was faced with something that required a different kind of effort than he was used to giving.

"We can't let this wait," I said, calmly. Evenly. Kindly. "It's not fair to Johnny."

Dad looked down the table to Mama. I glanced over at Johnny. He gave a faint shake of his head, as if to say I should drop it. I knew what he really meant. He intended to go on his own, whether they allowed it or not. Might even prefer it that way. And might even go that night. I gave him a look in return to say he wasn't going alone.

Nothing more was said about the matter that evening. We finished eating, cleared the table, and cleaned the kitchen, then went in separate directions. Dad to the den to watch TV. Mama to the living room to read. Johnny and I to our rooms to study.

When the house was quiet and settled, I crossed the hall to Johnny's room. "You can't go by yourself," I said.

He was reading and didn't look up. "You'll be in trouble if you go with me."

"We've done everything together. And Memphis is too far. Besides, you'll need help driving."

He looked over at me and smiled. "What about Mr. Ledet?" Herman Ledet owned the grocery store where we worked.

I took a seat on the bed. "We'll need a cover story."

Johnny looked puzzled. "A cover story?"

I nodded. "If we tell him we want off for a trip to Memphis, he'll mention it to Mama. He always talks to her when she goes to the store."

"I thought about that," Johnny replied. "Which is why I need to go by myself. If I go to Memphis and you go to work, you can explain what happened and maybe it'll be alright. If we're both no-shows, we'll lose our jobs. If we ask for time off, word will get out and your parents will know before we even leave. I have to go by myself. It's the only way."

"We could quit."

Johnny shook his head. "Bad idea."

He was right about that. If we quit, my parents would find out and we would have an argument about going to Memphis and about jobs and work and not sitting around the house. Then I thought of another way. "We could wait until graduation," I suggested. "Ask Mr. Ledet to let us off for the weekend to celebrate. He would probably go for that without saying too much and it would be something we could cover with Mama and Daddy. We're going over to someone's house. Last chance to see everybody. Something like that."

The idea seemed to resonate with him. "I'll think about it."

"Okay. But don't go tonight."

Johnny pointed to the book he'd been reading. "Can't. We have a test tomorrow."

"Okay."

A few months later school ended and we graduated. As planned, we arranged to take a few days off from our jobs at the grocery store. In the afternoon of graduation day, we loaded our clothes and toiletries into backpacks and stashed them in the cab of the pickup truck, then attended the graduation ceremony with my parents. Afterward, we went home with them and changed clothes. We were set to attend a party at the house of a classmate. Everything was going according to plan.

At the last minute before we left the house, I put a note on my desk telling my parents where we were really going, then I turned out the light, caught up with Johnny, and started across the yard toward the truck for the ride to Memphis. I felt bad about leaving like that, but I knew my parents would never let us go any other way and I didn't want to fight with them about it. This trip was important to Johnny and I was curious to find out how things went. We were going and that was that.

Neither of us said a word as we walked across the yard, but as we got about halfway to the truck, I saw Dad was standing by the front fender. Johnny muttered under his breath. "What is this about?"

"I don't know," I replied. "Just take it easy."

I expected the usual comments. "Don't drink. And for sure, don't drink and drive. And if you do get drunk, call me and I'll come get you." Dad often said things like that when we went out and he usually said them in the yard or somewhere away from the house so Mama couldn't hear. He didn't want an argument with her about how comments like that only enabled us to drink. Enabling was a key point in her assessment of handling teenagers and in her view of his relationship with us.

As we came closer to the truck, Dad stood up straight and I braced for what I knew was coming. Instead of talking, though, he took his wallet from the hip pocket of his pants, opened it, and counted out five hundred dollars—three in hundred-dollar bills and the rest in twenties. He handed it to me and said, "Take the highway through Liberty, and get on the interstate over at McComb. It'll be safer that way."

"Yes, sir," I replied as I put the money in my pocket. That's when it hit me that he knew we were going to Memphis. I really didn't know what to say. He pulled me toward him and gave me a hug. "And be careful," he whispered.

"Yes, sir," I replied. "Thanks." He hugged Johnny, too, and then we got in the truck.

Johnny had the first shift driving so he got in behind the steering wheel. Dad came to the driver's door and gave Johnny's arm a squeeze. "I hope you find her." He seemed on the verge of tears and I was, too. Until that moment, I had never been surprised by anything he ever did. That night, I was totally blown away.

A few hours up the road, the adrenaline of the venture wore off and we were both tired, but we pushed on through the night and arrived at Memphis a little after five the next morning. We located a café and ate breakfast, then bought a city map at a convenience store and turned our attention to the task of finding Johnny's mama.

The letter that Sadie mailed to Rufus from Memphis had been sent from an address on Madison Avenue. She talked about being in a drug rehab and we assumed the return address on the envelope was the location of the place where she was staying. We located it without much difficulty, parked the truck on the street, and went inside.

A receptionist was seated at a counter just beyond the door. When we told her why we were there, she referred us to Renee McCoy, the director of the program. "Her office is down the hall to the right," the receptionist said. She had a nice smile and from the way she looked at us I thought she was flirting. Johnny said we needed to focus on the task at hand. I wondered why the receptionist let us wander down the hall and didn't come with us to show the way.

After a few starts and stops, we came to Ms. McCoy's office. A plaque on the wall near the doorway made it obvious. The door was open. She was seated at her desk and looked up as we appeared. "May I help you?"

She was a pleasant woman, by appearance. About forty years old, probably. With blonde hair and a nice smile. We entered her office and stood before the desk while Johnny explained we were looking for his mother. "Her real name is Sadie Doucet," he said. "But she might have told you something else. Maybe Sarah Delaberta. Or Sally Landry."

McCoy gave us that disinterested look adults often give to teenagers. "I'm sorry. I—"

"Sometimes," Johnny interrupted, "she went by Rosie Fontenot."

McCoy's expression softened. "I'd love to help you," she said. "But I'm afraid I can't even confirm for you whether she was here or not."

Johnny didn't like that remark. "Why not?" His voice had an edge. "She's my mother."

"I understand." She seemed more interested than she did at first. "But confidentiality rules prevent us from sharing that kind of information with anyone."

"Not even her son?"

McCoy nodded. "I'm sorry, but that's the way it is."

Johnny wasn't finished. "Look," he said. "This isn't like some of those situations you might have dealt with before. I'm not an ex-husband or the law or anyone like that. I'm her son."

"But we have rules and I can't—"

"It was just me and her and then one day when I was in the eighth grade she got in the car with a guy and drove off and never came back. Never said goodbye." Johnny's voice cracked and I thought he was going to cry. "She never called. Never wrote. She just left. And I want to know where she is and what happened."

"I understand but—"

"Do you know what that felt like?"

"I can't imagine."

"All she said was, 'I'll be late. Supper's in the refrigerator.' And then she was gone. I've lived every day after that thinking she was dead, or tired of me, or never really wanted me in the first place. And then a month or two ago I found out she wrote a letter to my dad after she disappeared. The letter has this facility's address as the return." Johnny took the letter from his pocket and showed her. "She sent this to my father from right here. At this very place." He held the envelope for her to see and pointed to the return address. "Right there. That's your address."

As she studied the envelope, McCoy's forehead wrinkled in a frown. "Your father was an inmate at Angola?"

"Yes," Johnny replied.

"But he lived with us," I offered quickly.

McCoy seemed puzzled. "His father lived with you?"

"No, ma'am," I said, realizing the confusion. "Johnny lived with us."

She leaned back in her chair, propped her elbows on the armrests, and stared into the distance, as if considering the situation. Johnny sensed an opening. "Can you help me out? Please?"

"There was a woman here back then, but I don't remember...."

McCoy stopped mid sentence and lifted the receiver from a phone on the desk. She pressed a button and called someone on the inter-com. A woman appeared at the doorway. McCoy scribbled some-thing on a slip of paper and handed it to her. "Bring me this file," she said. The woman took the paper from her, glanced at it, then disappeared.

When she was gone, McCoy looked back to Johnny. "There was a woman here about the time that letter was postmarked. She came to us from the courts. I think she was listed under one of those names you mentioned."

"Which one?"

"I'm not sure." McCoy gestured for patience. "Just wait until we get the file. She'll be back with it in a minute."

"And you think it was her? You think the woman you remember might have been my mother?"

"We'll find out."

I spoke up. "You seem to remember her for a reason."

"Yes." McCoy smiled, as if thinking of something pleasant. "For one thing, she was very pretty. Or had been at one point."

"Had been?"

She looked over at Johnny. "If the woman I'm thinking of really is your mother, the things you'll learn about her might be unpleasant for you."

None of that seemed to matter to Johnny. "I need to know where she is," he said. "I don't care about all the rest."

"Well, she's not here. I know that much."

"Where did she go?"

"Let me look at the file before I answer that." McCoy scooted her chair closer to the desk and rested her arms on the desktop. "But here's the thing I was saying," she continued. "When we got her, she came to us from the court. She had been using crack and living on the street. The police picked her up on a drug charge. She was in bad shape."

"And that's why you remember her?" I asked. "Because she was in bad shape?"

McCoy smiled. "That and the fact that she made gumbo in a way I had never tasted before. I was not a fan of gumbo, but I became a big fan of hers."

Johnny grinned. "Mamou Kazoo."

"Yes." McCoy's eyes opened wide. "That's what she called it."

Johnny nodded. "She used to say that to me when I was a kid. She made gumbo in this huge pot—at least, it seemed huge to me at the time—and I'd smell that stuff cooking all day. I got so hungry I could hardly stand it. When I asked her what she was making she would say, 'Mamou Kazoo.'"

"Mamou," I explained, "was the name of a town in Louisiana near where his mother grew up." That was the truth. Mamou isn't far from Opelousas.

"Apparently, she liked the gumbo as much as you did," McCoy said. "After she'd been here a while she started doing better. Got clean from the drugs. Began eating regularly. Gained a little weight. And talked her way into the kitchen."

"She had a way of talking herself into a lot of places," Johnny noted.

"Well," McCoy said, "she got our cook to let her help and, not long after that, convinced someone to bring her some shrimp."

Johnny grinned. "That sounds like her."

"The cook wasn't sure we she should let her do much with the food, but when a guy came with five pounds of shrimp one day, I thought it would be okay to give it try." McCoy grinned. "She made the gumbo. We loved it."

Johnny's mood changed. "A guy? Did she have visitors?"

"Just the man who brought the shrimp. I think he came once or twice besides that."

"Do you remember his name?"

"No. But I remember he drove an older model Cadillac. A big one."

"A black one?"

"Yes."

Johnny and I glanced at each other. McCoy noticed. "You two

know the car?"

"That's the kind of car she left in," I said. "The day she disappeared."

The woman appeared with the file in hand and gave it to McCoy. She flipped through it quickly, then turned to a page with a photo attached. "This is the woman we knew as Rosie."

Tears filled Johnny's eyes as he glanced at the picture. I leaned forward to see. "Yes," I said softly. Johnny wasn't able to speak. "That's her." She was much thinner than when we saw her last and harder—the luster was gone—but the woman in the photograph was Sadie Doucet. Johnny's mama.

"You're certain she's your mother?" McCoy asked.

Johnny nodded. "Yes, ma'am," he said. "That's her."

McCoy looked back at the file. "She came to us in December 1983. Stayed here until March 1985."

"She completed whatever she was supposed to do here?"

McCoy leaned back in her chair again. "Yes," she said slowly. "She finished the program. Actually, she finished quite a while before she left. She didn't want to leave, and we weren't in a hurry to send her away. Everyone liked her, and not just for the gumbo. So, I found ways to keep her around. Let her live here and work as a volunteer. Hired her part-time. She was a good person to have. Great with the new people."

"So, why did she leave?"

McCoy looked over at Johnny. "You're certain you're her son?"

"Yes."

"Let me see your driver's license."

Johnny took his license from his billfold and handed it to her. She glanced at it. "You have a different last name."

"I have the same name as my father." He showed her the letter again. The one from Sadie to Rufus. She seemed satisfied.

McCoy leaned forward again and pressed her hands flat against the desktop. "Your mother...." She seemed ill at ease. "Your mother tested positive for HIV."

Johnny frowned. "HIV?"

"She had AIDS," McCoy explained. "Not an active case at the time, but she had the virus that causes it. Doctors told us it was only a matter of time before she started showing symptoms. Our board thought it would be best to send her somewhere else."

"Why was that?" I asked.

"They were worried about her being contagious. I tried to explain to them how the disease worked but there was so much we didn't know about it—and still don't—that they didn't want to take the chance." That's how it was back then. No one understood the disease. Everyone was scared.

"Where did she go? Back to the street?"

"No," McCoy replied. "We found a place for her at a home on Watkins Street. They dealt with AIDS patients."

"Are they still there?"

"Yes." She jotted down the address on a sheet of paper and handed it to Johnny. "I don't know if Rosie's still there, but the home is still in business. You could check with them, though. They might be able to help you. If she's not there, maybe they know where she went."

"Do you know if she actually even went there? When she left here, did she actually go to there?"

"Someone from our staff drove her over there," McCoy said. "I don't know if she stayed, but we made sure she got there. The person in charge over there is a woman named Mildred Adams. Older lady. Very kind. I know her. Feel free to use my name."

We turned to leave, then I thought of one more thing. "Do they know her as Rosie Fontenot?"

"That's the name she was using when she left here."

We thanked McCoy for her help, then retraced our path back to the reception desk and out the door to the sidewalk. Johnny looked sad and when we got to the truck I said, "We're making progress. We know more about her than we did before."

"But AIDS," he replied. "She had AIDS."

Back then, a diagnosis like that was pretty much a death sentence. No one held out any hope for survival. Only misery and agony and

OTHER PEOPLE, OTHER PLACES

humiliation. Gays and drug addicts were the ones who got AIDS the most and both were treated as outcasts. Somehow, though, knowing Johnny's mother was among them made it not so much of a stigma anymore. It was disease. And inside I felt inside like saying to everyone, "Shut up talking about people that way. They're sick, damn it. We need to help them." But I kept quiet to everyone else.

To Johnny, I said, "She's your mother. We'll find her, and we'll help her, and we'll tell anyone who doesn't like it to kiss our skinny white asses." We were young and slim back then.

He chuckled. "You have such a way with words."

"I mean it."

"I know." He reached across the seat and gave me a friendly nudge, as if to recognize the kindness of my intentions. "The first thing, though, is to find her." He started the truck and steered it away from the curb. I checked the map and gave him directions.

The place on Watkins Street was called Shekinah House—an old three-story house with wooden siding and a big front porch, just beyond North Parkway. It sat on a large lot with oak trees that cloaked the house and yard in shade most of the day. From the street it appeared cool and inviting. After driving all night and being up all day, I wanted to stretch out on the grass and go to sleep. We didn't, though. Johnny brought the truck to a stop at the curb and we made our way up the sidewalk toward the front steps.

The house had a wide hallway that ran from the door, past a staircase, toward a kitchen in back. Beyond the staircase, halfway to the kitchen, a counter had been added, creating space for a receptionist. From her perch on a stool behind it, she had a clear view of the doors in either direction. She looked our way as we entered. "May I help you?"

A young woman, maybe early twenties, she had short hair and tanned skin, as if she'd spent a lot of time lounging by a swimming pool. Unlike the other place, however, there was no suggestion of anything other than business. Not the least hint of a smile. We approached her in a similar manner.

Johnny said, "I am looking for my mother. Rosie Fontenot. I believe you have her as a patient."

A woman, older than the receptionist, approached the counter. By the receptionist's reaction, I assumed she was a person of authority. "We can't disclose the names of our patients."

"She's my mother," Johnny said.

"Doesn't matter. Unless you're on her visitor list, we couldn't even tell you whether she is or is not one of ours."

"Then how am I supposed to find her?"

"Write her," the woman said. "At this address. If she's here, we'll give her your letter."

"And if she's not?"

"I'm sorry. That's all I can tell you to do."

Johnny was frustrated and tired and I knew he was on the verge of exploding. So, I took him by the elbow and said, "Come on. Let's go. We need to eat lunch and maybe rest a little. We've been up all night." The last thing we needed was a fight.

As we turned to leave, the older woman stepped away from the counter. The younger one came behind us and caught up with us as we reached the door. "I'm sorry we couldn't be of much help." She handed me a brochure. "Perhaps you'll find something in here that will." I took the brochure from her and glanced at it, then caught her smile. "You can read it while you eat lunch," she added and did this thing with her eyes.

"Thank, you," I replied, but I was unsure what she meant.

We continued outside and made our way down the sidewalk. Johnny was a few steps ahead of me. "What was she talking about?" he asked.

"I don't know. She said something about this brochure might help us."

"Let me see it." He held out his hand and I gave it to him. He opened it to look inside. "What's this?" He pointed to the inside page. I took a couple of long steps and caught up with him, then looked over his shoulder. A note was written in the margin that read, "Try Peterman's on Alma Street."

Johnny glanced in my direction. "Did she write that for us?"

"I think so. She did something with her eyes when she gave it to me. Like she was sending me a message or something."

"What's Peterman's?"

"I don't know. We ought to be able to find it," I said. "But let's eat first. I'm starving."

From the house on Watkins, we drove to a hamburger joint and went inside to eat. While we were there, I checked the map for Alma Street. "It's not far from here," I said, pointing. "We can go up here to the corner and turn right and it's just a little way from there."

In no time at all, we were on Alma and not long after that we came to a house with a sign out front that simply said, "Peterman's." Johnny found a space for the truck and we made our way inside.

The building was angular in shape and appeared to be an institutional leftover from an earlier era. Its walls were made of concrete block and the roof was flat. Once inside, however, I saw that the part facing the street had been added as an addition to yet another of Memphis' older homes. It was not as nice as the first place, nor as inviting as the second, and it smelled. A blend of body odor, body fluids, and unpalatable food. I didn't like it, but Johnny seemed not to notice.

Instead of a reception desk there was a nurses' station positioned to control access from the front door. It stood in a spot that would have been on the front porch of the original house, but now was at the center of the re-configured first floor. A monitoring board with indicators for individual rooms was affixed to a column on one side. Stacks of patient files rested beneath it. Across from the station, shoved against the wall, was a metal cart that held boxes of various supplies—wipes, rubber gloves, disposable masks, and the like. A nurse was seated at the station and she glanced in our direction as we approached.

Johnny didn't wait for her to ask but stepped toward her and said, "I believe you have my mother as a patient here."

"What's the name?"

"Rosie Fontenot."

"And you are?"

"I'm her son. Johnny Tamburillo."

"Wait here." She came from the station and disappeared down the hall. We stood there waiting. Neither of us talked.

A few minutes later, the nurse returned and pointed to the left. "She's in the sunroom. All the way to the end of this hall."

Johnny started in that direction at a quick place. I thanked the nurse and went after him. His legs were longer than mine and I was nearly at a trot to catch up with him. "Are you ready for this?" I asked.

"Yeah," he said tersely.

"The other lady said she might not be in good shape."

"I know."

"If she's as bad as they seemed to say, she might not be eager for anyone to see her."

"She's my mama," he said. And I knew from the tone of his voice it was time for me to shut up.

A few steps farther and we were at the doorway that led into the sunroom. Two people sat in rocking chairs to the left. Two more were in padded chairs to the right. Neither of them was Sadie and I felt a twinge of disappointment. Then I looked across the way.

On the opposite side of the room was a row of large windows that looked onto a garden in back of the building. A woman lay on a chaise lounge beneath one of the windows. The sunlight fell over her in a marvelous way. Just enough light. Not too much glare.

Her hair was dark and thin. Her cheeks, gaunt and sunken. The bones of her wrists pressed against her skin, as if they might rip their way through at any moment, and the backs of her hands appeared frail, delicate, and on the verge of crumbling to dust at the slightest contact. But her eyes were alert and even from across the room I recognized her.

Johnny started toward her and in a few long strides he was by her side. They stared at each other a moment. Her on the lounger. Him standing over her. Then he dropped to his knees and rested his head softly against her shoulder. I saw her hand come up behind his head and she slowly stroked his hair.

After a moment, I came to where they were and stood behind Johnny. She looked up at me and smiled. "Taylor, you've grown up."

The mention of my name brought tears to my eyes at the sudden realization she recognized me. This really was her. After all this time. "Yes, ma'am," I replied. "I suppose I have. We both have."

"I remember when you used to come to the house. You and Johnny sat on the back porch and listened to football games on your little radio."

"Yes, ma'am," I said. Tears rolled down my cheeks. "That seems like a long time ago."

"It does for me, too," she said.

After a few minutes with them, I excused myself and walked back to the entrance. There was a breakroom near the nurses' station with vending machines and a couple of upholstered chairs against the wall to the right of the doorway. I chose the chair that looked softest and collapsed in it. The air was cool in there and pretty soon I was used to the smell that had bothered me when we first arrived. My body relaxed as I thought about all that had happened. Johnny's mother going missing for all that time. Meeting his father in the shack by the river. The letters. Dad giving us money for the trip. And finding her at last. A warm, pleasant feeling came over me. A feeling of satisfaction. Of triumph. Of accomplishment. Challenges lay ahead for Johnny. For me. For all of us. But right then, I was more tired than I'd ever been in my life and soon I was sound asleep.

Nashville

A Short Story

Hayden Carruth sat on the sofa. A worn, lumpy, food-stained sofa. In the living room of a double-wide trailer. A mobile home. A modular home. On a one-acre lot, three miles east of Cullman.

Resting gently across the top of his thigh was a Martin D-28 acoustic guitar. He strummed his thumb lightly across the strings. Listening. Trying to hear the chords. Trying not to disturb everyone. Saturday morning was their morning, too. He didn't want to wake them, but he couldn't resist the moment. Empty room. Television silent. Curtains drawn. No one awake.

All week long the songs, the chords, the melodies piled up in his mind, in his soul, in his heart, in his bones. Warm and comforting at first. Then burning like fire until he had to get them out. Play the music. Hear the chords. Write the lyrics. A notebook lay beside him. Dogeared. Frayed at the cover. A pen clipped to the edge.

In a little while, Reese, his wife, entered the room. House pants. Ragged t-shirt. Barefooted. She gave him a look. Not the one that promised pleasure. Not the one she gave just before her flesh touched his. Not the look he enjoyed, but the morning look. The one that said leave me alone. I need coffee. Leave me alone. I'm hungry. Leave me alone. I wish I was still asleep.

As she passed the end of the sofa, on her way to the kitchen—that's the only place she could go, there was nowhere else beyond the sofa but the kitchen. As she passed him, she ran her fingers through his hair. Gave his scalp a rub. To say she wasn't angry. It wasn't him. Just the morning. Not in the mood.

Hayden continued to play, and listen, and write. And the aroma of coffee drifted through the room. The clatter of a spoon against a bowl. A big bowl. A mixing bowl. Biscuits? Pancakes? Maybe.

In a little while, Lila Mae appeared in the doorway from the hall. Three years old. Curly hair. Blonde hair. She smiled at him and said in a playful, coy tone, "Isn't it Saturday?"

"Yes."

"Aren't we supposed to have the TV on now?"

Hayden chuckled. "We don't have to."

"But we should."

"Why is that?"

"Because the shows are on!" she shouted, then she raced across the room toward him, colliding with his knees, arms outstretched, laughing and giggling. He set the guitar aside and picked her up. "Where's the gamote?" she asked.

"Remote," he said, correcting her.

"Where is it?"

"We might have to look for it."

"Where?"

"Under there, maybe." He pointed to the opposite end of the sofa where clean laundry was piled from the day before. Perhaps two days before. Lila Mae giggled. Hayden helped her from his lap. She lay face down on the sofa. He pushed against the bottoms of her feet. She burrowed forward beneath the clothes. "See if you can find it," he said. They had done this before. Many times.

Lila Mae squirmed her way beneath the laundry, moving it from in front with her hands, piling it on top of herself as she went, and in a moment popped up with the remote in her hand. A towel on her head. "I found it," she announced proudly. She plopped down in the midst of the clothes, pointed the remote toward the television, and pressed the button to turn on the set. The screen came to life and an animated show appeared. Hayden reclined against the sofa. Lila Mae flopped over from the laundry pile and leaned against him. He removed the towel from her head.

In a few minutes, Hayden heard the clatter of a pan as it landed hard on the stovetop. Then he heard the oven door slam shut. Loudly. With a rattle. And a moment after that, Reese appeared in the doorway. "The oven's broken," she announced. Her voice was flat, lifeless. Almost sullen. Not quite angry. Not bitter, either. But dull. Emotionless. The spirit gone from it.

Hayden looked up at her. "When did that happen?"

"Just now."

"What happened to it?"

"How would I know that?" Now there was emotion in her voice. Shrill. Angry. "I ain't no damn repairman!"

Hayden moved Lila Mae to one side. "Let me see about the stove."

"Okay, Daddy. I'm hungry."

Hayden rose from the sofa and caught an exasperated look from Reese. He gestured for her to move into the kitchen and he followed her. With the flat of his hand, he felt the cooktop and found it was cold. Opened the oven door and knew immediately it was cold, without reaching inside. "Do you think the circuit breaker is blown again?"

"I don't know," Reese sighed. "But I can't keep living like this."

"Like what?"

"Like what?" Her voice was loud, and Hayden gestured for her to calm down. "Lila's sitting on the sofa."

"I don't care where she is." Reese's voice was low but angry. And she gestured with both hands as she spoke. "I can't keep living like this."

He frowned. "Like what?" A tone crept into his voice, too.

"Look around!" Reese was really loud now. "The washing machine's broken. I have to lug the clothes to your mama's house to wash them. The toilets won't flush half the time. The air conditioner in the car is broken. Now the oven won't work."

Hayden closed the oven door. "I'll get somebody to look at it."

"Somebody like who? Not Tommy. Last time he touched it he

tripped three breakers."

"I'll get somebody."

"Who you gonna get?"

"I said I'll get somebody." Hayden's voice was firm. Edgy. "Now just—"

"Just what?"

"Just calm down."

"Don't tell me to calm down! Our daughter's hungry. You're hungry. I'm hungry."

"We can go up to Bradford's and eat."

"Yippee!" Lila Mae called from the living room. "I like Bradford's."

Reese shook her head. "We can't keep—"

Hayden's cell phone rang. The sound interrupted them. He checked the number on the screen. The call was from his sister, Ramona. He didn't want to talk to her. She was three years older. Opinionated. Bossy. Usually pressuring him about something. Anything. Everything. History between them. Lot of history between them. But it was early. Even for a Saturday. Especially for a Saturday. Family calling early was a problem. Usually. He pressed the tab to answer it. "Hey," he said. "What's up?"

"Daddy's in trouble. They think it's a heart attack."

"Is he okay?"

"Just get up here."

"Is he okay? Is he—"

"Damn it, Hayden. Just get up here."

He heard someone crying in the background. "Alright," he said. "I'll there in a minute."

Hayden ended the call. Returned the phone to his pocket. "I gotta go." He kissed Reese and started toward the door. She trailed after him. "What's the matter?"

"It's Daddy."

"What's wrong?"

"She wouldn't say."

"Is it his heart again?"

Hayden pushed open the door and stepped outside. Reese went as far as the doorway and called after him. "Wait a minute. We can all go together."

He turned his head to one side and answered. "Take Lila to town for breakfast. I'll call you and let you know what I find out."

Hayden's pickup truck was parked on the driveway outside the mobile home. An old truck. A dirty truck. On a dirt driveway. With mud holes that still held water from rain the day before. Weeds dotted the front yard. Kids toys were scattered about. Reese refused to have a dog. Hayden climbed into the cab, started the engine, and turned the truck around between an oversized red and blue ball and a push toy that used to be inside, then started for the road.

Five minutes later, he arrived at his parent's house. A farmhouse. An old farmhouse. With white clapboard siding, a large porch all the way around. It sat atop a hill with lots of trees that covered it in shade. Oaks, mostly, but a few pecans. And one hickory.

An ambulance was parked near the front steps. The exterior lights were off, but the engine was running and as he came from the pickup, Hayden heard the chatter of the dispatcher from the radio. Something about a wreck on the interstate. He bounded up the steps and went inside the house.

From the living room he heard the sound of a woman crying. The same sound he heard on the phone. Now he realized it was his mother. He hurried down the hall and into his parent's bedroom. The only bedroom on the first floor. Windows faced the road. Soft morning light cast the room in gray. His father lay across the bed, on his back. Eyes closed. Mouth slightly agape. The life obviously gone from him. Hayden's mother lay atop him. Fingers in his hair. Her cheek pressed against his. Crying. Sobbing. "Not yet," she said. "Not yet. I need you a little longer."

Hayden's sister, Ramona, stood in the corner. Cheeks damp from crying. EMTs were at the foot of the bed. Solemn but not shaken. They'd seen this before. One of them noticed Hayden. Shook his hand. "I'm sorry," he said. His voice was soft. Subdued. Reverent. "We did what we could, but he was already gone by the time we got here."

Hayden's mother glanced up. Saw him. "He's dead," she said. Hayden felt emotion welling up inside him. Tears. Anger. Sadness. A sudden awareness of words never said. Meaning never shared. Love. Thanks. Respect. What could he do about it now? Nothing he could do about it now. Despair. He began to cry.

Ramona came from the corner and put her arm around his shoulder. "He loved you," she whispered. Hayden nodded in response. Buried his face in the soft spot below her collar bone. He hated being vulnerable, especially with her.

They remained like that—standing around the bed, staring, thinking, silent—but finally one of the EMTs looked over at Hayden and said, "I know this is difficult for you, but we need to move the body."

Hayden's mother lifted her head. Glanced around the room. Came from the bed. Straightened herself. Looked over at them. "Where will you take him?"

"To the hospital," an EMT explained. "They'll examine him and then the funeral home can get the body from there."

She nodded. "They'll know what to do, I suppose."

"Yes ma'am. You tell the funeral home and they'll take it from there."

She leaned down and kissed Hayden's father gently on the lips, then turned to Hayden and Ramona. "Come on, y'all. Let's get out of the way and let them do their work."

Hayden and Ramona followed her to the kitchen. "Y'all want some tea?" she asked.

A platter sat on the counter with a tin pie pan upside down atop it. Hayden lifted the tin and saw four biscuits beneath it. "Those were from last night," his mother said. "You can warm one in the microwave."

"I'll eat it cold," Hayden replied. He took a bite. His mother handed him a glass of tea. He took a drink. She made good biscuits.

His mother cut her eyes at him. "Reese didn't fix you breakfast?"

"We were just getting to it when the phone rang." He didn't

bother to tell them the whole story. Never told them all of it. Too many nuances. Too many questions. Too much to explain. They would never understand. Or accept. That was the worst part. The never accepting.

They stood in the kitchen, sipping tea. Ramona didn't want a biscuit. Hayden's mother didn't either. The sound of a zipper came from down the hall. Zipper. Body bag. Hayden gestured toward the door. "Let's sit on the back porch," he said. The others followed him outside.

The funeral was arranged for Wednesday afternoon at New Harmony Church where Hayden's parents attended. He used to go, too, but that was a long time ago and he hadn't been to church since…probably high school. For sure not since graduation. And not after he started at the mattress factory. Lila Mae wasn't baptized. His parents said it was wrong for infants. Reese's parents were Episcopalian. Or maybe Methodist. Hayden couldn't remember. They thought it would be fine to baptize Lila Mae. Maybe even required. Hayden had no opinion. He didn't know if Reese had ever been to church. Certainly not since she started seeing him.

A wake for Hayden's father was scheduled for the night before the funeral. The viewing, they called it. It was held at the church. New Harmony Church. Same place as the funeral. Ramona said it should be done the same day. The viewing, then the funeral. "Most of the people who come on Tuesday won't be back on Wednesday."

Hayden's mother cut her off with a look. A comment. A question. "Is that the way they do it in Decatur now?" She had a way of asserting herself.

"Everywhere," Ramona said dryly.

"Not here."

And that was the end of it. Wake on Tuesday. Funeral on Wednesday. Both events at the church. Those who meant something would be there. Those who meant the most would do both. Those who didn't. Well. Hayden's mother already knew who they were.

On the day of the funeral, Hayden lingered in the bathroom. Lingered in the bedroom. Lingered on the sofa. Lingered. Lingered. Reese was worried they would be late. "We need to go," she said. "We ought to be there early. Before people start arriving."

"I hate funerals," he said. "I only attend them because it's what we do. But if I had my way, we wouldn't even do them."

"You don't mean that. You're just saying that because he was your daddy."

"Is my daddy," Hayden corrected. "That hasn't changed just because he's dead." He was still feeling the weight of unspoken words. Unexpressed love. Admiration. Anger. Guilt.

"Right," Reese replied. Her tone said she knew better. It irritated him when she did that. Especially when she was right.

About thirty minutes before the service was to begin, Hayden walked with Lila Mae out to the car and placed her in the car seat on the back row. Then he and Reese got in and they started toward the church. They rode in silence until Lila Mae said, "Is Granddaddy gonna be here today?"

"Yes," Reese said. "His body will be."

"But that's not really him, right?"

"He's in heaven."

Hayden looked over at Reese as if to say, "You don't believe that."

She shrugged as if to reply, "What else can I tell her?"

"Then I could talk to him like I talk to God," Lila Mae said. And before anyone could respond, she began. "Granddaddy, it's a beautiful day down here. I wish you could come and play in the yard with me. You could push me in my wagon and Mr. Piggles could ride with us." Mr. Piggles was a stuffed animal she carried with her.

Hayden began to cry. Reese took his hand.

They arrived at the church fifteen minutes before the service was scheduled to begin. As they turned from the road, they saw the parking spaces were filled and cars were parked on the grass all the way from the fence on the right to the cemetery on the left. Mostly older cars. Well-worn. High-mileage cars. Like their own. And pickup trucks. Lots of pickups. Dirty. Unwashed. Working trucks. But to the left of the front entrance there was a gray Mercedes. A big one. Four doors. Long hood. Deep trunk. Not a speck of dust on it. Reese noticed it right away. "Whose car is that?" she asked, pointing.

Hayden shrugged. "I don't know."

"Any of your relatives have a car like that?"

"No." He gave her a sarcastic look. "Any of yours?"

"Most of my family can barely afford shoes."

An attendant from the funeral home came toward them. Noticed Hayden. Gestured for them to stop. "Drive around back," he said. "We saved you a spot."

"Okay," Hayden replied.

They continued slowly around to the back of the building. Reese said, "How did they know who we are?"

"Good at their job, I guess."

As they came around the end of the building, a second attendant waved them toward an open space next to Ramona's car. Hayden steered the car into the spot and switched off the engine. He took Lila Mae from her car seat and stood her beside the car. Reese came from the opposite side and stooped beside her. Straightened her clothes. "This is a solemn occasion," she said. "Be on your best behavior."

Lila Mae smiled. "Mama, I always b'ave."

"I know you do."

Hayden took Reese's hand in his, then held Lila Mae's with the other, and they walked around to the front steps. An usher saw them coming and opened the door. He held it for them as they went inside.

Hayden Carruth grew up on a farm outside Cullman, Alabama. A farm that previously belonged to his grandfather, Wyatt Carruth. Wyatt died. The farm passed to his son, William, whom everyone called Billy. Billy Carruth was Hayden's father.

Billy married Mary Elizabeth Raines, a girl from his class in high school. Everyone called her Libba. She was Hayden's mother.

By the time Hayden was old enough to work, the farm was five hundred acres. About half of it came from Wyatt and half had been added by Billy. They raised cows on the least tillable part. Divided the rest between hay and soybeans. Sometimes they grew corn instead of beans. And they had three chicken houses. Commercial chicken houses. Big ones. Thousands of birds. Grow off a flock, clean the house, get new chicks. Every two months. Cows had been Wyatt's idea. Chickens were Billy's.

As a boy, Hayden worked on the farm after school. Plowing the fields. Gathering hay. Tending the cows. Cleaning out chicken houses. But what he really wanted to do was sing. Country music.

Beginning in elementary school, he taught himself guitar. Played in talent shows at school. And caught the eye of a guy in town. Hubert Sholes. An old-time country music singer. Small time to the world. But big for Cullman. Sholes taught Hayden chords and combinations and techniques most people never knew about. Chord progressions. Augmentations. How to work them into a melody. Walk a tune up and down the neck of the guitar.

Sholes told stories, too. Of life on the road. Honky-tonks and bus rides and barroom brawls. The life. What a life. Hayden dreamed of it day and night. Of going to Nashville. Writing songs. Making it big.

But there wasn't much support for it from home.

"You need to think about a job," Billy said. "Maybe learn to farm better than I do. I'm doing it different from your grandfather. You can do it differently from me. Make a living right here." Honest work. Actual work.

One person who encouraged him was the school band director. Ole Miss graduate. Played in a jazz band. Back in the day. Hayden didn't care much for marching band. But the director was a music guy. Loved music. All kinds. He was glad to listen to whatever Hayden was trying to write. Grinned at the sound of it. Made Hayden think his dream wasn't crazy. That it might come true. One day. Some day. Hayden liked that. Enjoyed their meetings. Usually left singing.

That Wednesday, in his junior year of high school, Hayden came from one of those meetings with the band director. Singing the song he was trying to write. Walked up the hall. Guitar strap over his shoulder, body of the guitar against his back, the way he'd seen Johnny Cash carry his.

When he reached the side exit of the building, he pushed open the door. Still singing. And found a girl seated on the top step. Ali Martin. She was in his class. Prettiest girl, actually. Smartest, too. And unpretentious. He wouldn't have used that word. Not back then. Didn't even know that word back then. But that's how she was. Genuine. Honest. The door almost hit her as it swung open. He almost stepped on her but came up short. Caught the door. Stopped singing. She smiled. "Don't stop on my account," she said. "You sounded pretty good."

"Thanks." He felt awkward, but not embarrassed. Which was surprising. He liked it. Not being embarrassed for someone to hear him.

"Please," she insisted. "Keep going. I like the way it sounded."

He moved past her a step or two, then stopped. Glanced around. Saw no one else. Realized it was late in the day. Mr. Sparks, the janitor, would lock the building soon. He was curious. "Why are you still here?"

"A friend was supposed to give me a ride," she said. "I guess they forgot."

He grinned. "You missed the bus?"

"You know where I live."

"Yeah." It was true. He did know.

"And you know it's not far enough away for the bus to run." The school had limitations on that sort of thing. Had to be a certain distance away. The bus didn't run in the city limits. Maybe. Something like that.

"Come on," he said. "I'll give you a ride." He couldn't believe he said it. To her. The prettiest girl in class. In school. In town. Prettiest girl he'd ever seen. In his life. But he was feeling confident. Assured. And she said she liked his singing.

"I would really appreciate it." She gathered her books and purse. Effortlessly. Without a fuss. But immediately. Then followed him down the steps.

They walked over to his car. A 1967 Chevelle. Black with black interior. Chrome rims. Wider than normal tires. Slight rake in the setup—front lower than back. A little. A smidgen. Nothing gaudy. With an engine. A big engine. A powerful engine.

Ali went around to the passenger's side and got in. Hayden put his guitar in the backseat, then got in behind the steering wheel. She looked over at him. "So, you play the guitar."

"A little." He started the engine. It made that mellow rumbling sound. She seemed not to notice. "Maybe you'll play that song for me some time," she said.

"Which song?"

"The one you were singing just now. When you came out of the building."

"Sure." He put the car in gear. "Sometime."

They rode in silence through town. He turned the car onto First Avenue. Came to a stop in front of a two-story brick house. Judge Gidden's house. Built around 1900. Two-story with an attic. Which made it seem like three. It looked old, and a little tired, but the yard was mowed, and the bushes were trimmed. The Giddens had been dead a long time. Ali lived in the house with her father, Gilbert. A truck driver for Mid-South Distribution. Worked a fixed route from a warehouse in town. Still, it kept him on the road a lot. Ali stayed by herself often. They moved to Cullman the summer before Ali entered the ninth grade. Her mother was already dead when she arrived.

She looked over at him. "Maybe you could play that song now?"

"The song?"

"Yes." She gave him a playful tap on the arm. "Don't be silly. The one you were singing before."

He turned off the engine, came from the car, and took the guitar from the back seat. They stood by the rear fender as he played and sang. When he was finished, she said, "Who wrote it?"

"I did."

Her eyes opened wide. "You write songs?" He loved the look on her face. It was perfect. Everything about her was perfect. "I try to," he replied.

"You should get in the music business."

"Yeah." He grinned. Sheepishly. Almost embarrassed. "I would like to."

She nodded. Lingered beside the car. A look as if…As if hoping. For something. He wasn't sure. "Well," she said after a moment. "Thanks for the ride." She stepped up to the curb, then onto the sidewalk.

He called after her. "Listen, if you ever need a ride again, just meet me by the car. I'm usually parked in that same place every day."

"Sure." There was a note of unusual enthusiasm in her voice. "That would be great."

He wanted to say something. Many things. Everything. Can I hold your hand? Can I walk you to the door? Sit with you in the front room. Kiss you. Many times. Or one long one if you like. Instead, he said, "Okay. See you tomorrow." Then he put the guitar on the back seat, got behind the steering wheel again, and drove slowly away.

After school the next day, Ali was waiting by Hayden's car. "Did they forget you were riding with them again?" he asked.

She had a smile. A knowing look. "Something like that." He opened the door for her. Helped her inside. Drove her home. The house looked dark.

"When does your father get home?" She seemed startled by the question. He realized it at once. "I didn't mean it that way," he said. His cheeks were warm and red with embarrassment. "I just meant—"

"I know what you meant." She seemed amused by his discomfort.

Did she really know what he meant? Or was she just saying that for his benefit. "Is he on the road?"

"Yes."

Hayden gestured toward the house. "You must come home to an

empty house often."

"Too often," she replied. "But it's not bad. I get my homework done. Watch TV sometimes."

"Well," he said. "If you ever get lonely or scared or just tired of being alone, you can come over to our house and stay with us until he gets home. I can come get you or you can ride home with me from school. I have to work in the afternoons, but you can sit at the kitchen table and do your homework. Nobody will mind or bother you or anything."

"Thanks. I'll think about it." She opened the car door to get out.

He said, "How do you get to school in the morning?"

"I usually ride with a friend."

"Is that friend more reliable in the morning than in the afternoon?"

She shook her head. "Not really. I end up walking much of the time."

"Walk? That's a long way." Her house was too close for the bus to pick her up, but it was too far away for her to walk.

"It takes a while," she said, "but I leave early."

"Why don't I come by and pick you up."

"You mean, every day?"

"Yes. Every morning. A standing deal. You ride with me. Forget about whoever was supposed to pick you up before."

Her smile grew wider and she nodded. "Okay."

"Seven-fifteen sharp," he said. "I don't want to be late."

"Late? No one will be there at that hour of the morning."

There was a twinkle in his eye. "I make a stop on my way."

She frowned. "What kind of stop?"

"If you're riding with me, you'll see. It's not illegal or anything."

She seemed uncertain but finally nodded in agreement. "Okay. I'll see you in the morning."

The next morning, Hayden arrived in front of Ali's house a little before seven-fifteen. She was sitting on the porch waiting. They drove from her house to the parking lot at Bradford's Café. A farmer's cafe. Mostly pickup trucks and working men. She looked puzzled. "Why are we stopping here?"

"This is the stop I make."

"For what?"

"Breakfast. Come on." He led the way inside. Ordered a biscuit and iced tea for both of them. They sat at a table and talked. She asked more about music. He asked about her.

"I want to be a lawyer," she said.

"You'd be good at that. But I think you'd be good at anything you chose to do."

They talked about school. About home. About town. About everything. Then Hayden glanced at his watch. "Hey," he exclaimed. "It's seven-forty. We have to go." He pointed to the piece of biscuit on her plate. "Bring that in a napkin. You can finish it in the car."

They drove to school. Quickly. But without speeding. The first bell sounded as they came from the car. "We're going to be late," she said.

He glanced at her and smiled. "I don't mind. Do you?" A risky question, but not that risky.

"I could have sat at that table all day," she said. "But I thought you didn't want to be late."

"That was before we started talking." He bounded up the steps ahead of her and opened the door, then held it as she entered. "Meet me by the car after school."

"Okay," she said. And they went in separate directions to their first period classes.

That afternoon, Hayden drove Ali home. As she reached for the handle to open the car door he said, "I'll see you in the morning."

"Okay," she replied. "But no stopping for breakfast. We were too close to being late this morning."

He grinned. "Then I'll pick you up at seven."

She smiled. "Okay."

She came from the car and was about to close the door when he said, "There's a movie opening Friday. I want to see it. Will you see it with me?"

She grinned. Wider than before. "I would love to," she said.

On Friday night, Hayden and Ali went to the Ritz Theater, downtown. Watched a movie. Went to a drive-in restaurant afterward. Ate a hamburger. Drank a milkshake. Talked.

When they returned to Ali's house, Hayden walked her to the door. Through the curtains at a front window he saw Gilbert, her father, sitting inside. "I think he waited for you."

"I'm sure he did. Want to meet him?"

"Yes."

Ali led the way inside and introduced them. Gilbert didn't seem too happy that they were together. Hayden did his best to cover. "I'm sorry if I kept Ali out too late."

"No," Gilbert said. "It's okay. I just didn't know where she was."

Ali spoke up. "I didn't know you were coming back early today."

"I have a long weekend off. Don't go back until Tuesday."

Hayden, sensing the awkwardness of the moment, said goodnight. Walked to the door. Lingered a moment. His hand touching Ali's. He wanted to kiss her. Not sure he should. With her dad and all. Instead he said, "I'll see you on Monday morning."

"Okay." And she gave his hand the lightest squeeze. Was it really a squeeze? Sure it was. Wasn't it?

Hayden and Ali dated regularly and in their senior year became inseparable. Movies on Friday. Concerts on Saturday. Television at her house. Sunday dinner at his. And they talked. Of her becoming a lawyer. Of him writing music. Moving to Nashville. She, to study law. He, to write music, sell songs. Maybe perform. And they would find success. Dreams fulfilled. Visions made real. What a glorious future they would have. Together.

As might be expected, their conversation spilled over into talk. Gilbert was amused. A couple of young dreamers. Think they're in love. Starry-eyed. Blissfully ignorant of life. Billy and Libba listened in silence. Hayden knew what that meant. The look in his father's eyes. The way his mother twisted her lip on one side. His sister's exasperated expression. They were not pleased. Wanted him to stay right there. In Cullman. At home. On the farm. Working the farm. It'll be yours one day. But I like Ali. His mother avoided eye contact. Spoke in that tone of hers. A boy could do much worse, I suppose.

Billy stopped short of telling Hayden he couldn't go. Couldn't pursue his dream. Couldn't chase his vision of the future. Or the girl he loved. And Libba never quite said Ali was unacceptable. Not wanted in their house. But the message was clear. They were against it. Against Nashville. Against Ali. Against the future. Against the whole thing.

A month or two before graduation, Ali received an acceptance letter from Vanderbilt. Suddenly, talk became plans. Firm plans. Definite plans. A few weeks after that, she received a dorm assignment with a move-in date and the schedule for new-student orientation. Hayden contacted his cousin, Jeff, who lived in Nashville. Made arrangements to stay with him. Only for a month or two. Until he got settled. Found a job. A place of his own. Be there by the end of August.

A week before they were to leave, an afternoon thunderstorm chased Hayden from the hayfield where he had been working. He came to the house, poured himself a glass of tea, and sat on the back porch to cool off in the breeze while he watched the rain. He hadn't been there long when Ramona, his sister, arrived. He heard her car in the driveway. Heard her footsteps as she came through the kitchen. Knew something was on her mind. The heaviness of her step gave it away.

She pushed open the door, came onto the porch, and flounced down in a rocking chair next to him. A determined look in her eye. Yep. Hayden was right. "What is it?" he asked.

"I didn't say anything." She had a tone in her voice. Higher pitch than normal. Grating edge.

"You always have that look when you're determined to bend the world to your own ideas. So, what is it this time?"

"It's you," she blurted.

Anger wrinkled Hayden's forehead. "What did I do this time?"

She turned toward him. "You can't really be serious about running off to Nashville with that girl."

He glared at her. "That girl?"

"You know what I mean. Ali."

"She's not that girl."

"Look, I'm sure she's fine. But you have responsibilities here." She gestured with both hands while she talked. "Going off the Nashville is a crazy idea. You can't do this."

He cut his eyes at her. "Like you didn't have responsibilities when you and Pete ran off to Chattanooga?"

She slouched against the opposite side of the chair. "That was different." Her voice was lower. Sullen. A darker look on her face.

"Why?" Hayden retorted. "Why was it different? Because you're a girl and I'm a guy? Because you never had to clean the chicken houses, or bale hay, or even feed the dog? Because a different standard applies to you than to everyone else?"

She looked away. "That's not fair."

"It's more than fair. Especially when you come out here and try to tell me what to do. The only reason you could run off to marry Pete is because I was here to work. You ran off with him without telling anyone where you were going or what you were doing. And now you think that somehow gives you the privilege of coming out here and telling me that I have to trash my dreams, ditch my hopes, flush my future down the drain, and stay here so you won't feel guilty about running out on everyone."

Tears filled her eyes. "You can be so mean sometimes."

"Check yourself out first." He took a sip of tea. "You've got a lot of nerve trying to tell me how to live."

She stood, then leaned toward him. "Well I know this, they put a lot of money into this place on the belief that you would be here to run it when you grew up. And now you've finished high school and you want to skip out."

"No, no, no," Hayden retorted, waving his hands in protest. "They never consulted me about any plans they might have made. And they didn't believe I wanted to be here. They couldn't believe it because I've been telling them since I was ten years old that I wanted to be a musician."

She dismissed him with a wave of her hand. "That was just a childhood fantasy."

"To you, maybe, but not to me."

She smirked. "No one believed you."

"No one wanted to believe me," he argued. "They wanted to believe their own fantasy. Like you wanted to believe some fantasy about life with Pete. How's that working out, by the way?"

Tears ran down her cheeks. "You're impossible."

"And you're impossibly arrogant to come here and tell me how to live my life. You didn't want anyone's advice about yours. What makes you think I want your advice about mine?"

Ramona was sobbing as she snatched open the door to the kitchen and stomped her way through the house. Her heels hit the floor so hard they rattled the dishes in the cabinet. Then he heard the front door slam as she went out on the far side of the house. A moment later her car started, and she was gone.

Not long after that, Billy came out to the porch. Before he could speak, Hayden said, "Don't start on me. Ramona was here trying to tell me what to do. Since I bought my first guitar, I've been telling everyone I wanted to be a musician. I've been talking about going to Nashville for years. Nobody asked me if I wanted to work on the farm all of my life."

"I just want to make sure you've thought it through," Billy said. "Do you know how you'll—"

Hayden set his glass on the floor and stood, then started toward the steps.

Billy called after him. "I was in the middle of a sentence."

"I already told you I didn't want to hear it," Hayden shouted.

"But what about—"

"I'll figure it out for myself," Hayden shouted again. "I've been doing it that way my whole life. No reason for things to change now."

By then he was down from the porch, on his way to the barn that stood near the edge of the yard. Rain splattered against the bill of his cap. Hit the lower portion of his cheeks. Dabbled the tops of his shoulders. He walked with a determined gait but about halfway there he abruptly stopped, removed his cap, and tilted his head back, letting rain strike him full on the face. His hair quickly became wet. His shirt soaked.

The rain continued all afternoon. Hayden watched it from where he lay atop a stack of hay bales in the barn. He liked the smell. Of the rain. The barn. The hay. Organic. Damp. But not pungent. Rain falling in wind driven sheets, a constant stream of runoff from the roofline, puddling on the ground.

While he watched through the doorway, Hayden thought. Of Ali. Of moving to Nashville. Their lives. The things that lay ahead. And the thing he had realized earlier that year but refused to admit. Ignored it in his thoughts. Avoided it in conversation. All year long. Growing. Festering. And now, with their day of departure at hand, it was unavoidable.

The issue first presented itself at the beginning of the school year. His senior year. And it came as fear. Usually prompted by thoughts of another topic—all that could go wrong if he stepped out. Followed his dream. Pushed ahead. Rejection, for sure. But even more to the point, lack of ability. For all his interest in music. For all the notebooks filled with lyrics and melodies. He had never tried to sell even a single song. Never played with anyone other than Hubert Sholes. What if he wasn't as good as Hubert said? What if he wasn't any good at all? What if he didn't have it? The stuff. The ability to succeed. What if the things that meant something to him, meant nothing to anyone else?

Deeper down, though, something else bothered him even more. From the day Ali arrived at school, way back in the eighth grade, he had known she was the smartest person in the class. Not just the smartest girl, the smartest person. Perhaps the smartest in the entire school. He knew that. Everyone knew that. She must have known it, too, but it never showed. Until their senior year when she let slip that if he decided to go to college, there was always Corona State, on the opposite side of Nashville. He could always get a job, she said.

He was good at manual labor. He might have to drive a taxi to make ends meet. Or deliver pizza. What she said might have been true, but the way she said it seemed to reveal something more. Something about her opinion of his intellect. As if he wasn't as smart as she. As if he wasn't as capable as she. As if she would be carrying him. Letting him tag along. Have a ringside seat to her displays of her dazzling brilliance. As if she believed what others said. That she was prettier than the rest. Better than the rest. And could do better than tie herself to someone like him.

At first, he only wondered. Told himself, surely not. Not Ali. Maybe one of the others. One of the cheerleaders. One of the majorettes. But not her.

Slowly. Incrementally. Doubt crept in. Was she using him? Someone from home to help her make the move. Someone familiar for a date to the parties and events of the first year. Until she got herself established. Until she found her way. Were his parents' concerns valid? Was he being used?

The sound of footsteps told Hayden his father was approaching. A moment later, Billy appeared in the doorway. He came over to the stack of hay. Took a seat on a bale. Spoke without making eye contact. "What's bothering you?"

More than anything, Hayden wanted to talk. To say the things he'd been thinking. To unburden himself. To get it out. Rid himself of the angst. Instead, he took a surly tone. "Nothing, he replied.

"Doesn't sound like nothing."

"I don't want to talk."

"You need to talk."

"I don't want to."

"Tell me," Billy insisted. "What's the matter?"

"I'm scared," Hayden blurted. Tears filled his eyes. "Okay? I'm scared."

"Of what?"

"Of failing."

"Oh."

"Yeah."

"Is that all?"

"There's a little more to it."

"Like what?"

Hayden sighed. "All my life, all I ever wanted was to write music. It's all Ali and I have talked about since we started dating. Going to Nashville. And now it's here and...there's a big difference between going to law school and writing songs."

"Yeah. I suppose there is, but is that all there is to it?"

"It sounded like a great idea when we were talking about it before. But now, I'm not so sure it's the right thing to do."

"I came to this same point myself."

Hayden was caught off guard. "When?"

"After high school. I was set on leaving. Going to New York. Seeing the world. Couldn't wait to get out of here."

"So, what happened?"

"I got right up to the night before I was supposed to leave and I realized everything I really wanted was right here. Your mother. The farm. So, I unpacked my bags and went to bed. Next morning, I got up and went to work, just like usual."

"And Grandad never knew."

Billy smiled. His eyes were full. "Oh, he knew. He just didn't say anything."

"Ever?"

"Not for a long, long time."

Saturday morning came. The big day. The day they were leaving for Nashville. Hayden awakened early. The sun was just coming up. The house was still and quiet. He dressed in blue jeans and a t-shirt. Picked up his boots from beside the bed. Tiptoed down the steps. Eased the front door closed. Put on his boots at the porch step. Went out to the car and drove to town. He was the first customer at Bradford's Café. Ordered a biscuit and tea. Sat in the corner and ate alone.

About seven, he went over to Ali's house. Suitcases and boxes were everywhere. She was frantic. "I know it's a mess in here, but I've packed and repacked about ten times. I'm leaving so much behind I'm not even sure I have what I really need. But I think it will all fit in your car." She paused long enough to take a breath. "But I'm not sure yours will." She took another breath. "If we have to take some of your stuff out to get my stuff in, you can just leave it here. Daddy won't mind. He'll look after it. I'll have to come back on a weekend to get the rest of mine, too." She closed her eyes. "I need to calm down." She stood motionless a moment, then her eyes opened and she noticed Hayden wasn't dressed for a trip. Her face wrinkled into a sour expression. "You're going in that?" She pointed at his blue jeans and t-shirt, then glanced at his hair. "You haven't had a shower, either. Hayden, what's wrong?"

Hayden looked down at the floor. "I'm not going," he whispered.

Ali's shoulders sagged. Disappointment hung heavy in the room. Gilbert was standing nearby. His face became red with anger. "What do you mean you're not going?"

Ali's chin trembled. She was on the verge of tears. "How will I get to school? I have to be there for class in two days."

Gilbert spoke up. "I was counting on you, Hayden. You said you were going. That you would take her." He glanced at his watch. "I have to hit the road with the truck. I'm late now as it is."

Ali slumped onto a chair. "We had dreams," she sobbed. "Plans. We've been talking about this for years. What happened?"

Hayden knelt beside. "I...I don't know. I just can't go." He knew what happened. Time had passed. She had changed. He had changed. They had changed. While they were busy trying to graduate, racing to the end of high school, life had continued. They had continued. And they were different for it. But he couldn't tell her all of that. Not then. Not that morning.

She looked at him. Her eyes glistened. With tears. Anguish. Pleading. "What am I going to do?"

"Go to Nashville," Hayden said. He stood and took the car keys from his pocket. "Become a lawyer." He placed the keys in the palm of her hand. "The car's out front. Gassed and ready."

She looked down at the keys resting on her palm. "But it's your car." Then she looked up at him. "You love that thing."

"Not as much as I love you." He wasn't sure that was true but there was no use trying to address it then. He had promised her a ride to Nashville. Not in so many words. But in ways that were deeper than words. And a promise was a promise. "Come on," he said. "Let's get your stuff. I'll help you pack." He picked up the nearest box and started toward the door. Trying not to think about the car. Or her.

Hayden and Ali packed the car, squeezing as much as possible into every nook and cranny. When they were finished, she said goodbye to Gilbert, then Hayden walked with her to the street. They stood by the fender of the car, both of them crying. "I'll come up later," he said.

"Promise?"

"I promise." He wiped his eyes with his fingers and grinned. "I have to. You have my car."

She hit him on the shoulder. He grimaced playfully. They laughed. "You better get up there fast," she said. "I need you with me." He kissed her. They kissed again. Then she got in the car and started the engine. He stared at her through the driver's window. She looked wonderful sitting behind the wheel. Of his car. Could it be their car? Maybe he was wrong about her. Maybe going to Nashville wasn't such a bad idea after all. Maybe letting her go there alone was a big mistake. The worst mistake. Maybe he should stop her. Tell her to wait. She put the car in gear and with one last wave started up the street.

Hayden stood in front of the house and watched until the car disappeared from sight, then he turned away and walked toward home. It was a long way to the house. He wasn't worried. Someone would see him and give him a ride. Ask why he was out there on the road alone? He would dodge the question. Get to the house. His grandfather's pickup truck was in the barn. A 1974 Ford. Sitting right where Gaga left it on the day he died. He would get it out. Clean it up. Put it back in use. He liked the old truck anyway.

With every step toward home he felt lighter and lighter. Certain he'd done the right thing. Certain he was doing the right thing. And then he thought of his guitar. Standing in the corner. By his bed. And the notebooks filled with songs. That he had written. That might never be heard by anyone. Ever. And sorrow fell over him with a heavy weight.

At first, Ali came back to Cullman on weekends. Having driven the car down, she needed it to get back. He went up to see her a few times for ballgames. She came home for Christmas. They saw each other almost as much as before. They spent time together. They talked almost as much as before. Things between them seemed to be working. He was glad he let her use the car. Thought of it as the manly the thing to do.

After her first year, Ali remained in Nashville for the summer. Worked a part-time job. Attended summer school. Needed the car to get back and forth. As had become their custom, Hayden went up to see her. Met her friends. She told him of sorority life and parties. He talked about the few people from their class who were still in town. Gradually the distance between them—emotional distance, interests, events—became obvious.

During Ali's senior year at Vanderbilt, she and Hayden hardly spoke at all and in the spring her father died. Hayden went to the house to be with her. The living room was full of people, but he knew none of them. No one from their class. No one from town. And when Ali arrived, she came in a different car. A newer one. Driven by a tall, broad-shouldered guy she introduced as Mark. Handsome. Pleasant. Always at her side. She avoided eye contact with Hayden. Hardly said a word to him.

The funeral was held a few days later. Hayden attended and afterward, when Gilbert's body was in the grave and everyone was walking away, Ali came to Hayden and took him by the arm. "Listen," she began. "I know this is awkward, but it wasn't working with us anymore. We both knew that. Our lives have taken us in different directions."

"Right," he said. What else could he say?

"I'll bring the car back at the end of the year."

"Okay." He smiled. Nodded. Steeled himself against emotion. Determined to avoid a confrontation. But he had no intention of leaving the car in Nashville. No intention of letting that guy drive it. Not for a minute. He would go up one day next week. Find it on the street. Get in it. Drive it home. Let big boy take care of her transportation. Loan her his car. Ramona would help him. She would drive him up there. He hadn't talked to Ramona in…months. And he'd have to listen to her say "I told you so" all the way up there, but this was the kind of thing she went for. Payback. Gotcha. Abrupt. Rude. Effective.

A week later, Hayden was sick with the flu. He tried to work but after a day or two he was forced to stay in bed where he remained for the following week. While he lay there, staring at the ceiling, he had time to think about Ali. The car. The demise of their relationship. The situation he faced. Before long, snatching the car from the street didn't seem like such a good idea. Whatever happened to their relationship was as much his fault as hers. He could have gone up there to live, like he said. And even if he didn't travel with her that first time, he could have gone later, like he said when they were packing the car. But he didn't. And the fact that he didn't go left him feeling as much to blame as she. He would let things play out. She would bring it back at the end of the year. Despite the way things turned out, he was certain she would do that much. But which year? The calendar year or the academic?

A few months later, Christmas came. Then New Year's Day came and went. End of the calendar year. And Ali did not appear. He drove by the house in town. Walked up to the porch. Peered through the windows. Nothing but darkness inside.

That spring, Vanderbilt held its graduation. Hayden read about it in the newspaper. Even saw Ali's name. He was more certain than ever that she would turn up in town. Maybe stay for the summer. Maybe go out with him. Maybe they would get things back on track. Maybe. But May and June passed. And July. And there was no Ali. When he tried to call her, she never answered. He wrote to her, but never received a reply.

One morning that fall, on a trip into town, Hayden stopped at Bradford's Café for breakfast. A new girl was working there. New to the café, but not new to him. She had been a year or two behind him in high school. But what was her name? What was her— She saw him. They exchanged smiles. She started over to his table. Name. Name. Name. She stood across from him, coffee pot in hand. Reese Bennett.

"Hello, Reese," he said.

"Wasn't sure you'd remember my name."

"Never forget a pretty face."

"Or a silly cliché."

"That's me. How long have you been working here?"

"About a month."

Hayden frowned. "In the mornings?"

"Yes. Why?"

"I haven't seen you in here."

"You haven't been in here."

"Wow." He thought about it. "I guess not."

"Don't wait so long to come back." She turned to leave but he spoke up. "Hey, Reese." She looked back in his direction. "You want to go to a movie this weekend?"

"What makes you think I don't have plans?"

He felt embarrassed. "I'm sorry. I should have thought first, before saying anything."

She walked away. He ate in silence. But he watched her as she moved around the dining room. The curve of her hip. The movement of her top against her breasts. The playfulness of her smile. The sound of her voice.

When he finished eating, Hayden came from the table and started toward the door. Reese was nowhere in sight. He pushed open the door and went outside. Walked toward the pickup truck. Thinking of the things he had to do. The part for the tractor he needed from the store.

As he reached for the door handle on the truck, a voice called to him. He turned to see Reese coming toward him. She caught up with him. Stood close. Almost touching. "I'm sorry for what I said. I would love to go to a movie with you."

"Good," he said. "I'll pick you up around six." He didn't know where she lived. She gave him the address.

On Friday, Hayden borrowed his mother's car and went to Reese's house. She wasn't quite ready when he arrived. He sat in the front room with her mother and waited. When they finally came out to leave, Reese pointed to the car and said, "What happened to your pickup truck?"

Hayden said, "I wasn't sure you would like it."

"Actually," she said. "I was looking forward to riding in it."

"Well," he replied. "We could do that tomorrow."

She took his arm in hers. "That would be fun."

The next day was Saturday. Reese had the day off. He picked her up in the truck. They went to a spot out in the country. Walked. Talked. She remembered he liked music. "Didn't you want to be a singer?"

"Yeah."

"You were going off to Nashville with Ali Martin. That's all anyone ever talked about. What happened with that?"

He shook his head. "It didn't work out."

"Oh," she said. "I'm sorry."

"No need to be." He smiled at her. "It was for the best."

"Do you still sing?"

Hayden nodded politely. "I try to. Sometimes."

"Sing me a song."

"Okay. Maybe. One day."

"No. Now," she insisted. "Better yet. Make up a song."

"About what?"

"About anything."

"Well. Okay." He remembered she liked horses. "What about a horse?"

"And barrel racing," she added.

"Rodeo." He thought a moment. "Horses. Rodeos. Pretty

women. Probably a song in that." He paused, then said, "They have a rodeo at the fair every year. Rodeo. Fair. Women."

She laughed. "That's about a dozen country songs right there."

"Do you still ride at the fair?"

"No."

"Why not?"

"To be any good you have to get on the road. Ride as much as you can. That's what I was doing in high school. I was never around. We were always going to rodeos."

"So, what happened?"

"I graduated from high school. Barrel racing wasn't working out. Takes a lot of time and it's expensive. I did it a while, but then a few months ago I gave it up."

"Still have a horse?"

"Yes. He's at my grandparent's place."

"You'll have to show him to me."

"Sure."

By then they were back at the truck. He turned to face her. They kissed. She seemed to enjoy it. He was pleased. They kissed again. Longer this time. After a moment she leaned away and said, "You still owe me that song."

He grinned. "One day."

"No." She shook her head. "Days like one day never come. I want that song now." She pushed his arms away and propped against the front of the truck. "Let me hear it, songwriter."

Red sorrel pony
Charging from the gate
Girl on his back
Something or other with fate
Fast across the arena
Round a barrel tight
Back to the next one
Holding on tight

Hayden stopped. Shrugged his shoulders. "Spur of the moment. Best I can do."

"Add that line."

"What line?"

"That 'spur of the moment thing.' Round a barrel tight. Something about spur of the moment."

Hayden kissed her. "I'll work on it and get back to you," he said.

Hayden and Reese saw each other the next weekend. And the one after that. Then nights at her house during the week. Her parents liked him. He liked them. Finally, he took her to meet his parents. On a Sunday. At lunch. Hayden's sister, Ramona, was there. With her husband. And their children. Everyone was polite. Cordial. But Billy and Libba were reserved. Withdrawn. Unengaging.

Afterward, Hayden drove Reese home. She sat against the door on the opposite of the truck. "I don't think they like me," she said.

"Give them time," Hayden replied. "They didn't like me at first, either."

"They seemed to like you fine today."

"That's because I stopped talking about music and went to work on the farm."

"I think there's more to it than that."

"Not really. As long as I work and live like they work and live, they're fine."

"Well, I don't think they like me. And I'm not sure they ever will."

Despite Hayden's assurances, Reese's intuition proved more right than wrong. Billy and Libba were tolerant, but distant. Hayden ignored them. And suggested Reese do the same. "They've never liked what I liked. Or wanted what I wanted. They only wanted what they wanted and expected me to accept it as the wise choice."

"I bet they liked Ali Martin."

"No. They didn't."

"I don't believe you."

"They treated her the same way they're treating you."

"Why do they do that?"

"I'm not sure."

"Is that why she went to Nashville without you?"

"She didn't go without me. I sent her without me."

"What does that mean?"

"I put her in my car and told her to go."

"So, that's why it's not around."

"We were headed in different directions anyway."

"Well, I like you." She hooked her arm in his and leaned against him. "But I don't like the way they act."

A few months later, Hayden gave Reese an engagement ring. Libba cried. Billy shook his head. "I think you're making a mistake."

"Why?"

"Son, she's just not like us."

"What does that mean?"

Libba spoke up. "I heard she rides horses in the rodeo."

"Mama, have you looked out the window lately?"

Billy snapped at him. "Watch your mouth, boy."

"Seriously, Mama," Hayden continued. "Have you noticed what we do here?"

"Of course I know what we do here. We run a farm. Why are you talking to me this way?"

"Because you're talking like riding a horse at a rodeo is totally foreign to the way we live."

"I've never been to a rodeo."

"We have a rodeo every day," Hayden argued. "Right out there in the pasture."

"It's not the same."

Billy spoke up. "She's a waitress, son. Do you really want to marry a waitress?"

"I want to marry Reese."

Libba had that look. "You could have married a lawyer."

"Now wait right there." Hayden was beside himself. "Y'all were totally against that when it happened and insisted I not go through with it. Don't throw it up to me now as if you thought it was a good idea."

"We weren't against you seeing Ali," Libba said. "We just didn't want you moving off to Nashville to sing."

"And because I didn't go, the relationship with her had no chance."

"Well." Billy sighed. "Sometimes things like that are for the best."

"You two are unbelievable."

Billy scowled. "Show some respect."

"How about you show *me* some respect?"

"Well I never …" Libba's voice trailed off in a disapproving tone.

"I'm not a kid anymore," Hayden said defiantly. "I can marry anyone I choose."

Billy raised an eyebrow. "And we can dispose of this farm any way we choose, too."

Hayden was astounded. Angry. Incensed. "So that's it?" he roared. "If I marry her, I'm out with you?"

"I didn't say that," Billy retorted. "Your mother and I are just—"

"You damn sure did say it," Hayden fumed. "And you—"

Whap! Billy struck Hayden across the cheek with the back of his hand. Hayden winced in pain, then turned on his heel and went upstairs to his room. He took his clothes from the dresser and stuffed them in a suitcase. Put the rest in the pillowcases from the pillows on his bed. Grabbed two jackets and a coat from the closet, then headed downstairs.

As he passed the kitchen door, he noticed Billy and Libba were still standing by the kitchen table. He called to them. "I'll be back for the rest of my stuff tomorrow."

Billy called after him in response. "Hayden! Wait." But Hayden was past waiting. He pulled open the front door, stomped his way across the porch, down the steps, and across the yard to the pickup truck.

Hayden spent the night at a friend's house in town, then went back home the next day for the rest of his belongings. He stored most of it in a rental building. When he finished with that, he called a realtor about a lot he'd seen for sale on the highway not far from his parent's house. He knew the owner. They made a deal that evening.

Two days later, a mobile home dealer sold Hayden a double-wide trailer. The sale included a setup on the lot. By the end of the week the utilities were installed, and Hayden spent the night there on his own. The day after that, he went to the mattress factory on the west side of town and got a job. It wasn't the farm. It wasn't Nashville. It wasn't music. But it was a job that paid enough. Almost enough.

A month later, Hayden and Reese were married in a simple service in a pecan grove on her grandfather's farm. Her parents. Some friends. The minister from their church. No one from Hayden's family attended.

Not long after they were married, Reese became pregnant. Before it seemed possible, Lila Mae was born. Hayden was a father.

An attendant from the funeral home met Hayden and Reese as they came inside the church. "We saved a spot in front," he whispered. Reese went ahead. Hayden followed with Lila Mae's hand in his. The attendant led them up a side aisle to the first pew.

Hayden's mother sat on the far end, near the inside aisle. She glanced in his direction, then looked quickly away. Ramona was seated next to her, with Pete and their children. Hayden gestured for Reese to go first. He had no intention of sitting next to the others. Lila Mae went next. Hayden took a seat last. While he waited for them to scoot ahead, he scanned the crowded sanctuary. That's when he caught sight of Ali seated on the far side of the room. She was with a man who was next to her. Older. Noticeably older. Dignified. Accomplished. Ali's eyes met his. Flashed a sympathetic smile. Hayden acknowledged her with a nod.

When they were seated, Reese leaned over and whispered, "I

guess we know whose car that was."

"Probably so," he replied.

A gray casket sat in front. The lid was closed. Flowers lay on top. A picture of Billy was propped on an easel near the far end. Hayden had objected to using it. Garish. Gaudy. And his mother thought so, too. But Ramona insisted. That's how they're doing things in Decatur now. Libba relented. Hayden closed his eyes and tried not to think about it. Instead, he filled his mind with thoughts of the things that mattered to his father. Fields. Fresh-tilled soil. The smell. His father wearing work clothes and a cap.

Everyone said the minister did a good job. A fine sermon. Captured the essence of Billy Carruth. Great way to send him off. But Hayden heard little of it. When Reese nudged him, he glanced at his watch and noticed the service had taken less than an hour.

After the benediction, Hayden and Reese walked together with the family behind the casket as the pallbearers carried it from the church to the cemetery next door. Billy and Libba had grave plots reserved already. Marked out years ago with rocks to mark the corners, then with iron posts to make sure no one else got them.

An open grave was ready for Billy's casket. The dirt piled neatly to one side. A green mat over it. A tent over the grave. Chairs arranged in a row beside it. Hayden stood in back. His mother. Ramona. Reese. Sat in the chairs with Reese's children and her husband. Hayden held Lila Mae in his arms.

Ten minutes later, the graveside service ended and workmen lowered Billy into the ground. And he was gone. For a while, Hayden stood and watched as the workmen carried away the chairs that had been placed for the family. When those had been loaded onto the funeral home's truck, they removed the sheet of fake grass that covered the dirt they'd removed when digging the hole.

The irony of the moment was not lost on Hayden—a man who worked all of his life with dirt, laid to rest in the dirt. A smile came to him at the thought of it, then images from the past flashed through his mind. Just as they had during the service. Working on the farm. The conversation they had in the barn that day when it rained. And the one they had when he told them he wanted to marry Reese. That had been the last time they talked. At least, the last conversation of any consequence. After Lila Mae was born, Billy came to the house every Saturday to see her, but Hayden made sure he wasn't there and if he was, he went outside while they visited.

"That's the way it was with us," Hayden whispered. "I guess that's how—" A hand touched his. He glanced to the left and saw Reese standing next to him.

"Are you okay?" she asked.

"Yes," Hayden said bravely. "I'm fine."

"He was a good man."

"He was an asshole."

"He could be. But that's not all of who he was."

"You don't think?"

"Nah." She shook her head gently. "I saw him with Lila Mae."

"Maybe I should have been a girl."

She took her arm in his. "I'm glad you're not." She kissed his cheek. Tears came to Hayden's eyes. "Come on," she said. "Everyone else is gone."

Hayden looked past her and saw the yard around the church was empty. "Sorry," he said. "I didn't realize I had been out here that long."

Later that afternoon, when they returned home, Lila Mae took a nap. While she slept, Hayden and Reese retreated to the bedroom and forgot about everything else except each other. Naked. Warm. Intimate. Bliss. Release. Afterward, they dozed in each other's arms.

Sometime later, Hayden awakened and carefully moved aside the covers, then came from the bed. Jeans and t-shirt in one hand. Barefooted. Tiptoed down the hall. Dressed in the living room. Sat on the sofa. Thought about all that had transpired the past few days. The phone call. His father's body on the bed. His mother distant as always. Ramona trying to smooth things over. Keep the peace. Take charge. All at the same time.

Almost unconsciously, he lifted the guitar from its place at the end of the sofa, rested it on his thigh, and gently plucked the strings. Reese appeared in the doorway. "Not too loud," she whispered. "Lila Mae is asleep."

He looked up at her and smiled. "Sit here with me." Reese took a seat beside him and Hayden set the guitar aside. She ran her fingers through his hair. Pushed it from his eyes. "Are you sure you're okay?"

"I don't know."

She frowned. "What then?"

"It's just, things happen fast," he said.

"What do you mean?"

He slipped his arm in hers and rested his head on her shoulder. "I mean, one day you're talking to someone and the next day, they're gone. Really gone. And you can't get them back."

"Is that how it feels to you?"

"Yes."

"I'm sure he loved you."

Hayden felt the tears coming. "I don't know how he felt toward me."

"You don't really mean that."

"It feels like I mean it."

They were quiet a moment. Reese changed the subject. "Did you talk to Ali Martin?"

"No."

"She didn't come out there when you were standing by the grave?"

"No. Why?"

Reese shrugged. "I don't know. Just checking."

Hayden leaned closer and nibbled on her ear. "Anything else you'd like to check?"

"Didn't we already do that?"

"No reason not to again, though."

Reese smiled. "I would love to," she said softly. "But Lila Mae will be awake any time now."

"I don't think—" The rumble of an engine caught his ear. Smooth. Deep. Familiar. His eyes were alert. Reese looked over at him. "What is it?"

"I know that sound."

"What sound?"

"That car."

She listened. "That sounds close. Is it in the driveway?"

"I don't know." Hayden stood and looked out the window of the front door. Then he smiled. Glanced back at her. Nodded for her to join him at the window.

She hesitated. "What is it?"

"Come see," he said, and he pushed open the door. Started down the steps. Motioned for Reese to follow. "Look at this," he said, pointing toward the driveway.

Reese came from the sofa. He heard her footsteps behind him. Knew when she reached the front door. Heard her say, "What is—" Then she stopped short. "Oh." From the tone of her voice Hayden knew she saw. Knew she knew. Knew immediately that she felt intimidated.

Parked on the driveway was a 1967 Chevelle. *The* Chevelle. Black with black vinyl interior. Chrome rims. Wider than normal tires. Super clean paint. Slight rake on the setup. The car he'd owned when he was in high school. The one he lent to Ali for the trip to Nashville after graduation. The one he hadn't seen in…years.

Before Hayden reached the bottom step from the trailer, he heard the car's engine switch off, then the driver's door opened, and Ali Martin stepped out. Her petite body poured into a pair of jeans meant to impress. A top that fit like an oversized man's shirt. Ballet flats for shoes. She grinned at Hayden. "Better late than never." Her voice was light. Expectant. Upbeat.

Hayden walked toward her. "Yeah," he said. "I suppose it is." She seemed to expect an embrace. A greeting. But he continued past her and walked around to the opposite side of the car. Checking. Looking. Touching it lightly with the tips of his fingers. Nothing seemed out of place. No scratches. No dents.

"Sorry it took so long to get it back to you," Ali said.

Hayden was on the passenger side of the car. "Was it fun to

drive?"

"Yes." She came around the end of the car. Paused at the corner by the bumper. Seemed to strike a pose. Looked at him pensively. "It was nice having the memories with me, too." She stretched out her hand. Offered him the car keys.

Hayden took them from her and clinched his fist around them. "How will you get home?" he asked. At the moment, he didn't really care how she got home. She was with someone else now. A second or third someone else since him. She knew the car was his. She could have returned it to him a hundred times over since he'd seen her last.

"A friend drove down with me," she said. As if on command, the Mercedes they had seen at the church turned into the driveway. "This is him now." Ali pointed. "Want to meet him?"

"Sure," Hayden said. It was a reflexive answer. The cordial thing to say. He glanced in that direction. Saw the man from before. Handsome. Distinguished. Older. "Is he a friend or a friend?"

Ali shrugged. "I don't know. We haven't gotten that far."

From the look in her eye Hayden knew they would never get that far. He followed her to the Mercedes. Glanced back at Reese. Gestured for her to come. Wanted her to come. Needed her to come. She shook her head.

As he approached the Mercedes, the driver's door opened, and the man stepped out. Ali introduced them. Rick. Or Tom. Or… Hayden didn't quite catch the name. Didn't quite care, either. They talked for a moment, then Ali made her way to the passenger door. They said goodbye from across the hood.

When Ali and her friend were gone, Reese came from the trailer and met Hayden in the driveway. "Who was that in the car?"

"I don't know."

"Ali didn't tell you his name?"

"Yes. But I don't remember."

Reese seemed skeptical. "Why not?"

"I don't know. I heard her say, but I wasn't paying much attention." He pointed to the car. "She brought it back."

"About time."

"Right."

Reese walked over to the car. "He drove down here from Nashville with her?"

Hayden was puzzled. "Who?"

"That guy with Ali."

"Oh. Yes. That's what she said. A friend."

Reese seemed skeptical. "Spent the night with her?"

"I suppose," Hayden said. "I didn't ask."

Reese raised an eyebrow. "If he drove with her from Nashville. And spent the night with her. He's not just a friend."

"Maybe so." Hayden pointed to the car. "You want to go for a ride?"

Reese frowned. "A ride?"

He tapped the fender with his finger. "A ride."

She glanced at the car quickly, then shook her head. "You go."

"I want you to go with me."

"Lila Mae is still asleep. We can't leave her here alone."

"We can bring her with us."

Reese opened the door on the passenger side and sat on the front seat. Hayden got in behind the steering wheel. "Isn't this a great car?" He beamed like a proud father as he ran his hand over the dash.

Reese wrinkled her nose. "It smells like her."

"Like who?"

"Like Ali Martin."

Hayden put the key in the ignition and turned it. The engine came to life with the familiar rumble. A sound that took him back to high school. He grinned. Reese rolled her eyes. Hayden pressed the accelerator lightly. The engine ran faster. The rumble smoothed out. The grin on his face grew wider.

Reese touched the back of his hand. "I have to go inside." She came from the car and closed the door. "You can take it for a ride if you want to. I'll stay here with Lila Mae."

Hayden switched off the engine, came from the car, and closed the door. "You can use it for your car," he said.

"No, thanks."

"Why not?"

"I told you before, it smells like her."

"It's a better car than the one you're driving."

"I'm not driving that car."

"Why not?"

"Because it was her car."

"It was my car. It's always been my car."

"But she had it."

"Yeah. And now, we have it back."

"No." Reese pointed to him. "You have it back."

Monday morning, Hayden was due on the job at the mattress factory. As usual, he left the trailer early and drove to Bradford's Cafe to get a biscuit. He took the pickup and left the Chevelle behind.

As he stood in line at the pickup window, Ali arrived. An emotion hit him in the pit of his stomach. Fear? Anger? Guilt? A longing for the past? For her? No. Realization. Intrusion. Confrontation. She knew his routine. Knew he would stop there on his way to work. And if she didn't know it, she was certain enough to get out of bed and drive up there.

He acknowledged her with a nod. "Where's your friend?"

"At the house."

"He's not interested in a biscuit and tea?"

"I think he's still in bed."

When their food was ready, Ali said, "Do you have time to talk for a minute?"

Hayden checked his watch. "Yeah," he said. "But not long."

They took a seat at a table near a window. "Listen," she began. "I'm really sorry about your dad."

"Yeah. Thanks. Me too."

"I heard someone at the funeral say that you two weren't on good terms."

"It was complicated." He took a sip of tea. Changed the subject.

"Why didn't you bring the car back sooner?"

"At first, I was seeing someone and if I came back then, he would have come with me and I would have to explain it to you. And it would be a big deal and all that."

"And after that?"

"After that, he broke up with me and I didn't want to come back."

"Because you would have to explain about that."

"Yes. And then my dad died, and I had no choice but return."

"And you were with someone else."

"Yeah. And I didn't want to talk about it then, either."

"And now?"

"I didn't realize you were married until just the day before."

"So, you came back here to see me before you decided if this guy is the guy."

She had an embarrassed smile. "Something like that, I guess."

"Well, either he is, or he isn't."

"What does that mean?"

"There is nothing worse than a bad deal."

"Do you have a bad deal with Reese?"

"I have a great deal with Reese."

"How did you know she was the one?"

"Well, you made it rather clear that you weren't the one." Hayden glanced at his watch again. "I gotta go."

"Okay."

He stood. Paused a moment. Sighed. "Do you like him?"

"I suppose. Why?"

"If you like him, you can get through anything. If you don't like him, it's gonna be really tough."

"And you like Reese?"

"Yes." He grinned. "I like her a lot."

"I'm sorry about the car."

"I didn't mind you using it. I minded that when I tried to reach you, you didn't respond."

"Yeah. Well." She looked away. "I wasn't thinking too clearly then."

Hayden sighed. "It's okay, Ali. I have the car back now and that's that."

When Hayden returned home that afternoon, he found Reese sitting on the sofa, waiting for him. He knew from the look on her face that she was angry. "What's the matter?" he asked as he came through the front door.

"You know exactly what's the matter," she fumed.

"I don't have a clue."

"You were with Ali at the café this morning."

"I didn't go there to meet her."

She cut her eyes in his direction. "So, you admit you were there."

"Yes. I go there every morning."

"And you admit that she was there."

"Yes."

"And you sat with her."

"Yes. She wanted to talk. So, we talked. But I didn't invite her there. She just showed up."

"You knew she would be there."

"No. I didn't know it. She probably knew I would be there, but I didn't even think about it. I was just standing there, waiting for my biscuit and she showed up."

"You weren't thinking about her?"

"No. I wasn't."

"Then what were you thinking about? How hot she looked yesterday when she brought the car back?"

He grinned. "You're cute when you're angry."

She threw a pillow at him. "What were you thinking about?"

He took a seat on the sofa beside her. "I was thinking about selling that Chevelle."

She looked startled. "Why?"

"It's worth a lot of money," he said. "A lot to us, at least. We could get more than enough from it to buy a new washing machine. And a dryer. And get a new stove. And fix the toilets. More than enough for that."

She glared at him. "You weren't thinking about that."

"I was," he insisted. "I called a guy in Birmingham about it at lunch. He wants to come see it."

She folded her arms across her chest. "Everybody in town knows you were talking to her."

"Yeah," he replied. "They probably do. The place was full of people. They all know me. And they all know I go there every morning on the way to work. It's hardly the place to go to meet someone in secret." He nudged her. "That's how you found out."

She nudged him back. "Found out what?"

"Where I was."

She smiled. "A new washing machine would be great."

"Yes," he said. "It would. And a dryer to go with it would be even better."

She shook her head. "They won't both fit. Not enough room."

"They make stackable ones. Washer on bottom. Dryer on top."

She had a questioning look. "And you would really sell your car for a washer and dryer?"

"No." He took her hand in his. "But I would sell it for you."

They were quiet a while, then she said. "I don't want a new washer."

"You don't?"

"I don't want a dryer, either."

"What do you want?"

"I think we should use the money to go to Nashville so you can record a demo of those songs. Like you've been talking about your whole life."

"I would rather have the new washer and dryer."

"Your mother has a perfectly good one."

"We need a new stove, too."

"You can get your biscuits at the café." She leaned against him. "You've been talking about recording music all of your life. We're gonna make it happen. Who do you need to call to do that?"

"I wouldn't know where to begin."

"Hubert Sholes could tell you."

"He's pretty old now," Hayden said. "Been a long time since he was in a recording studio."

"He'll know. Let's give him a call."

"He doesn't have a phone."

Reese stood. "Then let's go find him and talk to him."

"We can't just—"

"Yes, we can." She stepped toward the hall and called in a loud voice. "Come on, Lila Mae. We're going for a ride."

Lila Mae came to the living room. Hayden was still seated on the sofa. "Come on, Daddy. Let's go for a ride."

Hayden stood. "Okay," he said. "But let's take the truck."

Other People, Other Places

A Novella

CHAPTER 1

After the party ended and everyone went home, I was too tense and excited to go to bed. The house was empty and quiet with only a few of us to clean up. Langston was there, too, in the kitchen helping with the dishes, as he always did when we had a party. But even without the noise and commotion of an hour earlier, there was no way I could get to sleep. Not then. Not after all the conversation and music and food and wine. People did that to me. People and eating and drinking and talking. Especially talking. I found so much energy in it.

The dining room table was littered with plates and silverware and napkins. There seemed to be a lot of napkins. Way more than the number of plates. And there was a bottle of Jack Daniels near where Craig had been sitting. I'm not sure how the bottle got to his end of the table. He never drank. It was there, though, and I noticed it was about half full, so I took a seat, found the glass from my place, and poured about two fingers worth from the bottle. I don't know why I did it. Something about the moment, I suppose. And curiosity. I had never tasted whiskey before.

It looked nice in that glass. The amber color catching the light from the chandelier that hung from the ceiling above the table. I turned the glass this way and that, noting how clean and pure the liquid seemed. I had already had several glasses of wine with dinner. That might have heightened my mood. Maybe. Finally, though, I touched the glass to my lips and took a sip.

The whiskey felt cool on my tongue, but it burned as it slid down my throat. "Not bad," I said to myself. But what I meant was, not as bad as I expected.

As I stared at the glass, I wondered what the next sip would feel like, then I remembered how actors in movies and television shows slammed a shot all at once. A smile came to me at the thought of it and I imagined myself in a scene from a western. Standing at the bar. Doing shots with John Wayne or Robert Duvall or Lee Marvin.

So I steeled myself with determination, took a deep breath, raised the glass to my lips once more, and gulped down the entire contents. All at once. No pause. No stopping to savor. No hesitation. I drank it all in a single swallow.

At first nothing happened, and I was disappointed. I thought there would be some great moment of insight. Some defining revelation. An occurrence. An entrance to manhood I hadn't yet found. I had been looking for it. A way to fix the father-son errors of my youth. The angst. The unfulfilled expectation. The missing validation. Whatever was necessary to find and live an authentic life. One with meaning and purpose. For which I didn't have to sell my soul. I thought perhaps swallowing a glass of whiskey in an instant might do that. I don't know why I thought that. It had been an incredible evening. With lots of wine. But when I drank the whiskey, nothing happened.

At first, I considered having another. Maybe a second shot would make a difference. Push me through. Carry me over to the other side. Maybe I would fill the glass halfway this time. Gulp it down nonstop. Might take several swallows but I was confident I could do it. Confident. Assured. After a moment to think about it, though, I decided to forgo that idea.

Instead of having a second drink, I scooted the chair back from the table and pushed myself up to stand. If I couldn't find manhood in a single gulp of whiskey, I might as well clear the rest of the dishes from the table. I could do that much.

As I reached for a plate, the top of my head exploded. I gasped for breath. My throat burst into flames. My stomach revolted. Someone's water glass sat nearby. I snatched it up and drank the contents, hoping it would help. It did, a little. But not much.

"Whoo!" I heard myself cry aloud. It was spontaneous. I don't know where the noise came from or how I forced it past the fire that burned my throat, my chest, my inner organs.

Then the room began to spin, and I dropped onto the chair. My body sagged against the back and I had the sense that I was sliding toward the floor. Melting. Oozing. Dripping. I stuck out my right foot in an effort to catch myself and, at the same time, latched onto the table with both hands. When that didn't seem to be enough, I leaned forward, rested my head on the tabletop, and closed my eyes. That only made the spinning worse and I felt like I was about to vomit, so I sat up.

Sitting up straight didn't help either but it was better than lying with my head on the table and my eyes closed, so I focused on keeping my eyes open. Holding my head upright. Forcing the contents of my stomach to remain inside. But the weight of my skull kept pulling me forward, downward, toward the table. I nodded once, caught myself. Nodded again. Then a third time. The back and forth of my head gave my stomach new problems. I focused. Caught myself, then gave up and allowed my head to proceed on its downward path toward the tabletop. It landed with a thud.

Sometime later, I came from the dining room and wandered into the front parlor. The house had two parlors, a front one and a back one, with a drawing room and dining room on the other side of the hall. We used the back parlor as an extra den and library. The front parlor was our music room. That's where the piano was and I made my way toward it in a non-deliberate fashion, drifting first to the chair near the window, then lingering at the window itself. A shelf beneath it was crammed with music books and after gazing out the window into the darkness for a few minutes I bent over and ran my finger from book to book, as if admiring the titles, before angling to the music stand in the center of the room where Langston's saxophone rested in its stand. I thought I was being coy about my intentions, but really I was feeling guilty about not helping Langston and hoping he wouldn't notice what I was doing and get mad at me before I had time to sit at the piano and play.

Moving to the music stand put me only a few feet to one side of the piano—the stand was positioned so Langston could use it with the saxophone while I played the piano—so once I was to the stand I was almost to the piano bench. It was only a step, and a step, and then I was there, seated at the keyboard.

The white keys were made of ivory—imported before the ban, if you're worried about that sort of thing—and felt smooth against the skin of my fingertips. I paused a moment to adjust my position, squaring up to the frame near the middle of the keyboard, then ran through a couple of scales, just because that's what I do before I play. Start with G. Up to A. Maybe modulate to a variant of A because it's my favorite. On to B, if I'm not already there. And up to C. Straight up, straight down with each one. Not too fast, but certainly not too slow. Except maybe for A.

After a little of that, a hymn came to mind—*Precious Lord, Take My Hand*. They played it at my grandmother's funeral—she died when I was six—and it has been stuck in my head ever since. That's why I was always singing it in school and always getting into trouble for it. Like right in the middle of a science test or when we were supposed to be reading silently. Boom! That hymn would pop into my mind and my lips would start moving before my mind had time to stop them. Some might have thought it was from a sense of religious devotion—none of my friends would have thought that, they knew me better—but the teachers might have. Some of them. Perhaps. I wasn't a religious person back then and the hymn had nothing to do with church. Only with Mamaw. That's what we called her. Grandmother was Mamaw to us. Her husband was Papaw, though he was her second husband. She never would say what happened to the first. I don't think even Mama knew.

Most of the hymnal arrangements for *Precious Lord* were too high for me but I knew the tune by heart so I found a key that was comfortable and started to play from memory, which is the way I like to play, transposing from one key to the next by the way a song feels and sounds. My fingers knew where to go. All I had to do was sing, which, as I already mentioned, came naturally to me. Especially for that song.

As my fingers moved to the second verse of the song, a noise came from behind the staircase and Elvis popped out. His hair was combed back on the sides, like he always kept it, but not with so much hair oil and wax anymore. And not so much hair, either. It was graying on the sides now, too, but in a dignified way that made him look accomplished, settled, no longer concerned with whether anyone liked him. He had a big grin, like all the other times when he showed up at the house, as if he was as glad to see me then as he was the first time, which was a long time ago, though Mama and them and no one else believed me when I said he came to the house. They still don't. Certainly not Mama. She's dead now. Mamaw believed me because she was there and saw it for herself, but they all thought Mamaw was crazy, so they didn't believe her either.

Elvis is a great singer and a wonderful entertainer, but totally predictable. If you ever attended one of his concerts or read articles about him in a magazine or saw videos of him, you might think he was spontaneous and carefree. He could be spontaneous with a group. But when it was only me and him together, he was totally predictable, and I knew what would happen next. So, without waiting for him to ask me or tell me I scooted over to one side of the piano bench. He took a seat next to me and said, "I love that song. Start it from the beginning."

Because Elvis was asking, and because I had the rest of the night to do whatever I wanted, I started the song over and Elvis began singing. Not the high, thin voice he had when he was young but the rich, mellow tone he developed later. I loved the sound of his voice, the way he began a phrase strong, forcing the sound up from somewhere below his chest, then squeezed it against the back of his throat in the middle, before letting the rest of the words out at full volume. Not actually words, like someone trying to pronounce them clearly or distinctly. More like an opera singer using his voice as an instrument to emit a musical tone. A chill ran down my spine that night at the sound of it and goosebumps appeared on my arms. They are there right now, merely from the memory of the moment.

Before we reached the refrain, Langston came from the kitchen and appeared at the parlor door. "Did you lose your place?" he asked.

Not wanting to interrupt Elvis, I responded with a shake of my head and kept playing. Langston thought he was being ignored. He didn't like being ignored. "Can't you answer me?" he asked. His voice had that insistent, demanding tone that makes me angry and usually leads to an argument, but I kept quiet and continued to play. Elvis kept singing.

Langston stood in the doorway, glaring at me the whole time. I couldn't see him but I felt him and when he put his hands on his hips in that prissy, motherly way he does sometimes, I used my kindest voice and said, "Let us get through the song."

"Us?" A frown wrinkled Langston's forehead from hairline to hairline on both sides. "Who are you calling us?" He stomped his foot as he demanded a response. I gave him one of my be-nice-to-me smiles and said, "Elvis and me." For added effect, I gestured with a nod of my head as I spoke.

Langston rolled his eyes and scoffed, "Not that again." He turned away in a huff and disappeared up the hall toward the kitchen. I kept playing. Elvis kept singing.

When we came to the end of the song, Elvis patted me on the shoulder. "Good job."

"Thanks," I replied.

"Let's do *Crying in The Chapel*." I knew Langston would be stewing really good by then. He always said, "Leave the dishes to me," but that only meant he wanted me to insist on helping. This time, though, I took him at his word. I knew he would be angry at me for it, but Elvis was there—right there—in our living room—and he wanted to sing. I never knew when he was going to pop in or how long he would stay or if he would be coming back. So, I started playing *Crying In the Chapel*. And Elvis started singing.

When we finished that song, we started another. That led to another. And then another. By the time Elvis left, the sun was coming up and I was hungry again—it had been a long time since dinner—so I walked into the kitchen to see if Langston was ready for breakfast. The dishes were done and put away. The counters wiped down and dry. But he was nowhere to be seen. "He must have gone to bed already," I mumbled to myself.

Rather than awakening Langston to see if he was hungry—we were set for a fight after all of that business the night before about Elvis and the dishes and me not helping and I was hoping to avoid all of that—I decided to take care of breakfast for myself. As quietly as I could, I lifted the latch on the back door and walked outside to the pickup truck, a five-window Chevrolet, then started toward town.

City Café on Main Street was my favorite place to eat in town. In fact, it was the only place to eat in town. Most weeks, I was in there four or five times. They all knew me—regular customers and café staff—and usually knew what I was going to eat before I asked, especially at lunch. I think they based it on the day of the week. Monday, meatloaf special. Thursday, hamburger and fries. Friday, chicken fried steak. Saturday was a tossup, depending on my mood and who was in there. And in the morning, I had a usual—two eggs over easy, toast, hash browns, sausage, and hot tea. Just about every morning.

The café had two cooks, but I only liked one of them. He worked four days each week. They were closed on Sunday. So, on Tuesdays and Wednesdays I never went near the place. The blonde waitress with a blue streak in her hair didn't work those days either and when she wasn't there the waitresses were all different. Grouchy. Glowering. Condescending. And they never smiled at my one-liners. Not that I had that many. And not that they were very good. The blonde always smiled. And sometimes she laughed. I don't know if she thought I was funny or witty or entertaining at all, but at least she had the courtesy to smile. At least she did that much. Which is why I only went there when she was there. And the cook, the good one. He worked the same days she worked.

By the time I arrived at the café, all the tables were full. It was noisy, too, with the clatter of forks and knives and spoons floating through the din of conversation. I stood at the door, watching and listening. It had been like that all of my life. Noisy. Crowded. A place of constant motion. A microcosm of the town. Everyone cliqued off with the same people they dealt with all week. Mechanics in the corner next to a table of car salesmen. They all worked at the same dealership. Farmers on the opposite side, seated at a table with the guy from the feed store. People from the courthouse and mayor's office, a short distance to one side. And the lawyers, loud and boisterous by the window. Trial lawyers, that is. The office lawyers sat near the cash register and were more subdued.

After a moment, I spotted an open stool at the counter, made my way to it, and took a seat between a delivery driver and a guy who worked at the car dealership down the street. The same dealership as the others, but he wasn't with them and I sensed from the way he positioned himself on the stool that he didn't want to be with them. And maybe they were glad for it.

Some people don't like sitting at the counter but sitting there was my favorite thing to do at the café, other than to eat. From the counter I could watch the cook—frying eggs, making hash browns, flipping hamburgers, working the toaster. He was like a machine. Or better, a one-man orchestra. Over here. Over there. Reaching. Getting. A bend of his arm. A flick of the wrist. And every time his arms moved his muscles flexed. It was an amazing thing to watch, and I couldn't keep my eyes off it. Or him.

The cook was about my age—maybe a little younger—but with

biceps that seemed as big as my thighs. They flexed as he moved his arms, pushing up against the sleeves of his shirt like a caricature from a cartoon, only these were big, pulsing lobes of real-life muscle. He had a well-defined chest, too. Noticeable from the counter. And even with the white apron draped over him. Bulky, muscular mounds that rose and sank with each move of his arms. He was a weightlifter, I think. He looked like a weightlifter, though I didn't know if that was true. We never talked but I heard his voice when he responded sometimes to the waiters when they called out an order to him.

Waitresses at the café always shouted their orders to the cook even though they wrote them on a ticket from an order pad and stuck the tickets on the carousel—a shiny stainless-steel contraption with the spin-around thing that sat on the pass-through. The cook could spin it around and read the tickets if he wanted to, though I never saw him do it. He cooked everything from memory and without a mix up, too. At least, I never knew of a mix up. He might have cooked everything wrong and no one complained and so I only thought he always got it right. Maybe. No one ever complained about anything at the café…except for that guy from the paint store. He complained about everything. "Coffee's cold. Coffee's too hot. Eggs aren't done enough. Eggs are too done." And the toast. No one ever browned the toast right enough to stop him from complaining about it.

Not long after I took a seat at the counter the guy from the dealership, who was seated to my right, finished breakfast and left. That meant there was an open stool beside me, and I began to wonder who might show up to take it. Would I know them? Would they want to talk? What would their voice sound like? What would they smell like? More to the point, what would their breath smell like? Not everyone remembered to brush their teeth in the morning and those who didn't—wow—it could be really bad.

Just then a waitress set a cup in front of me and placed a teabag on a saucer next to it. She turned away without saying a word, then came back with an urn of hot water. "You having a usual?" She spoke without making eye contact and in a tone that seemed to assume the answer.

"Yes," I replied. "I think I will."

She scribbled something on her order pad, then turned her head to one side and, in a voice that was way too loud for that early in the morning, shouted back at the cook. "Two eggs over easy, hash browns, toast, with a side of sausage!"

The cook shouted back. "Link or patty?"

"Patty!"

The waitress didn't bother to check with me first but shouted a response to the cook and kept moving. She was the older one with hair dyed deep red. Deep red. Like, so red it was redder than red. I didn't mind her, or her hair, but she wasn't the blonde with the blue streak. No. This one was all business. No smiles.

By the time my food arrived, the delivery driver who'd been seated to my left got up from the stool and started toward the cash register. No one paid the waitresses at City Café. Everyone paid the gray-haired lady at the counter by the front door. She was older than my mother would have been and sometimes she looked like she needed to be somewhere else, but she was there every day, early and late. Checking the tickets. Taking the money. She'd been there all my life but I don't think she ever said anything to me other than, "That'll be seven ninety-five," which was always the price no matter what I ordered or what day it was. But I wasn't ready to pay yet. I still had to eat.

As gently as I could, I slipped my fork under the eggs and moved them onto the toast. First one egg, then the other. When they were in place, I cut off a bite-size piece and placed it in my mouth. Yellow liquid flowed from the yolk, so I pushed some of the hash browns into it to soak it up.

Before I took a second bite, a man appeared beside me and took a seat on the stool where the delivery driver had been. He was an old guy—about my father's age—and ran the hardware business that was down by the Baptist Church. I never went there. We always used the one by the Episcopal Church that was run by my uncle. Even after my uncle died and his children sold the business to a guy who moved down here from Michigan, we still took all our hardware trade to that store.

As he got comfortable on the stool, the guy from the Baptist hardware store glanced in my direction. "You been up all night?"

"Yeah," I replied.

"Elvis again?"

I didn't know why he was asking me about Elvis, or how he even knew that Elvis came to my house sometimes. In all the time I'd been coming to the cafe—which was all of my life—he and I hadn't had more than three conversations. Four at the most.

"Yeah," I said, in a tone I thought indicated I wasn't interested in talking.

"I liked Elvis," he continued. "Had a nice voice. But I thought he could have chosen better songs."

"What do you mean?" Before, when he first spoke to me, I hadn't been interested in talking to him and wanted him to order, eat, and leave like the guy who sat there ahead of him. But after he made that comment about Elvis not recording good material, I was feeling the need to say something.

"You know," the man said. "Songs that actually had some meaning. That actually had something to say."

"I think they say something."

"But about what?" He said it as if he'd actually thought about the topic. "Walking through the rain to find some woman who left him? What's that? Nobody does that."

"You mean, *Kentucky Rain?*"

"Yeah." He shrugged. "What's that song about?"

"About a man, walking through the rain—"

"I know that," he said, cutting me off. "But it bears no relationship to reality."

I felt my forehead wrinkle in a frown. "What do you mean?"

"I mean, when's the last time you heard about someone walking from town to town, searching for a woman?"

He had a point, but I wasn't conceding it. "Elvis saw himself as a troubadour."

Now a frown wrinkled his forehead. "A what?"

"He liked ballads," I explained. "Songs that told a story."

"Even if they made no sense?"

"It makes sense."

"Not much."

"You remembered it."

"Yeah."

"And I bet you remember most of the words to that song, too."

"Maybe."

I gave it a try. "Seven lonely days …"

"And a dozen towns ago."

"I reached out one night …"

"And you were gone."

"See." I smiled over at him. "You remember."

"But it still doesn't change the fact that the song bears no relationship to reality."

I changed the topic. "Fly me to the moon. Let me play among the stars."

"Yeah." The guy nodded. "But that's a metaphor."

I gave him a look. "So, you cut Frank Sinatra some slack, but not Elvis?"

"I'm just saying. The songs could have been better."

That was true. Some of Elvis' songs were rather thin on message and meaning. But he had talent. He took a song like *Blue Christmas*—which has only two stanzas and a little bit of a bridge—and turned it into a standard that's played a zillion times every year from November to December. He made something out of it by what he brought to the song. He made the song. And that was true about many of the songs he recorded. The songs didn't make him. He made the songs.

By then I was finished with breakfast, so I said goodbye to the man seated beside me, paid the lady at the door, and drove back to the house. When I arrived, Langston still was in bed and I was tired, so I went to bed, too. I was asleep almost before my head hit the pillow.

CHAPTER 2

Sometime later, I was awakened by the sound of a bell ringing in the distance. Faintly at first, then louder and louder. It seemed to be part of a dream, but my eyes refused to open. When I finally succeeded in prying them apart, I saw that I was lying in bed and the noise was coming from somewhere below me. A doorbell. Maybe. From the floor beneath me, perhaps.

Before I could gather myself to get out of bed, the sound of the bell stopped and I lay on my side, staring at a wall that was only a few feet away. It was made of plaster and painted stark white. I remembered that the walls in the house with Langston were made of plaster, but I didn't remember them being so white. So stark. Or so close. Not in my room. I couldn't remember the color in Langston's room. But did we have a doorbell?

Still groggy from sleep, I rolled onto my back, then propped on my elbows for a better view of the room. A dresser stood at the far end of the room, positioned evenly beneath a row of windows that were wide and tall and beautiful. The glass was clean and clear and seemed to offer a commanding view of something. Through them I saw there were trees outside and behind the trees, slightly farther in the distance, a brick building. The sound of traffic filtered through the walls and I surmised a city street lay beneath my field of vision, perhaps. But where was I? And how did I get here?

To the left of the bed were more windows, equally as tall and wide and beautiful as the ones near the dresser. Broad shafts of sunlight streamed through them, falling in great swaths across the floor, over the end of the bed, and extending up the opposite wall, before bending onto the ceiling and coming to an end near a black fan that spun lazily overhead. I was in a bedroom. Lying atop a wonderfully comfortable bed. Bathed in beautiful light that shown through gorgeous windows. But it wasn't the house where I'd been with Langston. Nor was it any house I'd ever lived in or visited before.

From down below, the doorbell rang again. This time, the tones came quicker and continued incessantly, ringing over and over. One behind the other with a hint of insistence. A note of urgency. Or was it merely impatience?

Frustrated by the interruption and disoriented by the unfamiliar surroundings, I threw aside the covers and swung my legs toward the side of the bed. "Okay. Okay," I shouted. "I'm coming." My feet hit the floor with a thud as I hauled myself out and stumbled toward the door.

Outside the room was a hallway with hardwood floors and the same white walls. To the left, a staircase went in both directions. One led up to the floor above. Another led down to the floor below. The doorbell still was ringing from below, so I made my way in that direction, moving quickly but with a jaunty, deliberate gait.

At the bottom of the steps, I came to a stop opposite what appeared to be the front door. It had a window in the upper half with glass as clear and beautiful as the windows in the bedroom. Through it I saw a mailman standing on the stoop outside. He looked familiar. James or Bobby or…something like that, but I couldn't remember how I knew even that much about him.

Behind the mailman, brick steps led down to a sidewalk and past the sidewalk was a tree-lined street through a neighborhood of townhouses. Brownstones, actually. A name taken from the color of the sandstone used for the exterior surface. It all seemed strange and confusing—no rambling house with a main hall and parlors on either side, no piano near the staircase, no field across the road—and no road but a city street.

The urge to sort it out at once was all but overwhelming. I wanted to drop on the floor and lie there with my eyes closed, thinking of nothing, but there wasn't time for that right then. The mailman had

an impatient expression and gestured for me to open the door, which
I did.

"You gotta sign for this," he said. He handed me a scanner and
pointed to the screen. "Sign right there. Same as before." He continued to talk while I took the stylus and tried to remember my name.
"I knew you wanted it," he said. "And I knew you were here so that's
why I didn't give up on the doorbell." He smiled nervously. "Hope it
wasn't too much of an interruption."

A city bus rumbled past, belching black smoke from the exhaust.
The acrid smell of diesel fumes wafted toward us and stung my nose,
causing me to glance momentarily in that direction.

"Nah," I grumbled, still trying to remember my name. "I appreciate the effort." The first response came from frustration. The second was automatic and I had no idea why I said it.

"It's just, if I take it back," he continued, "they'll make me return
it. That's the rule. At least at this station. Deliver it or send it back."

Name. Name. Name. I struggled to remember and stole a glance
at the letter in his hand. It was addressed to Taylor Jones. A sense of
relief swept over me.

Taylor. That was my name.

When I was born, my father wanted to name me after his grandfather—his mother's mother—whose name was Monk Ewing.
Mama objected. "We're not naming him Monk." She wanted to
name me Taylor, after her brother. Daddy, who disliked her brother
immensely, objected but Mama insisted. Daddy held his ground
but when the nurse came around to collect the information for the
birth certificate, she sided with Mama. "It's the law," the nurse said.
"Mothers name their children."

Mama relented a little, though, and added Ewing as my middle name. Taylor Ewing Jones. When I was a child, people called
me Taylor, but my father persisted in calling me Monk. In the sixth
grade, a friend overheard him and after that, much to my mother's
dismay, I became forever Monk to any and all who knew me then.

Using the stylus, I scribbled my name on the mailman's scanner,
then handed it back to him. The machine beeped as he gave me a

letter, along with a stack of mail he'd been holding. "Thanks," I said as I took it from him.

By then, the smell of diesel from the bus had subsided and I caught the faint aroma of the mailman's sweat mixed with the scent of his freshly laundered uniform. "No problem," he said. "Just doing my job. And again, sorry to wake you up."

This time, I managed a smile. "You can wake me any time you have something. I don't mind. Just took me a minute to remember where I was." That was a lie. I remembered my name was Taylor, but I still did not know where I was.

The mailman smiled and started down the steps toward the street. I pushed the door closed and turned aside, too, then stood there in the hallway, thinking. "Taylor," I whispered. "My name is Taylor Jones." A glance at the mail told me I lived on 114th Street. A second glance told me the city. "I live in New York City."

Suddenly everything came rushing back and my eyes opened wide. "I teach creative writing at Columbia University." Panic seized me. I had a class to meet. "What time is it?" I hurried past the staircase to the kitchen and checked the time on the microwave. It was a little after ten. I was late and started back toward the hall, then came to a halt after only a few steps.

"What day is it?" My classes didn't meet every day. I needed a calendar. A date book. Something that would indicate....

The cell phone was upstairs on the table by the bed. It would have the date and day on the screen. I dashed up the steps, snatched the phone from the nightstand, and checked the screen.

"Monday," I said aloud. My shoulders sagged in relief and I sank to a sitting position on the edge of the bed. Monday was a free day. My classes were on Tuesdays and Thursdays. And they were at one in the afternoon, not ten in the morning. Ten was the previous semester. I'd lobbied heavily with the department to get out of morning classes. Afternoons were much better for me.

As I sat on the bed, my mind returned again to events at the house with Langston. The guests who'd come to dinner. Elvis, who showed up unannounced after everyone was gone. The people at the café in town. And even Langston. A smile turned up the corners of my mouth. Was he my housemate? My partner? I shook my head and sighed. "It was only a dream." But it seemed more real than the bed I sat on or talking to the mailman.

And the piano. Wow.

The smile on my face grew into a broad grin. I had always wanted to play the piano and I had read many books about it but sitting at the keyboard and making the right notes sound at the right time…. That was something I had never done, though I knew the tunes I enjoyed most. Sinatra. Coltrane. Brubeck. But I could never play. Only listen.

After a while, I got up from the edge of the bed, wandered into the bathroom, and took a shower, then dressed and prepared to leave for campus. It was only a few blocks away.

Even though I had no classes that day I was expected to appear in my office, in case a student wanted help. As I came from the house and started up the sidewalk, I remembered I had one appointment that afternoon. A girl. I never was comfortable alone in the office with female students. Too much at odds. Too much at cross-purposes. Too much could go wrong.

As I walked up the street toward the school, my mind returned again to the night before and my memory replayed scenes from the dream. Elvis, the piano, and the sound of his voice. The café and the people who were there—the man from the dealership, the driver from the delivery service. And the man from the hardware store. I knew him. I remembered the day he closed on the purchase of it from my uncle's estate. I was there when my cousins handed him the keys. I knew him. Didn't I? And Langston, my housemate…I think that's what he was…. Maybe. It was all so real. So vivid. So… so much like life. My life. Reality. Not a dream. Not then. Not when I was…living it. But now—

A dream. I never dreamed.

Not much.

Some of my friends had dreams every night and many of them repeated the same dream, night after night. A few had dreams with continuing characters. People who appeared in one dream, then re-appeared later in another. Pete, a guy I knew from a club in the Village, had a butcher from his childhood who appeared in a dream almost every month. And a guy I knew from the coffee shop down the street told me his first-grade teacher showed up in dreams every few days dressed in leather and in a weird role he tried to explain but I stopped him. None of them, though, ever had a dream one night, then returned the next night to finish the story. Some awakened in the night in the midst of a dream, then went back to sleep that same night and finished it. None had a dream one night, then came back the next night to continue it from where they left off when they awakened.

All of that meant, the dream I had with Langston and Elvis and the café, was all there was to that story. And all there would ever be. I would never see any of those people again. Ever.

A sense of loneliness swept over me at the thought of never seeing them again. A heavy sadness that sank against me, pressing down on my shoulders with a great weight. Making the process of walking, of simply putting one foot ahead of the other, seem like a laborious task. The weight of it. The heaviness of it. Was too much for one to bear and yet I bore it, trudging along with great effort in the direction of the building where my office was located.

As I continued, the thought occurred to me that, having existed only in a dream, the people I'd seen at the café didn't exist at all. Not really. And the loneliness ran even deeper still at the realization that they never existed. Not in reality. Only in my mind. Only in my dreams. Only in dreams that might never return. And yet, the notion that I knew them was inescapably real to me. So real that even then, after waking and greeting the mailman and remembering who I was, even then, I had moments when I wondered which was really real—the dream, or this, the streets and buildings around me. Was I really in New York, and dreaming of somewhere else? Or, somewhere else and dreaming of New York?

❖ ❖ ❖

Eventually, I reached the office and settled into the chair at my desk. As I was getting comfortable, there was a knock at the door. I responded and when the door opened, I saw the visitor was the student from my class who had made an appointment. Many of them didn't. Some didn't. I preferred the ones who did.

The student's name was Emily something—I could never remember her last name. A graduate student from Schenectady. Her father was a doctor. Her mother was a violinist who once gave lessons but now only gardened and kept an eye on her husband, who seemed to be getting restless in midlife. Several of the mother's students became professional musicians. One or two were members of the New York Philharmonic. Emily had a brother who was a student at Stanford where he studied physics. But for all of that, I couldn't remember their last name.

Emily had come to the office that day to talk about a piece of short fiction she was attempting to write. This was now the second or third time we'd met to discuss it, and things hadn't moved along much from the first session. She hoped her work would be published in one of the major literary magazines and advance her efforts to establish a career as a writer. I hoped it would be successful, too, but we had no leverage for a story like the one she was attempting to write and, from my experience, most of those magazines only published work from people they knew, or people who knew people they knew. I knew some people. And I was a known person. So, technically, we had leverage, though in a slightly different direction— my fiction wasn't like hers—but I didn't tell her that. Her writing wasn't that good. It might have been. Or, perhaps, could have been. Though not in its present form. It lacked that certain element of… honesty. More to the point, it lacked authenticity. It left me feeling she had something to say, that she wanted to say, but she was trying to say it without really saying. The piece needed a lot of work but something was blocking her from getting to the point of whatever it was she wanted to say and I'd been trying to get her to see that, but with little success.

As the office door opened and Emily entered, I was met with an overwhelming sense of tiredness. The weight of it pressed against me in every way—physically, mentally, emotionally—and I wanted to slide from my chair, stretch out my full length on the floor, and go to sleep.

Thankfully, Emily had questions—lots of questions—that filled up the time and made my distraction unnoticeable. I wasn't sure I had answers but that didn't matter. She started talking before she took a seat and talked nonstop the entire time, answering most of her own questions before I could respond. It was a strange conversation. Not really a conversation. More like an unloading. A disgorgement. And not merely an unloading of words but of energy and emotion that seemed to well up from somewhere deep inside her soul. I mostly nodded my head to acknowledge her presence while she kept talking. And talking.

By the time Emily finished I was ready for her to go, but from the way she looked at me I wondered if she wanted something more from the visit. School policy was clear about that sort of thing, as was my own policy. And besides, she was much too young for me—I think. I could have misunderstood the moment entirely about what she wanted, but I was certain there was something on her mind. Something she wanted to say but was unable to bring herself to say it, which was the fundamental problem with her writing, too. I made a run at getting her to talk, but she dodged my questions and finally I maneuvered the conversation to a conclusion, then rose from my chair and came around the end of the desk. She stood, too, and I ushered her to the door with a firm commitment to read her work and mark it yet one more time.

As I pushed the door closed behind her, I felt my stomach growl and realized I hadn't eaten lunch. Or breakfast. Eating in a dream didn't count—not to my stomach—and a check of my watch told me it was almost two in the afternoon. A little late for lunch by my regular schedule but I had a late start that day. And my stomach didn't care what time it was. It wanted to eat. So, I grabbed my sweater from the coat rack, came from the office, and made my way to the stairs.

When I reached the bottom floor, I stepped outside and started up the street toward Tom's Restaurant. It was located at the corner of Broadway at 112th Street, not far from the office. In only a few minutes, I arrived and went inside where I was greeted by the smiles of the waitstaff and the scent of grilled onions.

One of my uncles operated a restaurant back in the day, and he told me once that the first thing he did each morning was chop up an onion and dump it a cast iron skillet sizzling with hot grease. "The smell of frying onions makes people hungry," he explained. I thought of him every time I encountered that smell, including the moment I entered Tom's that afternoon.

Booths stood along the front wall where windows overlooked the sidewalk. Sometimes I sat there and watched the people out-side as they passed by, imagining where they had been, where they were going, and what they might be thinking. That day, however, I found myself drawn to the counter on the opposite side of the dining room and I started in that direction. Before I had taken three steps, I remembered the café from the dream and how I had been drawn toward the counter there, too—as if I was being compelled by some inner force to make that same choice.

At first, I was put off by that notion and wondered if I should resist the urge to sit there, merely because the desire of that moment coincided with the desire from the dream. Very quickly, though, I saw it was a ridiculous dilemma and rather than argue with myself over the memory, I followed my initial instinct and took a seat on a stool at the counter.

As I scooched into place on a stool, a waiter appeared. A young guy. A student at the university, perhaps. He looked familiar. "Hello, Professor Jones." He smiled at me and spoke with a friendly voice. "What could I get for you? Coffee and pie?"

I shook my head. "I think I'll have breakfast."

The waiter nodded approvingly. "Your usual?"

Usual. That word hit me hard. Like right out of the dream. "Yeah," I said slowly, wondering what that might mean. "A usual."

He cocked his head to one side, as if thinking, and said, "Two eggs. Two pancakes. And two sausage patties?"

"Yes," I replied. He was right. That was the breakfast I usually ordered.

"And ..." the waiter continued tentatively. "Hot tea."

"Right again," I said.

The waiter moved away and when he was gone, I glanced around, curious to see what else I might find that appeared similar to the things I had seen and experienced in the dream. By then, the earlier quandary of whether I was dreaming or awake had faded and I felt as confident in the surroundings of that moment as I had in the moment of the dream. Confident. Sure. Convinced the moment was the real one. What I noticed at first were not the similarities with the dream but the differences.

Unlike the café of the dream, the space and objects behind the counter at Tom's were tightly configured. Which is to say, it was cramped and...a bit cluttered. There was a pass-through that opened into the kitchen, but this one was smaller than the one in my dream. Not wide enough or deep enough for me to watch the cook as he prepared the food, but I had seen the afternoon cook in Tom's many times before anyway. He was an older guy. Heavier and softer. Nothing like the buff cook at the café. And the pass-through wasn't really used for passing anything, except sometimes plates and cups for the counter service.

In a few minutes, the waiter returned with a cup and saucer along with a small tea pot filled with hot water. He set them on the counter in front of me, then lifted the lid of the pot and placed a teabag inside. "I'll let you pour your own," he said.

"I can handle it," I replied, but he'd already moved up the counter to wait on someone else and was well beyond the range of my voice.

Steeping the teabag didn't take long and in no time at all I had filled my cup, sweetened it with sugar, and began sipping it gently. Before I'd swallowed much at all, the waiter came back with my food.

While I ate, a deliveryman entered with an oversized envelope.

There was a flurry of activity near the front with this one asking that one as if they were looking for something or someone, then the driver waited alone by the door while someone rushed off in the direction of the hallway that led to the office. When no one came immediately, the driver took a seat in a chair near the window by the door. The envelope rested on his lap while he sorted through items on his phone.

Presently, an older woman emerged from the hallway and the deliveryman stood as she approached. He seemed to recognize her and offered a stylus for her to sign on his remote device, much like the one the postman had given me earlier that morning. She signed for the envelope and took it from him, then turned toward the counter, briefly facing in my direction. At the sight of her, my heart skipped a beat. She looked exactly like the woman who ran the cash register at the café in the dream.

After the driver was gone, the woman opened the envelope and removed the contents, a framed photograph, which she held for those around her to admire. They gathered closer, pointing and commenting and smiling, speaking among themselves in low, almost reverential, voices. I was too far away to hear what they said, but from the look on their faces they seemed pleased to see it. Satisfied. Relieved, actually. As if they'd been waiting for its arrival and worried that it might not make it, but there it was at last and now everything was suddenly right again.

Finally, the woman laid the photograph gently on its back in an open spot on the counter near the register. "Leave it there for now," she said. "Let everybody have a good look at it. We'll hang it somewhere later." Then she disappeared down the hall toward the office.

The cash register was at the end of the counter, halfway down from where I was seated and when I finished eating, I walked down there to pay. The photograph was lying where the woman left it and I saw that it was a picture of the café's staff. As my eyes moved slowly from face to face, I was overwhelmed by the strangest emotion I'd ever felt. As if something was pulling at me away from myself. Loosening me from my internal sense of being. Drawing me from my body, from my mind, from my soul, from all that it meant to be me.

All of the people from my dream were right there in the photograph. The buff morning cook with the muscles that rippled when he flexed his arms. The waitress with a shock of blue in her hair. The one with red hair that was redder than red. They all were right there in the framed photograph that arrived from the delivery man. Right there in Tom's Restaurant—not in the City Café in the town from my dream, but in New York. Hardly six blocks from my office at Columbia University.

The waiter who helped me seemed to notice my confusion and through the turmoil in my mind I heard him say, "Are you okay?" That's when I realized I was gripping the edge of the counter with both hands. My knuckles were white, and the muscles of my arms were tense. I released my grip on the counter, lifted one hand, and pointed to the woman in the photograph who had a blue streak in her hair. "Who is that?" I asked.

"That's Jennifer," the waiter replied. "Jennifer Graham." His voice sounded sad and when I looked up at him there was sadness in his eyes, too. "Do you remember her?" he asked.

The question hit me hard and I started to explain, then thought better of it. No one would believe that, even though I had never seen her before, I dreamed about her the previous night. "What happened to her?" I asked instead.

The sadness in his eyes deepened. "She died," he said softly.

"What happened to her?"

"She was stabbed to death by the ex-girlfriend of an old boyfriend."

The comment struck me as ironically humorous, but I suppressed the urge to smile. "An ex-girlfriend of an old boyfriend," I repeated.

"Right."

"An ex-boyfriend's ex-girlfriend?"

The waiter smiled and his mood seemed to change. "It sounds better when you say it that way."

"So, what happened?"

"She went home to visit her parents. Saw an ex-boyfriend. From what I heard it wasn't a romantic encounter or anything. They just ran into each other at the store."

"And the guy had an ex-girlfriend."

"I think the guy had recently broken up with his girlfriend and the girlfriend didn't take it very well. She was really mad about it. Somebody told her they'd seen him talking to Jennifer. So, Jennifer was staying at her parent's house and the doorbell rang. She answered it and the ex-girlfriend was there. Stabbed her six times."

My eyes were wide. "The ex-girlfriend stabbed Jennifer?"

"Yes." He nodded his head. "It was awful. She bled out right there on the steps."

"What happened to the girlfriend?"

"Ex-girlfriend," he corrected.

"Yeah. What happened to her?"

"They caught her. From the reports we heard, everyone knew who she was. They all knew each other. Jennifer knew her, too, I think. And she wasn't the first person the girl had attacked."

"But they arrested her?"

"Yeah. I think she's in prison now."

"Where did this happen?"

"Texas."

There was much I could have said about that, but I kept it to myself and asked, "What town?"

"Giddings, I think." He frowned. "Is that a place?"

"Yes," I replied. "Giddings, Texas. It's northwest of Houston."

Giddings wasn't far from Round Top, the town where I grew up. I had relatives who lived in Giddings. He was a doctor. And as I stared at that picture, thinking about Jennifer the waitress from Tom's, I remembered that Giddings had a café like the one I dreamed about. We went there a few times when I was younger—my uncle, my father, some of the cousins. My cousins still lived there and I wondered how much they might know about this.

I pointed to the muscular cook in the photograph. He really was good looking, better than the guy in the dream but still, it seemed uncanny. "What about him? Does he work here?"

"That's Steve. He's the morning cook. Do you know him?"

I ignored the question and pointed to a man in the background of the photo. He was seated at the counter but visible between the cook and the person standing next to him. "He works for an auto dealer?"

The waiter nodded. "Down the street. I don't remember his name. Do you know him?"

Again, I ignored his question and pointed to another man in the background. "He runs a hardware store." It was a statement, not a question, and the words sounded odd. Hardware store. In Manhattan. No one thinks of hardware stores when they think of the city. Bars. Shows. Broadway. Those things come to mind, not hardware stores, but there was Garcia's on 109th Street. And there was another one on Columbus Avenue.

The older lady had come from the office again and was standing behind me. I didn't see her. "That's Bob Swan," she said.

I glanced in her direction. "Do you know him?"

"Yes," she replied. "He's been coming in here for a long time. Has breakfast with us every morning." She pointed to the picture. "All of the people in this photograph work the morning shift." The implication was that I didn't come there in the mornings, but that wasn't true. I came there enough that the waiter who helped me knew what I usually ordered without being told. But I let it slide.

"Worked," someone corrected.

"Right. Worked," she acknowledged. "Jennifer is dead now, but they already told you that."

I gestured to the picture. "And all of the people in the background are morning customers?"

"Yes," she said. The photograph still lay on the counter but as she spoke, she reached over me and picked it up, then turned to someone and said, "Let's find somewhere to hang this." I had the sense she didn't care for my questions.

After paying, I went outside and stood on the sidewalk a few feet beyond the door, thinking about what to do next. It was late in the afternoon—later than I had planned on coming from the café—but not late enough to simply call it a day and walk home. Which posed a dilemma. Walk back to the office and sit there a while—classes would end for the day in less than two hours—or find something else work-related to do. A dilemma.

Finally, a sense of duty won out and I started on my way back to the office, but before I reached the next corner, someone tapped me on the shoulder from behind. In Round Top, Texas, a tap on the shoulder like that wouldn't have been a problem—people did it all the time, but back there we knew everyone, and everyone knew us. In New York, more often than not, a tap on the shoulder meant trouble. The kind of trouble no one wanted. So, I hesitated at the touch and felt a sense of panic over what to do, then I caught sight of someone from the corner of my eye. The waiter who had helped me at the café. Relief swept over me.

"Hey," he said. "I just wanted to say, don't take it personal."

I knew immediately what he meant. "She really didn't care for my questions, did she?"

"She's like that about us," he said. "You know. Protective."

"Us?"

"The people who work for her."

"What's there to protect?"

"We get all kinds in there. And Jennifer was…special to her. To all of us."

"How so?" I had the impression that he liked her. As in, he really liked her. But I chose not to mention it.

"I don't know." He shrugged. "It's hard to explain." It wasn't difficult for me to explain. Boy meets girl. Boy likes girl. Boy senses girl likes him back. But I kept that to myself and let him continue. "She came here from Texas to make it big. Wanted to be an actor, I think. Or maybe a dancer. I can't remember which. Started working at the restaurant to pay the bills. At first, she went on auditions and everything, like what you read about in the stories, but after a while she just worked."

"The city was bigger than her dream?"

"It wasn't a sad thing for her, I don't think. Not like she was giving up. She just liked working with us more than what she came here to do. That's why she was like that with you this morning. She wasn't feeling mean toward you. Just protective about Jennifer."

"Even though she's dead."

"Well." He shrugged again. He did that a lot. I think it was a nervous response. "I guess now she's protective of the memory." As he turned away and started back toward the café, he added, "Just wanted you to understand." I watched him until he reached the door and paused as he opened it, then glanced back at me and waved before disappearing inside.

Something about the conversation seemed odd. Phrases from what the waiter said began playing in my head. She. And she. And she. He switched back and forth between the same pronoun—she, and she, and she—using it as a reference to Jennifer and also to the older woman. And then it hit me. He never called them by name. And he never said his name, either. Then thought of the conversation about the picture. No one used names then, either. Not the cook's name. Not the ex-boyfriend. Not the ex-girlfriend. Only Jennifer.

Still standing there on the sidewalk, where I'd been when the waiter stopped me, I recounted the events of my day—from the time I awakened when the mailman rang the doorbell to the time spent in the office with Emily, my student. And I searched my memory for names.

The day began with the mailman. I knew his name, sort of. And I knew Emily's name, though I couldn't remember her family name. But that was all since waking. No mention of the department secretary's name—a woman I passed every day going to and from my office—or the custodian, or any other person I passed that day. And right at that moment, even, I couldn't remember any of their names.

In the dream there was a lack of names, also. Only Langston and Elvis. Not the waitress with the blue streak in her hair. Not the redhead whose hair was really red. Not the muscular cook whom I liked. And not any of the people seated around me, though I knew many other details about them. Even the man who sat beside me and asked if Elvis had been to the house, even he remained nameless.

In the dream, there was an unstated, underlying consciousness—an assumption—that I knew everyone who appeared. As if I were swimming in a context of familiarity and their names were part of that context.

In New York, there was no such assumption. No such context. I knew no one—other than to recognize several as employees I had encountered during previous visits—nor did I expect to know them. I did not know their names, and I knew that I did not know them. And in that regard, the café in the dream and the café in New York were distinguishable. In one, the names were unstated, but I was certain that I knew them. In the other, I did not know, but I knew that I did not.

Was that enough to distinguish the two? Was it by the number of people who were assigned names? Is that how we interact with life when we are awake? I knew two names from the dream, and thus far, three from the day in New York. Was that enough? Was that the validating distinction? That one included more names than the other and so was reality? Or was it the certainty with which I engaged the moment?

If the number of names was the deciding factor, then New York was reality. But if certainty was the key, then the house with Langston and the events at City Café prevailed. In that set of circumstances, I was immersed in certainty of person and place...except for the name of the town. I was comfortably familiar with the surroundings of my dream, but I had no idea of the name of the town.

A quote came to me from somewhere. I don't remember where. "Memory saves us from the tyranny of time." Memory. Saves us. How could memory save one from the tyranny of confusion between waking and sleeping? Dreams are created from memory, aren't they? And the disorder of confusing the two comes from within. A corruption, as it were, of memory. The disorder resides in the very place from which hope might otherwise spring.

And the thought came to me. A name. A single name. Elvis. He died. It's a fact. One could easily verify it. Standing right there, I took my smart phone from my pocket and searched his name. The search engine listed thousands of results. The most obvious showed the highlights of his life. Born in 1935. Died in 1977. Yes. There. He was dead. Which meant he couldn't have appeared to me from behind the staircase in the house. Which meant all of that was a dream.

Relief came over me. I wasn't crazy. I was standing on the sidewalk in Manhattan. Really standing. On a real sidewalk. Alive. Breathing. Thinking. Once again in touch with reality. Memory saved me from the corruption of memory. Unless…unless I was dreaming and the article about Elvis on my phone was only a fabrication of my mind.

Just then, a passerby banged hard against my shoulder. Hard enough that it jarred me from my place, forced me to take a step to maintain my balance, and made me immediately aware of my surroundings. I was standing on the sidewalk, in the midst of pedestrian traffic, staring blanking ahead. My mind lost in thought. My eyes glazed over. Surely, anyone who noticed me must have thought I was delusional. But it was New York, and no one said anything, except for the person who bumped into me who offered the perfunctory, "Sorry." Not as an apology, but as an acknowledgment of the contact.

Prodded by the moment, I started on my way and retraced my earlier route back to the office, though I moved at a slow, plodding pace. As I made my way, I thought about the moment I referred to as the dream, and the moment I now referred to as the present—the one I referred to as reality. And I wondered further about the distinction between the two. In literature the use of dreams as an alternate reality is all but cliché—the man whose dreams are so real and vivid he can't distinguish between the world of sleep and the world of wake. There must be a—

At once, a realization came to me that I could organize my thoughts that way. Not to separate them as lesser and greater, real or unreal, but to think of them as separate worlds. Two worlds living in me. Two worlds that I inhabited. The world of sleep and the world of wake.

For the next few minutes, I tried out the idea to see if it suited me and quickly found myself wondering: is it possible for one to inhabit an alternative milieu—an alternative context—one that exists only in one's mind, and to do so with such all-consuming completion that it becomes a frame of reference—the frame of reference—equally valid with all others for one's sense of self and reality? That, once entered, it becomes reality to that person without reservation. Could I become so deeply involved in my dreams that the question of whether it was, in fact, a sphere of sleep or of wake no longer mattered? Could I enter it as my world and then emerge from it to this world, and never worry about the distinctions between the two?

And then, I was right back at the question I'd posed earlier about whether and how there was a difference. Several things came quickly to mind.

People involved in role playing games sometimes lose their grip on the difference between the world of everyday occurrences and the world of occurrences in the context of the game. But that dichotomy seemed to miss the point. Is there a distinguishable difference between the reality of a game and the reality of typical everyday life? Is one better or more real than the other? Is one valid and the other invalid? All of one's life exists within the frame of one's self and of others, and the two are not the same. We never perceive ourselves as others perceive us. And we never perceive them as they perceive themselves. So, is there ever a real world?

Is there a distinction between a world that exists only in my mind, versus the world of bricks and mortar? Does the difference stem from the quality of the space inhabited, or from the quality of the way we inhabit it?

When I reached my office I hoped for a few moments of quiet to gather myself and adjust to the reality of the school, but after only a few minutes, another student dropped by to discuss something that was mentioned in class. At first, I was disappointed by their appearance but very soon we were drawn into a complex discussion. The give and take of it relieved me from my current dilemma of the mind more completely than anything else I could have done.

Two hours later, I walked home in peace and when I arrived at the brownstone I put on water for tea. While it heated, I listened to a news broadcast through the radio app on my phone. Eventually, the water boiled and while the tea brewed, I cut slices of cheese and placed them on a plate with crackers and grapes.

When the tea was ready, I poured myself a cup, added sugar but no milk, and sat at the table, eating and thinking of the conversation with the staff at Tom's Restaurant, while the news played in the background. My body was physically seated at the kitchen table, but my mind was at Tom's, and, in a short while, far away in Giddings, Texas.

The story they told at the restaurant of how Jennifer Graham died seemed bizarre and I wondered if the incident really happened. Something about it didn't seem right. It was too bizarre. Too strange. As if someone made up the story and tried too hard. And why did the guy from the restaurant tell me? I didn't even know him. Why did he chase me down to tell me? And why the excuse of trying to explain the older woman's attitude?

Why was I even interested in this? Part of me wanted to drop the matter and move on to something else. Whoever the girl was, whatever happened to her, was none of my business. I didn't even know her. Either of them—the girl from the dream or the girl from Tom's. But their similarities in appearance were compelling and I knew those similarities, along with discrepancies in the story they told me about her, would nag me and bother me until I got to the bottom of it and figured out who the girl with the blue streak in her hair was, what happened to her, and why she appeared in my dreams.

In order to do that—to sort through the details of the story and get to the truth—I would need an objective source. Someone other than the guy who flagged me down on the street as I left the restaurant. Someone other than the older woman at the restaurant who signed for the picture from the deliveryman. I would need someone who lived in Giddings—the town where they said Jennifer died—who knew everyone and who was attuned to daily gossip. Only one person fit that description: Andy Russo, my cousin. He had been born in Giddings and lived there all of his life, except for the time he lived in Austin while attending pharmacy school. If anyone knew what actually happened, Andy would.

When I finished eating and when the last sip of tea was gone, I closed the radio app on my phone and called Andy. We talked for a while, catching each other up on the latest family news, then I told him about what I had heard, recounting the details about Jennifer as accurately as I could—a young girl, not more than twenty-one, went off to New York to become an actress, returned to Giddings to visit her family, stabbed to death on her parents' front porch. Finally, I asked, "Is it true? Did that really happen?"

"Wow," Andy replied. "That's a strange story."

"Yes, it is," I acknowledged. "But is it true?"

"I don't know."

His answer wasn't what I expected. "You've never heard of anything like that?"

"No. I don't think I have."

"Do you know someone named Jennifer Graham?"

"Yeah," he replied. "There was a girl from here by that name. I think one of Loraine's children went to school with her."

Loraine was my cousin from another of my mother's siblings. Her family lived in Giddings, too, and we used to see them when we went up there, though we always stayed with Andy's family. Back then, we made fun of Loraine's name—it sounded so old and odd to us. Our humor was rather biting and cruel and it upset her that we laughed at her expense. I've apologized for it many times since and she seems not to be upset about it anymore but that's the reason I called Andy and not her. I wasn't sure how she felt toward me, and I didn't want to find out right then, though from Andy's response it sounded like I might be forced to.

"Which one of Loraine's children are you talking about?"

"The youngest one," Andy said. "I can't remember her name."

"Becky."

"Yeah. Becky," he replied. "I think she might have known that girl you're asking about."

"Jennifer Graham."

"Lots of Grahams live around here," Andy noted. "And I think one of them might have gone to New York for a while, now that you mention it. But if she's the person I think she is, she's back here now. Works at the café down the street from the store."

Café. My heart skipped a beat. "She has a blue streak in her hair?"

"I don't know about that part, but the girl I'm thinking of works at the café."

Talking to Andy did little to clear up details about the story of the girl with the blue streak in her hair, but I liked the sound of his voice, so our conversation continued a while longer. When we finished, I loaded the dishes into the dishwasher, turned out the lights in the kitchen, and went upstairs. I have a chair in the corner of the bedroom where I read at night and after changing clothes, I settled into place with a novel, but I had trouble keeping my mind on the page.

For one thing, the story they told about Jennifer at Tom's was so awful that someone like Andy would have heard about it. People didn't get stabbed to death that often in Giddings. Not in broad daylight. Not on the front porch.

And only one person at Tom's told me that tale—the guy who followed me out to the street. Not only was the story strange, he was strange, too, and I had doubts about whether he was trustworthy.

As I sat there in the chair, the thought came to me that I should return to the restaurant and talk to some of the others who worked there. Not mince words. Not dance around the subject. Walk up to one of the waiters, unannounced, and say, "What happened to Jennifer Graham?" That was the thing to do. Go there early for breakfast. Talk to people who might have worked with her.

The plan seemed like a good one and I attempted to count backwards in my mind to figure out how early I needed to wake up the next morning to make it work, but I was tired and before I determined the time to set my alarm, I drifted off to sleep.

CHAPTER 3

A shaft of brilliant sunlight bounced off the wall in the hallway and caromed through the open doorway into the studio. Strong and intense, it would have drawn my eye in that direction, but I had learned to use a lamp positioned on the opposite side of the room to equalize the pull on my eye muscles. Not at first. Back at the beginning I went home with my right eye aching every day. But eventually I figured out what I needed to do to put things right. So, one day, I brought a floor lamp from home, parked it on the left side of the control board—the side opposite the door where the light came through—and turned it on. Worked perfectly for what I needed, but our engineer didn't like it. "The microphone will pick up the buzz from that light bulb."

He was a good co-worker, but I didn't really care what he thought or said. "I can't work with the light the way it is," I replied. "You want to work around the lamp and filter the noise or announce the show yourself?"

"Just close the door." He said it with an arrogant, superior smirk. That'll block all the light from the hall."

I didn't care for his attitude. "That's fine when you're here with me," I said. "But when I'm alone I like to see who comes and goes."

According to the regular schedule, I was supposed to work the mornings from six to noon, but sometimes I worked in the afternoon and lately I'd been there for the overnight, too. No way I was going to shut myself in that windowless studio and not know when someone came in the front door. We tried broadcasting with the lamp that first day and it didn't cause a problem. The engineer never said another word about it and the strain in my eyes disappeared.

The studio wasn't much. A control board, a couple of turntables, and a rather large collection of records—long-playing albums we called LPs and two-sided singles known as forty-fives because that was the speed they played on the turntable, forty-five rpms.

The control board had a panel with a couple of needle gauges that told me the strength of the signal we were sending to the transmitter. And a button to press that muted the microphone when I was about to cough or sneeze, or if Patsy needed to talk to me. Patsy was the station owner's daughter who worked part time. She did the bookkeeping and correspondence. There wasn't much of either for her to do.

We were a small station located in a building that stood off the highway about a mile out of town that had once been a two-bedroom house for a family from Mexico. Hardworking people. Husband worked on a ranch. Wife was a secretary. A few years ago, they moved to Amarillo. The station owner bought the house from them and put us out there. Before that, we were using a room over the old feed store so the house by the highway was a step up for us. Patsy's office was in the living room. A large picture window near her desk let in the sunlight that bounced off the wall and caused the problem for me.

One of the bedrooms had been converted into the announcer's studio—which is where I sat. The control board was in the middle of the room facing a wall that backed up to the kitchen, which was now the engineer's office. When I sat at the board, I faced it with my back to the front where Patsy was. Once there had been a window on the exterior wall to the left, but it leaked noise into the room. Someone removed it and nailed up unfinished drywall in its place, then covered the spot with a Hayride poster. The Hayride was a music show—the Louisiana Hayride—that broadcast from an auditorium in Shreveport. We carried it on Saturday nights. People really liked it.

The other two walls—from the door to the front corner of the room and from that corner back to the wall where they removed the window—were lined with bookcases. LPs on one section. Forty-fives on the other. All of them arranged in alphabetical order by performer. Most of the LPs were out of date, but we used them sometimes for oldies shows and several of the overnight guys liked big band music. We had a lot of that.

A table stood behind me, positioned between me and one of the bookcases, with two turntables on it. Around the turntables were stacks of forty-fives and a rack that held recorded discs for commercially produced advertisement spots—the slick kind with a jingle for name brand products. We only did a few of those. Most of our ads were live reads—the announcers reading ad copy on the air.

A third turntable sat to the right of the control board with more forty-fives stacked beside it. Most of the new music—Elvis, Buddy Holly, the kind of music people called in to request during the day and early evening—came to us as forty-fives. Record companies could press those by the thousands in no time at all. They sent copies to us for free and sometimes the bands dropped by to help convince us to play their music.

In between the stacks of records was a folded paper napkin that I used as a place to set my coffee cup. It takes a lot of caffeine for me to sit in one place for hours at a time without nodding off. I preferred coffee. The others usually had a soft drink. Bert, the regular afternoon guy, liked Royal Crown Cola and peanuts. He ate a lot of peanuts.

That afternoon, I was in the studio alone when I heard the front door open. A song was playing but I could mute the speaker in the hall, and I did. I heard one voice. Someone talking about whether anyone was there. The sound of it made me think he really was talking to someone, not talking to himself, and the shuffle of feet sounded like it, too.

A few seconds later, a head popped around the doorframe and I saw an eager young guy with nice hair and an even nicer smile. He gestured to the board and I realized he wanted to talk so I held up my hand for him to wait, introduced the next record to the broadcast, then closed the microphone. "Could I help you?" I asked.

He came into the room and behind him were two more men. Tall, but not as handsome. "I'm Johnny Cash," the first man said. "And these fellas with me are the Tennessee Two." They nodded politely.

We shook hands and I said, "If you're from Tennessee, you're a long way from home."

"Yes, sir, we are," Cash replied. He looked eager, the way only the young and untried can look. "We're on our first tour of the South and Southwest, playing music and hoping to get radio stations like yours to play our record."

"You have a recording." I said it as a question, but it really was a statement.

"Yes, sir," Cash said. "We have one and we're working on making more. Hope to have another one coming out real soon."

"What's the label?"

"Sun Records," he said proudly.

"Oh. The same one as Elvis Presley." We had a couple of Elvis records from Sun and played them frequently.

"Yeah," he said. "Elvis is on the label. As are some others." He seemed willing to acknowledge the label had a catalog but not interested in promoting it or the label. I assumed that was because he wanted me to focus my attention on him and his music, which I understood.

"Your name is Cash you said?"

"Yes, sir. We're billed as Johnny Cash and the Tennessee Two."

"I don't think we have your record."

"Well, I thought that might be the case." Cash turned to one of the men, who handed him a forty-five in a paper slipcover. "We brought one with us." He offered it to me with a grin I found hard to refuse.

The second man with him was wearing a jacket and he reached inside it. For an instant I wondered what he was going to bring out but then I saw it was a piece of paper folded lengthwise down the middle. He handed it to Cash, who handed it to me. "These are the lyrics for the songs on the record, and a little bit of information about us."

I was holding the forty-five when he offered it to me, so I set the record aside and took the page from him, then glanced over it quickly. The first song was something called Hey Porter. Cash pointed to the lyrics. "*Hey Porter* is on the A Side," he explained eagerly. "*Cry, Cry, Cry* is on the B."

The song playing on the turntable ended. Another record was ready to go on the turntable behind me, so I turned in that direction and started it, then glanced up at Cash. "Do you have your instruments with you?"

The question seemed to catch him off guard. "Yeah," he said. "They're in the car."

"Why don't you bring them in and play these songs for us."

"Live?"

"Yeah."

"On the air?"

"Is that a problem?"

"No, sir," he grinned. "That's not a problem at all."

"You play this first song. *Hey Porter*," I said. "And then we'll talk about it. I'll ask you a few questions. Nothing you can't handle. And then—"

"You mean like an interview?"

"Yes," I replied.

"Live?"

The naivete in his voice was both charming and amusing. "That's the best way," I said. "I think you can handle it."

"Okay."

They seemed excited as they left the room, and I heard the door open when they went outside to their car. While they were gone, I ran a commercial from the turntable beside me and loaded the other turntables with commercial discs, too.

A few minutes later, Cash and his companions returned to the studio. He carried a guitar, as did one of the others. The third man had a bass. I ran one more commercial while we positioned a microphone for them, then played a second commercial while we found a second microphone. When the last commercial ended, I was seated at the control panel and opened the announcer's microphone.

"We have a special treat for you today, listeners. Here in the studio with us is a new singer, Johnny Cash. He's traveling the country with a band known as the Tennessee Two, and they've recorded a couple of songs for Sun Records in Memphis. They're live in the studio, and they're going to sing for us right now. So here they are singing their new song, *Cry, Cry, Cry*."

Cash and his men seemed surprised by that announcement and I realized I had gotten the order of the songs backwards, but they adjusted quickly and began singing.

Everybody knows where you go when the sun goes down
I think you only live to see the lights of town
I wasted my time when I would try, try, try
When the lights have lost their glow you're gonna cry, cry, cry.

Soon your sugar-daddies will all be gone
You wake up some cold day and find you're alone
You'll call for me but I'm gonna tell you bye, bye, bye
When I turn around and walk away you'll cry, cry, cry....

The song continued for several more verses and when it ended, I said, "That's a good song."

Cash smiled and nodded. "Thank you. We like it and it seems to be doing well for us."

"It's a song about a girl who is unfaithful to a guy."

"Yes, sir."

"And you wrote it?"

"I surely did."

"Is it biographical?"

"You mean, is it about my own experience?"

"Yes."

"Well, I think everyone has experienced that sort of thing," Cash said, "in one way or another, at one time or another. The hurt and confusion of loving someone who doesn't really love them back. At least, not in the same way."

Radio interviews tended to be glib and perfunctory. I wanted to go a little deeper, so I said, "Are you the one staying at home, or the one leaving at night?"

A puzzled look wrinkled Cash's forehead. "I don't understand."

"Are you the one remaining faithful, or the one going off to be with someone else? Going off to be with a woman, in your case."

Cash's puzzled look turned angry. "I don't think my personal life is any of your business."

I wasn't letting him off that easily. "When you write a song about infidelity, and you ask me to play it, don't you make it my business? And the business of everyone out there who's listening."

One of the Tennessee Two gave him a nudge and Cash took a deep breath. After a moment he said, "Life on the road is tough. There are a lot of temptations. But so far, I haven't had a problem with that. I've seen others have it, but I haven't."

"And at home?"

The anger faded from his face, but the look in his eyes told me he didn't like my question. "What about at home?" His voice sounded defensive.

"Is your wife faithful to you when you're away?"

Cash's face turned hard. "You're asking a lot of questions."

"You wrote this song, right?"

"Yes, but—"

"So, the lyrics had to come from inside you."

"Yes. I suppose they did, but—"

"And you chose this topic."

"It's what came to me." His voice was curt. Not dismissive or angry but he was not interested in exploring his inner feelings. "The lyrics came to me. The tune came to me. I wrote it down and it sounded good to me. It sounded good to Sam Phillips at Sun Records, too. So—"

"Like I said," I interrupted. "It's a great record. This song is going to be big for you and big for us, too. We'll get a lot of requests for it. I'm just saying, you sat down with your guitar, and started strumming around, and these lyrics came to you."

"Yes." Cash nodded. "That's exactly what happened."

"And they came from somewhere inside you. So, what's going on inside you that when you looked into yourself, this song was there?"

"Well," Cash replied. "I guess I'll have to think about that a while and get back to you on it."

They turned aside, as if to gather their things to leave so I spoke up and said, "Well, play that second song you were telling me about. *Hey Porter.*"

Once again, my suggestion seemed to take them by surprise, but Cash recovered quickly and said, "Yes, sir. I believe we will."

They started singing and as their voices wafted through the air, the room transformed seamlessly from the cramped studio in the house by the highway to a big, familiar space and in an instant, we weren't in the radio station anymore but in the front parlor of the house where I lived with Langston. I was seated on the piano bench. Johnny and the two men with him stood between the piano and front windows. They weren't eager young men anymore, either. Particularly Cash, whose face was the wrinkled one I'd seen on album covers after he was dropped by Columbia. The tired Cash who languished until picked up by Rick Rubin and his American Recordings label.

Langston was in the hall, arms folded across his chest, his shoulder propped against the doorframe that led into the room. He stared at me with that strange look he always gave me when someone showed up to play. Johnny and the boys were singing.

Hey, Porter, Hey Porter!
Would you tell me the time?
How much longer will it be
'Til we cross that Mason Dixon Line?
At daylight would you tell that engineer to slow it down;
Or better still, just stop the train
'Cause I want to look around.

Hey, Porter! Hey Porter!
What time did you say?
How much longer will it be
'Til I can see the light of day?
When we hit Dixie will you tell that engineer to ring his bell;
And ask everybody that ain't asleep to stand right up and yell....

When they finished, I said, "This one's about a man returning to the South. Returning to Dixie."

"Yes, it is," Cash replied.

"Dixie refers to the area of the country that's south of the Mason-Dixon Line."

"I suppose so."

"That's the area where slavery was permitted," I noted. "South of that line was Dixieland. Slavery."

Cash shrugged. "It's just a point of reference for the song."

"Not for some," I continued. "And the porter would have been Black. An African American."

"Not all of them."

"But most."

"Yes," he conceded with a sigh. "Most were."

"So, this is a song about a White guy returning to the Old South and he's asking a Black porter to help him."

"Look." Cash sounded irritated. "I wrote this song in 1954. The situation described in it was the given of the day. I traveled on a train many times back then. And yes, the porter usually was Black. That's how it was. I was thinking about someone who'd been a long way from home, coming back home, and glad to be back to familiar surroundings. That's all. The porter being there was just the given of the day."

"The given."

"Yes."

"But that given is long gone now."

An amused smile came over him, as if he knew something I did not. "You've got some givens of your day that are destined to be long gone, too. Things that will be obvious to later generations that aren't obvious to you right now."

"Like what?"

"That's difficult to say. I'm here now, too, so I can't really say."

"Give it a try," I insisted.

Cash thought for a moment. "Well," he said finally, "one thing might be the hollow religion of American individualism."

"Religion?"

"We think of American individualism as the thing that makes us great. And I reckon it did for a while. But individualism ends its course in selfish hedonism. I think one day people will see it that way."

My forehead wrinkled in a skeptical expression. "But a religion?"

"Think about it." He was insistent but not overbearingly so. "We go to church and sing and do whatever we do, and we call it Christianity, but it's nothing like what Jesus preached."

I smiled. "That sounds like the lyrics to a song."

"Yeah." His eyes lit up. "It does." His guitar was still hanging from the strap across his shoulder and he strummed a chord. "Call it Christianity, but it's nothing like what Jesus preached. More akin to vanity than what he had to teach."

Someone else spoke up. "Chasing money, power, and gold, sacrificing to the gods of old."

I tried a line. "Greed and wealth. Fortune and fame. Nothing like the things he told."

Cash laughed. "It needs some work, but we might have an idea we can work with."

It did need work, but I heard myself say, "How does this relate to the girl?"

The question seemed out of place and I had no idea what prompted me to say it, but he seemed to know what I meant. "The one with the blue hair?"

"Yes," I said. "How does this fit with her?"

"I don't know." He shrugged his shoulders. "You'll have to find her and ask her. If you do, I think she'll tell you what you want to know."

CHAPTER 4

All at once, my eyes popped open and I awakened with a start to find I was seated in the chair in the bedroom at the brownstone, where I had gone to read the night before. It was morning, but the light was soft and subdued, coming at a low angle through the windows that looked out onto the sidewalk, the street, and the townhouses on our block. It was early, too. Not yet six. Maybe not even five. Perhaps. Most mornings, I slept until seven, so I lacked a clear point of reference, but I knew it was early.

My shoulders were stiff from the way I was propped in the chair and my legs ached from being bent at the knees all night with pressure on the backs of my thighs. The worst part, though, was the buzzed feeling in my head. I hated it when I fell asleep like that. Even if I awakened after only a few hours, my body was off schedule and I felt it the next day. Already, I knew I would need a nap after lunch.

As I sat there, staring out the window, trying to pull myself together enough to stand, the words Johnny Cash had said to me when I asked about Jennifer played in my head. "I think she'll tell you what you want to know."

There was little doubt Cash's appearance had been a dream. Like Elvis, who came the night before, Johnny Cash was dead. I knew that. And the way the scene changed from a radio studio to the front room of that big, rambling house, and then the mention of Jennifer without context. All of that confirmed for me that I had experienced a dream. Unlike the day before, I had no confusion about the world of sleep and the world of wake. But I was confused about what to do next.

"You'll have to find her and ask her," Cash had said. "If you do, I think she'll tell you what you want to know." But find her where? And ask her what? What did I want to know?

After a moment I remembered the idea that came to me right before I fell asleep about going back to Tom's Restaurant and asking again for details about Jennifer. That was a good idea and if the hour really was as early as I thought, I could go there now. I took my cell phone from my pocket and checked the time. It was six-thirty. Not quite as early as I had assumed, but plenty of time to get to Tom's and have breakfast before my first class convened.

Though stiff and out of sorts, I came from the chair, crossed the room to the dresser, and put the phone on the charger, then started toward the shower. An hour later, I was dressed and on my way to Tom's.

The walk from the townhouse loosened me up and I arrived before eight o'clock. As I expected, the restaurant staff was completely different. With only a cursory survey of the room as I entered, I noticed none of them looked familiar. About the time I reached that conclusion, a waitress caught my eye. "You can sit anywhere," she said.

She was older, maybe ten years older than I, but I liked the way her white waitress uniform followed the curve of her hip and the contour of her buttocks. She noticed where my eyes had been and smiled at me in a knowing way. I acknowledged her with a nod, but instead of finding a seat I checked the wall to the left of the door, where I had seen the woman from the day before considering a place to hang the photograph.

Sure enough, there it was. Squeezed between an autographed picture of Jerry Seinfeld and one of Suzanne Vega. As I gazed at the photo, the same waitress who greeted me appeared at my side. "They just put that one up yesterday," she noted, pointing to it.

Without taking my eyes from the picture, I said, "Did you know these people?"

"That's me right there." She pointed to a spot on the photograph. "Everyone here this morning is in that picture."

I leaned closer, as if examining her image, then pointed to Jennifer Graham, the one with the blue streak in her hair. "What about her? Is this person here today?"

"No." There was a tone in her voice and from the corner of my eye I noticed the expression on her face had turned dark. I wasn't sure if she was upset with me for noticing someone else, as if noticing her earlier meant she had some kind of prior claim that obligated me to her, or if there was something else to the story. But before I could ask, she said, "Jennifer doesn't work here anymore."

"You knew her?"

"Yes."

"She was your friend?"

"Yes.

"What happened to her?"

"She went back to Texas," the waitress said. "That's where she was from."

"But she's still alive?"

"Oh, yes. She's alive." She looked over at me, her eyes not quite as dark as the moment before but this time with a hint of anger. "Did someone tell you she wasn't?"

"Yes." So, there was more to the story.

"Must have been Jimmy." Her voice had an edge and when I looked at her full on, I saw that what I had previously taken for anger was really disgust.

"Jimmy?" My forehead wrinkled in a frown. "Who is that?"

"Works in the afternoons. He's the one who told you Jennifer was dead. He's been telling everyone the same thing."

"I don't know his name," I said. It was true, I didn't know his name, but the real reason I said it was to keep her talking. I wanted to know more about Jennifer and why she wasn't there.

She cut her eyes at me. "Tall guy? Curly hair?"

"Yes."

"That's him." She nodded her head defiantly. "Jimmy Hughes. He's the one whose been spreading that story about her getting stabbed."

"It's not true?"

"No." She shook her head. "He came in here one day and told us that had happened to her. Said he learned it from an email. It sounded like a tale, so I called down to Texas to find out for myself."

"You talked to Jennifer?"

"No. To her mother. I had her mother's number, so I just called her and asked her. She assured me Jennifer was very much alive."

I was curious about how she came to have a phone number for Jennifer's mother but first I wanted to know about Jimmy and the story he was telling. "So, why was Jimmy saying that?" I spoke of him now as if I knew him. As if I knew all of them and we were all friends. Jimmy, Jennifer, the waitress standing beside me. Friendly and familial. As if we were part of the same group.

"Supposedly," she said, "he got an email from Jennifer's mother telling him that story."

"Did he really get that email?"

She shrugged. "I don't know. I didn't explain everything to her mother. I mean, you can't just call someone up and say, 'We heard your daughter got stabbed on your own front porch.' So I just told her we'd heard something happened to Jennifer and she said, no, that nothing had happened to her."

"Have you talked to Jennifer herself?"

"Nah." The tone in her voice said there was more to it, more to all of it. Jennifer. Jimmy. The waitress.

"I take it, you don't think much of Jimmy."

"Well..." She wrinkled her face in a sour expression. "Jimmy liked Jennifer. Wanted to go out with her. Tried to get her interested in him. And I think they went out maybe once or twice. But Jennifer was interested in a girl." She said that last part in such an offhanded way I almost didn't catch it.

I looked over at her. "A girl?"

"Yeah. And when Jimmy found out she liked women more than men, he couldn't handle it."

"What did he do?"

"He started telling her things like if she went out with him, she wouldn't want to date a woman anymore. That a woman dating another woman wasn't right. That people would find out about her and it would ruin her life. And he was loud about it. And rather obnoxious."

I nodded thoughtfully, then asked, "But she's alive?"

"Oh, yeah," the waitress said. "She's very much alive."

"Wow."

"Exactly."

"Do you know how to reach the girlfriend?"

"Who?" The waitress looked puzzled. "Jimmy's girlfriend? I don't—"

"No," I said, cutting her off. "Jennifer's girlfriend. The one you mentioned when you said Jennifer was dating a girl. Do you know how to reach her?"

"No." The waitress shook her head quickly. "I don't think I ever knew her name." She turned away, but again it seemed like she knew more than she'd said. Before I could follow up, she gestured to the room and said, "You can sit anywhere you like," and she kept walking in the opposite direction.

As she moved away, I took my phone from my pocket and captured an image of the photograph, then found an open booth by the windows next to the street and ordered breakfast. While I waited for my food, I stared at the image on my phone and thought about all that had transpired in the last two days. Dreaming about Elvis. Finding connections between the people in that dream and the people at Tom's. And then the dream with Johnny Cash and him telling me to find Jennifer and ask her what I wanted to know. But what did I want to know? I was curious now, having dreamed and experienced a world of sleep as vivid and real as the world of wake, but was there something else? Was there something beneath the dreams that produced them?

Ideas and concepts from undergraduate psychology courses flittered through my mind. Bits and pieces. Freud. Jung. Dreams as meaningful. Dreams as meaningless. A place to work out the tensions of one's conscious mind. A place to work out the tensions of the subconscious. Stories from Sunday school of prophetic dreams. Old men dream dreams. Young men see visions. Joseph was a dreamer, though, and a young man. It had been a long time since I was in Sunday school. A long time since I was in church.

Before I pieced that string of thoughts together into something meaningful, the waitress arrived with my food and I began to eat, but my mind quickly returned to the dreams, Elvis, Johnny, and Jennifer.

All of them were people I had never known personally. Music. Piano. Music history. Stories. They were topics I enjoyed. I had built a career on stories and I especially liked the ones from the dreams, which led me to a curious observation. In the dreams, I knew the stories of every person involved without being told those stories by someone in the dream and without recounting them to myself as a narrator during the dream to remind myself of the content. I knew everyone's story and I knew that I knew, and I lived and moved through my experience in the dream with them immersed in the essence of knowing. Rather like a pure state of knowing. A context of knowing without the conscious repetition of the things I knew.

Which, as I thought about it, was rather like the way one lives each day. I know that my student Emily is from New York and a hundred other things about her, but I don't recount those things to myself each time I see her in order to refresh my knowing of her. Those individual pieces of information simply get folded into the sense of Emily that I have when I encounter her. She becomes, as it were, the essence of Emily and I encounter the fullness of who she is based on the things I know about her but without having to consciously recall each of those things every time we meet.

Beneath all of that, however—beneath the dreams and the knowing and the pleasure of knowing, beneath the novelty of Elvis and Johnny and Jennifer and all the others—there was an unspoken restlessness that I had not noticed until right then, while seated in the booth next to the window at Tom's. An unsettledness that was buried beneath the surface of my conscious self-awareness. Not deeply buried but buried nonetheless and now it was working its way toward the surface. Who knew what that might bring?

After breakfast, I walked to the office and spent the morning reviewing and marking student papers. When I finished with that, I took the papers to the office and placed them in a box for my graduate assistant with a note about which sections to photocopy. I planned to distribute copies to the class and have the students read selected passages from their compositions. It was an exercise like an art school critique—show the class what you have created and let them react to it. I had used it previously with great results and hoped it would work well with this group.

From there, I went down the hall to the office of a colleague who had recently returned from a stint in England. I was considering a similar trip and wanted to know how hers went. Our conversation lasted longer than I expected and a little before noon I suggested we have lunch, but she had a meeting to attend.

When the class ended, I returned to my office and found a message from the department secretary taped to the door. One of those yellow preprinted forms that was folded in half and stuck to the door with a piece of clear tape. The secretary insisted that folding them that way insured the contents remained private. I was equally adamant that it did not, but despite our long running argument over the matter, she persisted in leaving them that way.

Not content to accept her explanation, I took my complaints to the department chairman where I was met with only a smile in response. When I continued to complain about it, a colleague took me aside and suggested the greater issue lay with the fact that the department secretary and department chairman were more than mere co-workers. Then my eyes were opened, and I put the matter aside, but it continued to bother me every time I found one of her notes on my door.

The message that morning read, "Call your brother," but there was no name or phone number. I had two brothers. One older, who lived in Dallas, and a younger one who lived in Louisiana. Both had my cell phone number and I wondered why they hadn't called me directly, but when I reached in my pocket for my phone to return the call, I found the phone wasn't there.

A check of my desk turned up nothing and I retraced in my mind the events of the morning from the time I left the house until I arrived at the office. That's when I realized I had left the phone at Tom's. I had laid it on the table so I could read the screen and study Jennifer's image while I ate.

Knowing the phone was at Tom's told me my brother had called, probably more than once, had been unable to reach me, and had phoned the office thinking that someone there would be able to reach me. That meant he was serious about having me return his call. Or, he was worried after having tried to contact me and been unable to reach me.

A dilemma formed in my mind—whether to call him back immediately from the office phone or walk back to Tom's, hope to find the phone, and call him from it once it was retrieved. After a moment spent going back and forth between those options, I decided to return to the restaurant. The phone held far too much information to risk someone else finding it. Besides which, neither of my brothers lived close enough for me to do anything about any situation they might face. Calling them back immediately offered no advantage to calling half an hour later. Immediacy was of no advantage and delay posed no increased risk that immediacy could avert. So, once more that day, I started towards Tom's Restaurant.

From the office, I walked quickly downstairs, then continued up the street at a brisk pace. I reached the restaurant a few minutes later. The waitress I had talked to earlier greeted me with a smile. "Looking for this?" she asked, and I saw my phone in her hand.

"Yes," I replied. "Thanks for keeping it for me."

"You have some messages."

A frown wrinkled my forehead. "You read them?"

"No. But I heard it ding several times."

Rather than wait to step outside, I took the phone from her, entered the biometric information, and opened it to find four missed calls from my brother Ryan, the older one who lived in Dallas. My heart sank.

Our father, who was in his eighties, lived with Ryan. If he called that many times, it must have been about Dad. The waitress seemed to notice my reaction. "Bad news?"

"Maybe," I said. The expression on her face indicated she wanted to talk and I had the feeling she was interested in more than talk, but I had other things to do that day and I wasn't interested in her like that anyway.

"Thanks again," I said, gesturing with the phone as I turned toward the door.

Noise on the street made a phone conversation impossible so I waited until I was back at the office to call my brother. He answered on the first ring. "Where have you been? I've been calling you all morning."

"I was teaching a class," I replied. I had no intention of telling him I left the phone at a restaurant. He would remind me of it every day for the rest of my life.

"You didn't hear it while you were in class?" His voice had that older brother tone that always got on my nerves. I wanted to move on with the conversation. "What's up?" I asked.

"It's Dad." Ryan's voice had a somber tone.

"What's wrong?"

"He had a heart attack."

I had expected the call was about Dad but that didn't make the news any easier to take. "How bad is it?"

"He's in ICU. They don't think he'll make it through the night."

This was Dad's third heart attack in two years. The implications were obvious. He was about to die. If I wanted to see him before he was gone, I better come quick. "Okay," I replied. "I'll get the next flight out of here and be there as soon as possible."

After talking to Ryan, I notified the department chairman that I needed to be away for a while, I wasn't sure how long, then checked for flights leaving from La Guardia. I found space on one leaving at three that afternoon and bought a ticket through the airline's website. Departing that soon left me barely enough time to return to the brownstone, pack a bag, and get to the airport, but I wanted to see Dad, so I moved quickly. I made the flight but with only a few minutes to spare.

When I arrived in Dallas, I rented a car and drove to the hospital. It was located in Plano, where my brother lived. As I came through the doors at the front entrance, I was met with the smell that I hated more than anything. Hospital smell. That awful blend of cleaning agent, sweat, excrement, vomit, blood...and sick people. I wanted to turn around immediately and go back to New York, but I also wanted to see Dad, so I pushed on to the elevator and rode upstairs. Ryan had already texted me the room number.

On the doors to the ICU there was a sign that gave the visiting hours. I ignored it and made my way around to Dad's room. Ryan had texted me the number. The nurses at the nursing station noticed me but I avoided eye contact with them and kept moving. Dad's room was on the far side of the unit.

Each of the rooms had a glass wall that faced the nursing station, affording a clear view of the patients. From the hall I saw Dad lying in bed, looking as pale and tired as I had ever seen him. So pale, in fact, that I wasn't sure he was still alive, though as soon as that thought entered my mind I replaced it with the assumption that if he were already dead he wouldn't be lying in a bed, hooked to the machines that surrounded him.

Dad's eyes were open, and we made eye contact as I came around the end of the bed. He smiled. "You made it." His voice was little more than a whisper.

"Yes, sir," I replied. "I wanted to see you."

"Once more, before I go?" He had a wry, and sometimes morbid, sense of humor.

I forced a smile. "They tell us you may be scooting on soon."

He had a contented expression. "Are you afraid, Monk?"

"No, sir." That wasn't true. I was scared to think of him not being around anymore. Of facing life without him there, even if I had moved on to live somewhere else and even if he was older now and wasn't involved with me each day. But I didn't want the moment to be about me, so I asked, "Are you afraid?"

He nodded. "Sometimes." Dad was refreshingly honest most of the time.

"Mama is there." That was the way we talked about death. Heaven awaits. Those who had died would be there to greet us. None of us was sure what lay in store beyond death, but we'd been faithful church members most of our lives, and we'd been believers even in moments of personal doubt and skepticism.

"I know," he said.

"What do you think she'll say?"

He smiled broadly. "Where have you been?" Tears filled his eyes.

"Ha." I laughed. That sounded like something she might say. "Put on a clean shirt," I added.

"Yeah," he agreed. "That, too."

She told us that all the time. If we were going over to Brenham, or to a friend's house, or down the road to the store she would say, "Okay. But put on a clean shirt."

I leaned closer and lowered my voice. "Thank you, Dad."

"For what?"

"For being honest." A lump formed in my throat. "For being you."

He looked at my chin to keep from looking straight at me. "I don't know how honest I was."

"You were always honest," I insisted. "Like right now. Instead of saying, 'Oh, it'll be alright.' Or 'I'm not scared,' you said how you feel."

"Too late to start telling lies now."

I took his hand in mine and kissed the back of it. "You made my life possible."

"It's okay, son." He had a reassuring tone and his voice seemed stronger than before. "I knew what you were going to say before you got here and you coming here said it all without you saying a word.

When you walked around the end of the bed, you said everything there was to say between us, just in that simple act." Tears came to my eyes and I could not stop them running down my cheeks. He gave my hand a shake and smiled at me again. "I'll tell your mama you're doing fine. She used to worry about you." He was trying to ease the tension of the moment.

"She never understood why I wanted to go to New York."

His eyes opened wider and his voice sounded a little stronger. "Oh, she understood completely. She just worried something might happen to you."

Ryan came into the room and the doctor was with him. I turned to move out of the way, but Dad wouldn't let go of my hand. The doctor noticed and rather than forcing the issue, took a position on the opposite side of the bed. "This is your son, Mr. Jones?" He gestured with a nod in my direction.

"This is the middle boy," Dad replied.

"The one from New York."

"Yes." Obviously, they had talked about me during their visits.

"Let me have a listen to your heart." The doctor placed his stethoscope on Dad's chest, and I watched to see his reaction, but he closed his eyes as if concentrating on the sound. I wondered if he was listening that intensely or hiding a look of panic at what he heard from Dad's heart.

After a moment, he moved the stethoscope aside and felt along Dad's arms, then pressed his fingertips against Dad's neck. Finally, he stood up straight. "Your heart is a little stronger this afternoon, Mr. Jones. Much better than it was this morning."

"I feel better right now," Dad said.

"We'll keep hoping for the best." The doctor gave one of those thin, tight professional smiles and spoke in a pleasant manner, but the sound of his voice told me he had little hope that Dad would recover.

When the doctor was gone, Dad looked over at me. "He's a nice guy but a hell of a poor liar."

The comment made me laugh. "He's not optimistic?"

"He wasn't giving me much of a chance before any of this latest stuff happened."

"Does he plan to operate?"

Ryan came back to the room. "He says you need surgery, but he doesn't want to do it while you're in the shape you're in right now." It was as if Ryan had heard my question and was answering it but from the look on his face, I knew it was just good timing. He planned to tell us that whether we had asked or not.

Dad grinned. "He's been saying that for years, but I don't want him doing it, either. Not right now. Not ever."

The three of us talked a while, but it was late in the afternoon and Dad was getting tired. Ryan's wife was an attorney and they had a teenage son who still lived at home. He needed to get home to check on them. And besides, he had been at the hospital all day and I could see he was tired, too. I said I would stay with Dad a while and suggested Ryan take a break. He agreed and when he was gone, I sat in the chair next to Dad's bed. It was one of those chairs they have in hospitals that are wider than normal and reclines. I kicked it back all the way, scooted out the footrest, and relaxed. Before long Dad's breathing slowed, and I watched as he drifted off to sleep.

For a while, I sat in the chair and stared at the darkened screen of the television that hung from a bracket on the wall beyond the foot of the bed. In my mind, I recalled the dream with Elvis about the girl at the café, the discovery that she was actually a girl who worked at Tom's, and the words I heard from Johnny. "Ask her. She'll tell you what you want to know." But recalling those words only brought me to the same point of frustration I had reached before and to the same question—what did I want her to tell me?

With nothing else to do right then, I began forming a list in my mind—a scratch list—of everything I could think of that I might ask her if I had the opportunity. The obvious came first. Do you know me? Have you ever seen me before? And then from what I had learned so far—why did you leave New York? Why does the waiter at Tom's think you're dead? Where you romantically interested in a girl and what was her name? I didn't care about the girl, personally.

Her romantic interests weren't of my concern. But knowledge of that had come to me in the context of the dreams and it seemed like a question I should ask, if I had the chance.

Beyond that, my mind was blank. Except for the questions from Monday about the difference between dreams and reality. The qualities by which we inhabit one versus the other. The consequences of our actions based on the difference between them. And whether events in one enhance the other.

I knew about dreams as a region where conflict in the waking world got resolved in the dreaming world, thus enhancing the waking world. But what about the other direction. Was the dream world merely a washing pool where the dirt of our conscious life got rinsed out, or could the quality of the dream world find improvement, too? Or, as my theological colleagues might ask, did redemption extend to the world of dreams? Were my dreams in need of a savior?

That thought brought a smile to my face. Some of my dreams has been rather deviant at times, though not recently. Still, I was intrigued by the question and tried to explore it further, but drowsiness overtook me and soon I was asleep.

CHAPTER 5

Early in the morning, I came from the hallway and walked into the kitchen where I saw Langston standing by the sink. That caught me by surprise because normally, he wasn't awake before ten. Without looking at me, he seemed to sense my presence and he pointed to the window. There were three windows above the sink and through them we had a wonderful view of the porch, the yard, and the barn. "Someone's on our back porch," he said.

"Who is it?" I asked as I crossed the room towards him.

"I don't know. Some old guy. With long hair pulled back in a ponytail."

By then I was at his side and I could see out the window for myself. We had two rocking chairs out there and the person Langston had noticed was seated in the one to the left. I recognized him immediately and grinned at the sight of him. "That's Willie Nelson," I exclaimed. "I didn't know he was coming over today."

Langston responded with that disgusted sigh he always gave when someone showed up. Especially someone who enjoyed music as much as I. "Not that again," he said. He turned away from the sink and started toward the hall, shaking his head as he went. "Maybe we should see about getting you some medicine."

"But you saw him yourself," I insisted playfully.

"Maybe we both should get some medicine."

The door to the back porch was at the far end of the counter. I reached it in three steps and went outside. Willie smiled at me from the chair and gestured with a nod toward Langston and the house. "He didn't want to join us?"

"Not this time," I replied.

Willie nodded. "Same as last time."

"He's like that," I said as I took a seat in the chair next to Willie. "A little afraid of what he sees and hears."

"But you're not."

"No," I said. "I'm not."

A guitar rested across Willie's thigh and he strummed it aimlessly, the way pickers do when they're thinking about something, or anything, or nothing at all. I watched the movement of his picking hand for a while, then shifted my attention to the hand that formed the chords on the neck. After a moment my eyes wandered from the guitar and I looked across the yard to the truck and the barn, with the sun shining down on them and the clear blue sky above while the mellow sound from Willie's guitar settled gently in my ear.

Willie noticed I was staring off into the yonder and he looked that way, too. "I like your truck," he said with a nod toward it.

"Thank you. It's a pleasure to drive."

"My cousin had one of those five-windows once." The truck in our yard was a five-window Chevrolet. "We used to take it rabbit hunting at night on his daddy's farm."

"I've never done that." Ryan, my oldest brother, went rabbit hunting at night with some of his friends when they were in high school, but they never invited me, and I wasn't interested in going, though I enjoyed hearing them tell stories about it when they returned.

"You ought to give it a try," Willie suggested. "That's one of those things a person should do. Somebody drives. Somebody else stands in the back with a shotgun. Headlights from the truck shine in the rabbits' eyes. People in back shoot them."

"Sounds illegal."

Willie chuckled. "It is," he said. "In most places."

I nodded toward the guitar. "What are you playing?"

"Just picking around a little." He looked over at me. "Want to give it a try?"

"On Trigger?" That was the name of his guitar and the suggestion that I should play it caught me off-guard. I had my own guitar, propped against the piano bench in the front room and the times when he came over in the past I always went inside and got it. He'd never offered to let me play his.

"Sure." He grasped the guitar by the neck with one hand and the body with the other and passed it to me. "Here," he said, offering the pick too. "You'll need this."

As carefully and gently as I could, I took the guitar from him and rested it on my leg like I'd seen him do, then took the pick and held it between the thumb and index finder of my right hand. "Stroke it nice and easy. Up and down," he suggested. "Let the strings do the work."

The guitar was a Martin N-2, with nylon strings. Well-worn from years of play, the wood had a luster that made it look like Willie. A hole had been worn in the top from the rub of the pick against the surface while he played which made it feel like Willie and sound like Willie, too. It wasn't a beginner's guitar but one a professional could use to make a living. A professional like Willie could coax it into making any sound in the world.

With a little concentration, I configured the fingers of my left hand to press the strings for a D chord—it required three fingers—and strummed the pick gently across the strings. I liked the sound it made and as I continued to play, my right hand fell into a rhythm.

A few strokes later, I moved my fingers on the neck to make an A chord, also three fingers. Then G. All of those were easy for me and I transitioned between them without breaking the rhythm of my right hand. The next chord, though, was a B minor, which was a bar chord and I was clumsy getting to it.

"Take it easy," Willie said. "It's just us. We aren't in a hurry." I tried it again and the movement went better. "It just takes practice," he added. "And time."

After a few more progressions through that sequence of chords, Willie pointed to my left hand and said, "Lift that second finger once in a while. Maybe on the upbeat." I gave it a try and noticed how it augmented the tone of the chord. "That's good," Willie said, and a chill ran down my spine. Willie Nelson. Telling me I was doing good.

While I was playing his guitar. On the back porch of my house.

After a few more strums and chords I was back to the D chord again and he said, "Keep it right there a while, and don't forget to lift that finger every now and then."

I did as he said and kept strumming that chord over and over, my right hand stroking the pick, up and down across the strings, lifting the finger of my left hand in time with the upbeat. He listened intently for a moment and I could see his head nodding in time with the rhythm and knew he was about to sing. He caught the chord just right.

> *Livin' on the road my friend*
> *Was gonna keep you free and clean*
> *But now you wear your skin like iron*
> *And your breath is hard as kerosene*
> *Weren't you mamma's only boy?*
> *But her favorite one it seems*
> *She began to cry when you said*
> *Good-bye, sank to your dream ...*

Somehow, I sensed the timing for the chord changes and, though I missed the first one, I moved through the rest of the song without dropping a single one. When we finished, he looked over at me and said, "You're coming right along with that. I might have to take you on the road." He was kidding, of course, but it made me feel good to hear him say it.

"That's a good song," I said. "Did you write it?"

"No." He shook his head. "Wish I did, though."

"Who wrote it?"

"Townes Van Zandt."

"Oh. He was from Texas." I knew a little something about Townes.

"Yeah," Willie said. "Grew up in Fort Worth, I think. Lived in Houston a while."

"Did you know him?"

"Not very well. I recorded a song or two with him, appeared with him on television once or twice. I can't remember if I did more than that or not. But I knew him, and I knew of him. He and Guy Clark were good friends."

"You knew Guy Clark?"

"Better than I knew Townes, but not as well as I knew others. Waylon. Johnny. Kris. I spent a lot of time with them. But I did a few shows with Guy Clark. He came to the picnic a couple of times." Willie's Fourth of July picnics were immensely popular in Texas.

"Who brought you *Poncho and Lefty*? Did Townes ask you to record it?"

"No. My daughter brought me that song. She heard it on an album by Emmy Lou Harris and thought Merle and I should do it."

"Merle Haggard."

"Yeah." Willie nodded. "Merle and I were doing an album and needed one more song to finish it and she suggested we give that a try. So, we did."

"And it went to number one."

He smiled. "We had a lot of success with it."

"A friend of mine said his older brother used to see Van Zandt at the Jester Lounge in Houston."

"Might have. He used to play there some; I think. A lot of people did."

"Did you?"

Willie shook his head. "I don't think so. I played a lot of places around Houston, but I don't think I ever played at that one."

I handed him back the guitar and noted the hole that had been rubbed in the top of the sound box. "That guitar has seen a lot of use."

He smiled. "I like the feel of it."

"That extra hole doesn't change the sound?"

"I don't know." He shrugged his shoulders. "If it does, I never noticed."

"You've taken good care of it, though. It's just a hole from use, not abuse."

"Mark over in Austin looks after it for me."

Willie began to play the guitar again. Strumming from one chord to the next, the way he did when I first came out on the porch that morning. I liked the sound of it. Easy. Rich. Full.

"You've written a lot of songs," I said after a while. "I don't know if I could do even one."

"It's nothing but telling a story." Willie looked over at me. "Speaking of which, you have a story to tell. Maybe it's time you talked to that girl and figured it out."

My forehead wrinkled in a puzzled frown. "That girl?" There was no way he could know about the girl from my dream or from the photo on the wall at the restaurant in New York.

"The one at the café," he added. "With the blue streak in her hair."

"She's not there anymore."

"You'll have to find her." He stopped playing and looked over at me. "I wouldn't wait for her to find me. I'd go now and get on with it."

For a moment I thought he was going to help me figure out what that story might be, so I asked him, "You think she has a story for me?"

"I think if you ask her, she'll tell you what you want to know."

The hope of help from him vanished. Replaced by a familiar sense of frustration. What he'd said to me was the same thing I had heard before only now, having heard it from him, I found myself thinking that I must be dreaming. And then I was sure of it. Certain that I was dreaming and that I was aware of it within the dream itself. But I had heard this twice now—ask her and she'll tell you—so I pressed the matter further.

"That's just it," I said with an insistent tone. "I don't know what I want to know from her."

Willie chuckled. "Ask her and find out."

That suggestion only increased my sense of frustration. "How do I ask her a question if I don't know what I want her to say?" A whiney pitch crept into my voice and I didn't like it but I didn't back away, either.

Willie tapped me on the top of my thigh with his index finger. "Just get her to talk." He spoke in a matter of fact tone. Like an uncle or an older friend giving advice. "You get her started," he said. "She'll do the rest."

At once, my body jumped, as with a spasm, and my eyes popped open. Startled by the suddenness, I glanced around the room and saw that I was seated in the chair next to Dad's bed in the hospital. A check of the window told me it was nighttime, then I looked over at Dad and he smiled. "Having one of those dreams?"

We had talked about them before, but I never told our mother or either of my brothers. "Yes, sir," I said.

"When did they start this time?"

"A few days ago."

"Bobby used to have dreams like that." Bobby was his brother. My uncle. He had told me that many times before. "He woke up sometimes the same way you did now."

"A family trait?" We had said these things to each other, also. So much, in fact, the exchange became a litany of sorts.

"Yeah," he said.

Usually, the conversation about my dreams ended there, except for the few times I explained the details to him. But that was on those few occasions when I knew what the dreams meant. This time, I didn't know what they meant, and I wasn't ready to discuss the details, but I was curious about Uncle Bobby. We had never discussed the details of his dreams before.

"Did he ever tell you about his dreams?"

"Sometimes," Dad replied. "I remember they were very vivid."

"Did he tell you anything else?"

"I don't remember what they were about, if that's what you mean."

"Well, just in general. What else did he say about them?"

"He said that sometimes the things that happened in the dream happened in life."

This was new information. I had not heard this before. "Things happened before he dreamed them, or after?"

"Well, sometimes I think it was both. Something happened and he dreamed about it. But once in a while he dreamed about it before it happened in real life. He dreamed about it, and then it happened."

That suggestion opened a new aspect I had not considered. A spiritual aspect. A mystical element. That I might dream prospectively. That I had been given these dreams to point me toward things that had not yet occurred. Toward something that had been conceived but not yet made real in the space and time of the awake. Which meant the thing I wanted to know, the thing I was supposed to ask the blonde waitress with the blue streak in her hair, wasn't about the past, but about the future.

Not what I expected. Not the intellectual endeavor I wanted. A professor. At Columbia. Almost no one in our department even believed God existed, much less that he might open the future to someone through a dream. A series of dreams. Dreams fraught with meaning and laden with significance. Knowledge. A sense of knowing that could not come from books or lectures or equations. But from revelation. A Sunday school class came to mind. Something about Daniel. Dreams. Their interpretation. About the future belonging to God alone. None of my colleagues would believe me. I knew that without consciously thinking it and made a decision never to tell them. But I wanted to know. To see the thing through to the end. To find out what the blonde waitress with a streak of blue in her hair had to say to me. I was determined to hear her speak.

Over the following two days, Dad continued to improve and near the middle of the week the doctors moved him to a regular room. By the end of the week they transferred him to a rehabilitation unit for extended care. Everyone was amazed that he recovered at all and confounded that he did it so quickly.

With Dad doing well, I made plans to return to New York and said goodbye, promising to return during the summer for an extended visit. Before leaving Texas, though, I drove down to Giddings. It wasn't too far from Plano, by Texas standards. About a four-hour drive for me. Ryan could have done it in three and a half.

Locating Andy's drugstore was easy enough, I'd been there before and Giddings was not very large, about a third the size of Brenham. Working outward from it, I succeeded in finding a café that seemed to fit the description he had given me. More to my amazement, it was City Café—the very café from my dream. I parked the car on the street out front and went inside.

And sure enough, there was the waitress with the streak of blue in her hair. Only now she was a teenager and as I came past the woman at the cash register, I caught a glimpse of my own reflection in the window behind her. I was a teenager, too. The waitress turned to look at me and our eyes met, and she nodded to an open table in the corner, as if she knew me. I made my way to it and took a seat.

In a few minutes, she came over to where I was and took a seat in the chair across from me. "I think there was something you wanted to ask me," she said. A smile turned up the corners of her mouth as she spoke and her eyes seemed to twinkle like the stars.

"Yes," I replied. "There is."

"Then why don't you ask me?"

"I don't know what you'll say."

"Do you really think I would disappoint you?"

"No."

"Then say it."

"Jennifer, will you marry me?"

"Yes," she replied. "One day."

CHAPTER 6

From deep in the recesses of my mind I heard a voice calling to me. "Taylor. Taylor."

A second voice, a male, barked in an authoritative tone. "Monk! Wake up."

Slowly, my eyes blinked open and I saw that my head was resting on the table in the dining room. A white napkin, rumpled and stained with brown splotches, lay a foot or two away. A sour smell wrinkled my nose and the same brown liquid that discolored the napkin was spread out before my face like an ocean, this one dotted with bits of chicken, peas, and shards of lettuce.

A hand, soft and kind, brushed through my hair, then a voice that was sweet and melodic spoke to me. "Taylor, you're sick. We need to get you cleaned up."

Carefully, slowly, the hand that brushed my hair pressed against my chest. Another hand braced against my forehead and eased my head up from the table. I leaned against the back of the chair.

From my position, I noticed the plates had been cleared but the napkins still lay about. And the bottle of Jack Daniels was sitting where it had been when I took a drink. The glass was there, too, only it was empty and the sight of its empties brought a smile to my face.

Then the one who had held my head and lifted it from the table appeared in my line of sight and I saw that it was Jennifer. Blonde, still, but without the streak. I nodded to her. "You changed your hair."

She seemed puzzled. "What do you mean? It's the way it's always been."

"The blue streak is gone," I noted.

She grinned. "It's been gone since before we married. And you're drunk."

"Yes," I nodded. "I'm drunk." Just then, a spasm hit the muscles in my stomach. "And I'm about to be sick," I chortled. Only this time, I bolted from my place at the table, stumbled my way to the hall, and made it to the bathroom just as the contents of my stomach found the freedom they sought.

Behind me, I heard Langston and Jennifer laughing. But inside, my heart laughed loudest. The house from my dream existed. It was the house where I grew up in Round Top. There really was a City Café, just down the street from Andy's drugstore in Giddings, where we had gone as children many times. And it was the place where I met Jennifer, who now was my wife.

Wackenhut Halfpipe

A Novella

CHAPTER 1

Winston came from the sidewalk by the street and made his way into the park. A city park. A grand park. With a lawn stretching before him. Down a gently sloping hill, up the hill beyond the first, over the top of that one, in a seemingly endless expanse. Lawn. Grass. Thick and green and lush. Dotted with trees here and there. Large trees. Smaller trees. Pruned. Trimmed. An urban likeness. Controlled.

The day was bright and clear. The sky, blue and cloudless. A pleasant day. Not too cool. Certainly not hot. A day when one could walk across the park without breaking a sweat. Walk across anywhere. Never feel the heat. Noticing only the beauty of the grass. The trees. The moment.

Except for the fact that his gray suit was rumpled, his white shirt wrinkled, and his muted tie stained, Winston seemed like any other businessman or professional. Except that his shoes were scuffed and needed new heels, he could have been a lawyer or doctor or judge. A preacher, even. And his fingernails were unevenly trimmed. And he had an ink stain on his right index finger.

Not far behind Winston was Bromley. Similarly dressed. Similar in appearance. Middle age, perhaps. With thinning hair. Lines ran along his forehead, tiny wrinkles at the corners of his eyes. Permanent. From a lifetime of frowning. And smiling. And frowning again.

Then holding it. As if considering. As if worrying. As if…he did a lot of worrying. A lot of ifs. Especially that day. Of all days.

Winston led the way. Bromley tried to keep up. Intermittently. Closing, falling back. Lagging. Catching up, only to lag behind again. On their way across the lawn toward the woods on the opposite side of the park. Some distance away. Far enough that it wasn't close. But close enough not to appear far at all.

Bromley called out. "Where are we going?"

Winston glanced over his shoulder. "Like I told you," he said. "We have to see the guy."

"What guy?"

"The guy." There was a hint of impatience in Winston's voice and he gestured in frustration with both hands. "You know. The guy."

"No." Bromley sounded equally impatient. "I don't know. I haven't the slightest idea who you're talking about."

"The guy," Winston repeated. "The one. The one who has all the answers." He glanced over his shoulder again, this time with a look of disdain. "Come on." He gestured with a wave and a scowl. "Keep up."

"But I have no idea who you're talking about or where we're going."

"We're going to see that guy." Winston, even more frustrated than before, flailed with his hands. "That guy…Wacken-something. We met him the other day." Then at once his eyes opened wide and a look of realization came to him. "Wackenhut," he said, suddenly remembering. "That's it. Wackenhut. Wackenhut Halfpipe."

"Who?" Bromley sounded more confused than ever. "Who are you talking about?"

"Wackenhut. Wackenhut Halfpipe."

"Ah," Bromley scoffed. "You're making that up."

"I am not," Winston insisted. "Wackenhut Halfpipe. That's his name. He told us himself. You were there. You heard him."

"Oh." Bromley smirked. "You mean, Walter Haffenburger."

"Well." Winston sighed. "I don't know. I guess. Maybe they're the same."

Bromley hurried to catch up and came alongside him. "Why didn't you say so?"

"I did."

"No. You said we had to see Bracken Calotype."

"I said no such thing," Winston sniped. "This is no time for word games."

"Then what did you say?"

"I said we had to see Wackenhut Halfpipe."

Bromley shrugged. "Same difference."

"You always say that."

"Walter. Wackenhut. The guy who knows everything. Right?"

"Yes."

"They're both the same."

"Except that they're different."

"Similar.

"In appearance, perhaps."

"Not in substance?"

"I've never met Walter," Winston said. "I don't know if he is or isn't."

"Then how do you know we have to see him?"

"I don't."

"Then what are we doing?"

"We're going to see Wackenhut."

"Oh." Bromley looked puzzled. "And why should we see him?"

"He's the one with the answers."

"But this isn't that kind of situation."

"What kind of situation?"

"Walter is a mathematician," Bromley explained. "He doesn't know anything about what we're facing."

"Maybe so for Walter, but Wackenhut isn't a mathematician."

"Then what is he?"

"A man with answers." Winston spoke in a matter-of-fact tone.

"But does he understand our situation?"

"We'll explain it to him."

Bromley looked surprised. "You can explain it?"

"I can try."

"We can try."

Winston gestured with his hands again. "We have to try."

"Even if we make mistakes?"

"Especially if we make mistakes."

"Risk."

"Yes," Winston said. "Risk is the key. Risk and reward."

"Who taught you that?" Bromley asked.

"Who taught me what?"

"Risk and reward."

"The same person who taught you, I guess. Besides, everyone knows that. It's common knowledge. A basic assumption."

"Ah," Bromley said. "Wherein we come to the assumptions of a capitalist society. Isn't that what got us in trouble?"

"The assumptions of a ballgame."

"Yes, but life's a game."

"Life is life. A game is just a game. We should have known that."

"You mean merely a game. People misuse that word."

Winston frowned. "They misuse what word?"

"Just. They misuse the word just."

"Then, only," Winston said. "Life is life. A game is only a game."

"You're saying these associations are the assumptions of life?"

"The assumptions are the same for both, but the meaning is very different."

"Because of the context."

"That's the way it works," Winston said. "Meaning is contextual. Context is meaning. We forgot that, too."

"Our context didn't work so well for us."

"That's the risk we took when we forgot to assume the context."

"But will Walter know this?"

"Wackenhut," Winston corrected.

"Will he know?"

"Wackenhut knows everything."

"Then he'll know what we're saying before we say it."

"Maybe."

"Then why do we have to see him at all?"

"Because that's how it works."

"That's how what works?"

"Finding out what we need to know. Fixing the mess we're in. Fixing the mess we made. That's how it works." Winston's sense of frustration returned. "We see him. We tell him. He tells us. We do what he says. Everything gets straightened out."

"But is this his area of expertise?"

"He has a PhD.," Winston replied.

"Is that enough?"

"It's a PhD. Doesn't that mean he knows everything?"

"PhDs don't know everything."

Winston was concerned. "They don't know it all?"

"They only act like they know it all," Bromley said.

"Well, for a guy who doesn't know everything, he sure has a lot of people fooled."

"He has himself fooled. I would guess."

"Wackenhut is no fool," Winston argued. "And you should stop guessing. We have guessed too much already."

"We need some certainty."

"We need lots of certainty."

Winston and Bromley walked in silence a moment, then Bromley said, "They're just like everyone else, you know."

"Who's just like everyone else?"

"Walter and...that other guy.

Winston scowled. "I assure you; Wackenhut is like no one else." He spoke with more than a hint of incredulity. "No one is like him."

Bromley looked surprised. "He's different?"

"He's certainly different from that Walter guy you keep mentioning. As different as night and day."

"Hot and cold."

"Plenty and lack."

"Happy and sad."

"We'll explain our situation to Wackenhut," Winston said. "He'll ask a few questions for clarification. Then he'll tell us what to do and we'll be on our way."

"But we'll still have to do it," Bromley replied. "Whatever he tells us to do, we will still have to do it."

"Everyone has to do something."

"Nothing comes from nothing."

"Sometimes."

"Sometimes what?" Bromley sounded perplexed.

"Sometimes nothing comes from nothing."

"You mean, sometimes nothing comes from something, don't you?"

"Yes. That too. But sometimes, it comes from nothing."

"Impossible."

"Improbable," Winston said.

"There's a difference?"

"One can't happen, no matter what," Winston explained. "The other might happen but isn't likely."

"So, when the improbable happens we say it's a surprise," Bromley mused. "But when the impossible happens we say it's a miracle?"

"A gift."

"Benevolence."

"Yes. Benevolence."

"We could use some benevolence right now. Where does it come from?"

"Wackenhut will tell us," Winston assured.

"You mean Walter."

"Same difference, I think. I hope."

"You always say that."

"From being around you so much," Winston quipped.

"Too much?"

Winston glanced over at him and smiled. "Never enough, my friend. Never enough of you."

A bench was just ahead. Bromley slowed as they came to it. "I'm tired. We should stop right here and rest a while."

Winston kept walking. "It's not that far," he said. "We can rest later."

"I need to rest now."

"Later." Winston gestured insistently. "Come on. Keep up."

"But I want to rest now. I might not be tired later." They were at the bench and Bromley plopped down onto it. Winston continued a few paces ahead, noticed Bromley was no longer with him, and came back to the bench. He loomed over Bromley. "We can't rest now. Get up. We need to keep moving. Time is of the essence."

"Rest is of the essence when you're tired," Bromley replied.

"We have to see Wackenhut today." Winston checked his watch. "This afternoon. Now. You heard what they told us. Tomorrow will be too late." Winston checked his watch again.

Bromley looked up at him. "Why do you do that?"

"Why do I do what?"

"Why do you check your watch?"

"To see the time, of course. Why do you ask such a silly question?"

"No one uses a watch anymore. And besides, that watch of yours hasn't worked in years."

Winston glanced at the wristwatch again. "My father gave it to me," he said.

"I thought you wore it to tell the time."

"I wear it to remember him."

"You might forget him?"

"I might forget to remember him. I have at times. I do at times. Then I glance at my wrist and there he is."

"Does Walter remind you of him?"

"Remind me of whom?"

"Your father."

"No. He reminds me of the things my father never was, and never said, and never did."

"Your father lacked?"

"Everyone lacks."

Bromley stared at him a moment, then asked, "What does that mean?" His voice sounded distant, and he had a faraway look in his eyes.

"What does what mean? That everyone lacks? You know perfectly well what that means."

"Not that," Bromley replied. "The other thing you said."

"What other thing?"

"The thing you said before. About being the same."

Winston was puzzled. "What are you talking about? You're making no sense at all. You can't possibly be that tired. What are you talking about?"

"You said that people who knew everything were just like everyone else. What does it mean to be like everyone else?"

"You're not making any sense."

"You said they were just like everyone else. Which means they're just like us. But if they're just like us, how can they help us?"

"They're like us, but they know more."

"Then they aren't like us at all."

"They're like us, only different."

"They know more."

"It depends on who you ask." Winston put his hands on his hips. "Are you coming now?"

"Not yet," Bromley replied. "I'm tired. And since we're all alike, you must be tired, too. Maybe you should take a seat." He patted the bench beside him. "Join me."

Winston sighed. He stood there a moment longer, looking at Bromley, then reluctantly plopped down on the bench. "There," he snapped. "Are you satisfied?"

Bromley ignored the question. "So, it's true?" he continued. "We're all alike. Us and them. Them and us. We're the same?"

"They're like us in that we are all playing a game."

"A role in the play that unfolds in our minds. The play of life. Day to day. Night to night. Each with his part."

"Except no one plays all the roles," Winston said. "At least, no one who is sane."

"We all have different roles to play. Is that the part your father lacked? He never had a role in his own play?"

"He played. Everyone does."

"But his games were different."

"Very much so."

"Bad different?"

"Not bad," Winston said. "Just different. But it was enough to make an impression and the differences are with me still."

"A gift?"

"He didn't mean it as a gift."

"A curse, then?"

"No. He didn't mean it as a curse, either."

"Then what?"

"He gave me what he had."

"That's good."

"Yes, but he also gave me what he didn't have."

Bromley had a questioning look. "I thought you were getting that part from Walter."

"Wackenhut," Winston corrected. "I got the lack from my father. I get the meaning of the lack from Wackenhut."

"The meaning for the play that unfolds in your head?"

"Yes," Winston said. "The meaning of the play. And sometimes, the meaning of my role."

"Life is a play."

"All the world's a stage."

"Everyone is an actor."

"Something like that."

Bromley nodded. "We are a play unto ourselves."

"A role unto ourselves, certainly."

"Self-actualization."

"I suppose."

Bromley frowned. "But if we actualize ourselves, wouldn't that make us God?"

"We are like Him, to a degree."

Bromley looked surprised. "Really?"

"Yes."

"How so?"

"He created. We create."

"Yes." Bromley nodded once more. "But His creation is very different from ours."

"Very different," Winston noted. "And yet very much the same."

Bromley had a questioning look. "How so?"

"His creation reflects his character. Our creations reflect ours."

"But we are limited."

"And He is not."

"Do you really believe that?" Bromley asked. "Or are you just repeating something you read in one of those books you love so much?"

"If I only read it, it wouldn't make it less true."

"Only if it were true."

"It is true."

"Because you say so?"

"Because it is so." Winston stood. "Come on. We need to get going."

With a loud and heavy sigh, and in a melodramatic manner, Bromley stood. "What sort of game would you like to play?"

"What are you saying?"

"If everyone is playing a game, what game would you like to play?"

"No game at all."

"I don't know that one."

"No one does."

"Does Walter know that game?"

"You can ask Wackenhut when we see him."

"I don't know anyone named Wackenhut."

"Come on." Winston gestured. "Try to keep up."

"It's tough walking in these shoes."

"Take them off."

"I can't take them off."

"Why not?"

"The ground is too rough."

"What do you mean it's too rough?" Winston gestured to the

lawn around them. "There's grass everywhere. Even right here where we're walking."

"My feet are tender."

"Which part?"

"Do what?"

"Which part is tender?"

"My feet."

"You said that already. Which part of your feet is tender?"

"Are tender," Bromley corrected. "Feet is plural."

"Is that the way it goes?"

Bromley stopped again, this time with his brow furrowed in a look of concentration. "I don't know if that is correct or not. But it sounds better."

Winston waited. "So, which part is, are, were tender?"

"My feet."

"The tops?"

"No," Bromley said. "The bottoms."

"The soles."

"Yes."

"Why didn't you say that in the first place?"

"I did."

"You said your feet hurt."

"Doesn't that imply my soles?"

"Not really."

"That's the part I step on."

"And how are your ankles?"

Bromley shook his head. "Ankles aren't part of the feet."

"Don't tell my podiatrist."

"What would he know? He's not really a doctor."

"He charges me like a doctor."

"My mother thought they were the best."

"I suppose they serve a purpose," Winston said. "Otherwise, they wouldn't exist."

"Only things of purpose exist?"

"Trivial things come and go. Things of lasting value remain."

"My mother doesn't remain."

"Al things end, too."

"Not according to the preacher."

"You don't go to church."

"But here's an interesting question. If a preacher preaches in a church, and there's no one there to hear him, does he make a sound?"

"We were better off talking about doctors."

"PhDs are doctors."

"Sort of."

"Do PhDs charge like a real doctor?"

"Only in aggravation."

"They get aggravated?"

"They are aggravating."

"You're aggravated. Are you a PhD?"

"Why would I be aggravated?"

"Because Walter doesn't have the answers we need."

"Ahh. But we aren't going to see Walter."

"Why not?"

"It's not his area of expertise."

"Maybe we should let him speak for himself."

"I'm all for that. But we aren't going to see Walter."

"Wackenhut?"

"Yes."

"He's not the guy who knows everything and that's why you're angry."

"I'm not angry."

"I can hear it in your voice."

"Why would I be angry?"

"Because you thought Wachita knew everything and now you know he doesn't."

"Wackenhut," Winston said. "His name is Wackenhut. And why would I be angry if he doesn't know everything?"

"Because you thought he did and now you know he doesn't. But you wanted him to so he could tell us what to do and now that you know he doesn't, and can't, you're aggravated."

"I have no idea what you mean."

"You feel duped."

"I feel duped?"

"Yes."

"Why would I feel duped?"

"Because you thought PhDs know everything and now you know they don't."

"They act like they know everything."

"That's my point," Bromley said triumphantly.

"If they don't know everything, they shouldn't act like they do."

Bromley stopped again. "So, what do you want to do now?"

Winston turned to him, waiting. "Like I told you before, we have to go see Wackenhut Halfpipe. He has the answers."

"And like I told you, he can't help us."

"I thought it was some PhD. That Walter Halfaburger fellow who couldn't help us."

"Haffenburger," Bromley said.

"Maybe Walter Halfaburger can't, but Wackenhut Halfpipe can."

"There is no such person."

"Halfaburger? You just said you knew him."

"My guy's name is Haffenberger and, yes, I know him."

"Then why did you say you didn't?"

"I didn't say that."

"Then what did you say?"

"I said the other guy didn't. Your guy. He's the one who doesn't exist."

Winston frowned. "You're saying Wackenhut Halfpipe doesn't exist?"

"Yes. That's what I'm saying."

"Sure he does." Winston smiled. "I saw him last week."

"No. That was—"

"And you even said so yourself. You were there. You saw him."

Bromley looked perplexed. "I saw him?"

"You've been talking about him the whole way."

"I said Walter exists."

"But Walter doesn't know what we need to know."

"Right."

"So, we go see Wackenhut."

"Why?"

"Because he has the answers we need," Winston said.

"But I thought you were talking about Walter."

"Then it's good for you that I'm talking about the person who knows everything."

"I told you, he doesn't know everything."

"If you don't know him, how would you know he doesn't know it all?"

"No one does."

"I'm not talking about Walter Half-of-something."

"You're talking about Wackenhut Halfpipe."

"Exactly. Now come on." Winston insisted. "We need to get moving."

CHAPTER 2

At the far side of the park, Winston and Bromley came to the edge of the lawn and faced a well-managed wood. The trees were large with branches that formed a web overhead. The trees were in full leaf, so thick they blocked most of the light from the ground beneath, making the woods appear dark and mysterious. A broad, well-worn path, clearly marked and paved with shredded bark, led into it. Winston started forward as if to continue down the path. Behind him, however, Bromley came to an abrupt halt and stood motionless. "We're going in there?" he said.

Winston stopped, too, and turned to face him. "We must," he insisted. "This is the way to Wackenhut."

Bromley shook his head. "I don't like it."

"You don't like it?"

"No."

"It's a trail," Winston said. "Merely a trail."

"A path."

"A trail. A path. What's there to like or not about it?"

"It leads into the woods."

"And?"

"It's dark in there."

"Not that dark. Not once you're in there. Your eyes will get used to it."

"But I don't want to go in there."

"You're afraid of the dark?"

"I'm afraid of that dark," Bromley said, pointing.

Winston gave an encouraging gesture. "Come on," he said. "I'll be right here with you all the way."

"On the trail?"

"It's a wide trail and a small wood."

Bromley looked scared. "I don't like it."

"You don't like the trail? Or you don't like the woods?"

"Neither."

"Neither?"

"I don't like neither."

"You mean either."

"That's what I said."

"You said you don't like neither."

Bromley turned to look him in the eye. "You know perfectly well what I mean."

"You dislike them both."

"Yes."

"Well, I can't do anything about them."

"I can," Bromley said, defiantly.

"You can change them?"

"I can do something about them."

"What can you do about them?"

"I can avoid them."

"And that's how you intend to change them?"

"That's what I can do about them," Bromley said. "I can avoid going in them or down them or on them."

"In them or down them or on them?"

"In the woods," Bromley explained, "or down the trail, or on the path."

"That's not changing them. That's changing you."

"Isn't that enough?"

"It doesn't get us to Wackenhut," Winston said.

"And that matters?"

"That's the point."

"That's your point."

"Come on," Winston said. "Let's go. It's getting late. We don't have far now, but we must get moving."

Bromley wrapped his arms across his chest. "I'm not going in there."

"Then why did we come all this way?"

"You led me."

"You followed."

"Same difference."

Winston gestured again. "Wackenhut lives on the other side," he said insistently. "We have to keep going."

"The far side."

"Yes. The far side of the wood."

"But we are on this side."

"He has the answers."

"So you say."

"Yes, I do," Winston answered. "And the only way to get to him is by going through these woods."

"And then what? We go through the woods and then what?"

"Why do you think there's more?"

"There's always more. Always a then what. Always something else. So tell me now. After this, what else is there?"

Winston sighed. "We take the bus."

Bromley's eyes opened wide. "We take the bus?"

"Yes. The bus. We go through the woods and take the bus to Wackenhut."

Bromley had an accusing expression. "You never said anything about a bus."

"You never said anything about your feet hurting until just a few minutes ago. And you didn't say anything about the woods until now."

"My feet didn't hurt until a few minutes ago. And we weren't at the woods until now."

"So."

Bromley jabbed the tip of his finger against Winston's chest. "You knew about the bus before we left. And you knew about the woods then, too."

"You knew it was a long way from where we started."

"I had no idea where we were going."

"I told you we had to see Wackenhut. That he has the answers we need."

"And?"

"If you didn't want to know the answer to our problem, why did you come?"

"You said you knew what to do."

"I still do."

"Which is?"

"Talk to Wackenhut."

"But to do that," Bromley said, "we'd have to go through the woods."

"Yes."

"And take the bus."

"Yes."

"But the problem we have isn't even in Wackenhut's area of expertise. How can he help us?"

"He knows things."

"He has knowledge of our situation?"

"He has knowledge that will help."

"He has truth."

"I suppose." Winston shrugged. "If you want to call it that."

"What else would we call it?"

"Help."

"Knowledge?

Winston nodded. "That, too," he said.

"Don't we need truth? They say the truth is best."

"Knowledge is applied truth."

"You're just making that up."

"All expression is made up. Knowledge is truth applied to a particular situation."

"I thought that was wisdom."

"No." Winston shook his head. "Wisdom is experience applied to a situation. Knowing which truth applies. Truth applied, and the result observed, yields knowledge. Experience remembered yields wisdom."

"You sound smart when you talk like that. Are you sure you don't have a PhD?"

"I'm too old."

"PhDs expire?"

"The person expires, perhaps," Winston said. "Not the degree."

"The person definitely."

"Excuse me?"

"All things end. You said so yourself."

"Ahh. Yes." Winston gestured. "Come along, then. Let's get going."

Bromley shook his head. "I'm not going through the woods."

"Yes. You are."

"Why would I do that?"

"Truth has a price. Going through the woods is the price. You want the truth; you pay the price. Let's go."

"To get applied truth."

"That, too. All of it lives beyond the woods."

"And to reach it, we have to walk through the woods. Take the bus. Talk to Wackenhut. Get some applied truth."

"Some wisdom," Winston said. "We get some wisdom."

"Through the woods."

"Yes."

"That's a high price to pay."

"It's only an illusion."

"An illusion of truth?"

"An illusion of a high price."

"You just said it comes at a price."

"Yes. But you can't buy it."

"A price you must pay, but you can't buy it."

"Precisely."

"That doesn't make sense."

"Which is why few people obtain it."

"They might have better success if it were more obvious."

"Obscurity sharpens the effect."

"More like hide and seek," Bromley opined. "Were you suggesting this is the game people play? Tell you it costs, but no one can buy? Demand a price, but no one can pay?"

"Not every cost is a price."

"How does that...ah," Bromley smiled. "Not every cost is a price. That's good."

"Got it now?"

"Got it," Bromley said, confidently. But almost at once, a questioning look clouded his eyes and a frown wrinkled his forehead. "Then what's the price?"

"Trust."

"Faith."

"Faith in the truth," Winston said. "Faith in wisdom."

"That seems like a very, very high price."

"It's only in how it seems."

"I'm not sure I want to pay it at any price."

"The true price is paid in loss of comfort."

"I can see that," Bromley said, gesturing to the woods.

Winston took him by the elbow. "I'm sure you can. Now let's—"

Bromley resisted. "But is it really worth it?"

"That's an age-old question."

"But it is a question."

"It is *the* question."

"*The* question?"

"Yes."

"Really?"

"Sometimes you hit upon the important things."

"Not all the time?"

"No," Winston said, with a shake of his head. "Not all the time."

"Sometimes, not all the time. Why is that?"

"It's that way for everyone. I didn't make the rules."

"You don't live by them, either."

"Not always."

"Like the time you—"

Winston cut him off. "Enough of that," he said.

"You don't like hearing those things about yourself."

"No one does."

"Then why do you say them about others?"

"It's a weakness."

"Doesn't change anything."

"Never said it did."

"And it doesn't make it right."

"Never said that either."

"If you had followed the rules, we wouldn't have gotten into—"

Winston interrupted again. "You've made your point. Rules exist and I don't always live by them. Now come on. We need to—"

"Which is how we came to be in this predicament, you know."

"Yes. I know."

"And now you want me to go down that trail, into the woods, into the darkness, for you."

"For both of us. To find the answers."

"If I don't want to go, but I go only because you insist, isn't that the same as you making me? The same as you making the rules and forcing me to abide by them?"

"Like I said, I don't make the rules."

"But you make me abide by them, even if you say you don't."

"It's not for me."

"What's not for you?"

"Going through the woods."

"It's for the truth."

"It's for you. It's for us."

"So you say."

"Yes." Winston sighed. "So I say."

"Very well." Bromley started forward down the trail into the woods. Winston followed. "So, now you're willing to go," Winston said. "After all of that, you're willing to go?"

"Yes," Bromley replied. "Of course."

"Of course?"

"You convinced me. Anything for the truth. Anything for me. Even if it's also for us." Bromley gestured with a wave. "Come on.

Keep up. We don't have all day, you know."

CHAPTER 3

Bromley and Winston continued down the path into the woods. Deeper and deeper into the shadows that lay beneath the thick canopy of foliage. The shade was heavy and cool. Dampening the sound of their voices. The sounds of the city. Muffled and hushed.

Bromley, who had the lead, glanced around warily. "It's getting dark," he said. "We should go home to eat."

"It's just the shade," Winston replied. "From the trees." He pointed. "See."

Bromley glanced up, then quickly back to the floor of the woods around them. "It's still dark. We eat when it gets dark."

"It's the middle of the afternoon."

"It's darker than it was," Bromley noted.

"It's not as light as before," Winston said.

"Same difference."

"Why do you say that?"

"Say what?"

"Same difference."

"What's the same difference?"

"Why do you use that phrase?" Winston asked.

"You know what I mean."

"I know what you say. I have no way of knowing the idea you intended to convey."

"Yet still we talk."

"And you have no way of knowing what I think it means."

"I could ask you."

"And I could tell you."

"And then I would know."

"Then you would know the words that I use."

"Same difference."

"Not really."

"We're still talking."

"What do you mean?"

Bromley smiled. "Can you really know what I mean?"

"Try me."

"If you didn't know what I mean, you and I wouldn't be having this conversation."

"Perhaps we're talking about two different things, but don't know it."

"Like, if I say apple and you say apple, but the thing I see when I say apple is really a strawberry to you? And the thing you see when you say apple is really a peach to me? Only, you can't see it?"

"Yes. A to me is B to you, but when you say A we both grab the same object from the bowl."

"The way I said it sounds smarter."

"Only because you said it first."

Not far down the trail, a man stepped out from behind a tree. He was dirty and grimy, and his clothes were a ragged mess. The man moved into the path, blocking the way. He was only a few feet away from Bromley. "You got any change?" It was a demand, not a question.

Bromley shrank back, a sour look on his face. "You, sir, have been drinking."

"Everyone drinks," the man said. "Give me your—"

Winston interrupted. "He means, you reek of intoxicating spirits."

The man frowned. "I reek?"

"You smell intensely of alcohol," Bromley said.

"It ain't alcohol," the man snarled. "That stuff will kill you." He grinned. "But strawberry wine's something else altogether."

Winston spoke up. "That's what you do all day? You loll about the woods drinking wine and accosting strangers to demand money?"

The man struck an indignant pose. "I ain't never 'costed nobody in my life."

"But you do solicit money on the threat of menace."

The man looked confused. "What's a menace?"

Winston took Bromley by the elbow. "Never mind all this. Let's be on our way."

The man moved to cut them off. "But I already asked." He had a determined look.

"Asked what?"

"You got any change?"

"Change would be great," Bromley said. "If we could get it. And a really good idea if we could implement it. But I think we're stuck with the present for now."

The man glared at him. "Not that kind of change," he said.

"What other kind is there?"

"The change in your pocket."

"He means money," Winston noted.

Bromley nodded. "Coinage."

"Yes."

Bromley turned to the man. "Look at us." It was a rhetorical gesture. "Do we look like the sort to carry money?"

"You're a better sort than me," the man said.

Winston shook his head. "No one is better than anyone."

The man looked irritated. "You know what I mean."

Bromley smiled. "He means we're all alike in a sense."

"He's right." Winston nodded again. "I know what he means."

The man was growing frustrated. "If you know what I mean, then you know what I want."

"You want change," Bromley said. "The seasons change without a struggle. The trees change without a fight. But you mean to make change happen." He smiled. "Very noble indeed."

"Not that change," the man growled. "Your change."

Winston took offense. "So, now you're demanding it?"

"You're in better shape than I am," the man answered. "So, give it up."

Bromley glanced in Winston's direction. "Give up our better shape?"

"Give up our money," Winston said.

"But we haven't any money. That's why we're—"

"He doesn't appear to believe us."

The man shook his fist. "Stop playing games."

Bromley smiled at Winston. "Games again?"

"Not like that."

"Then what?"

"He thinks we sound clever."

"So, people who play games are clever?"

"They want to be. And sometimes they sound like it."

"But they aren't?"

"No."

"Do you think that's what makes him think we're better than he—the cleverness of our words?"

"That's not what I mean," the man shouted. "And I don't care how clever you are. I only want—"

"Ah," Winston interrupted. Then still to Bromley, said, "He only wants a drink of strawberry wine."

"Not a drink," the man said. "I don't want no drink. A drink won't do me no good. A drink only—"

"Makes you want another," Bromley suggested.

"Yeah." The man seemed to relax. "You're familiar with the experience, are you?"

"Not with strawberry wine," Winston said.

The man looked at them. "Do you two always answer for each other?"

"Only when we are together," Bromley said.

"In the same place."

"At the same time."

"Shut up!" the man shouted. "Give me your money, now!"

"You've moved from asking for change to demanding money," Bromley noted. "Isn't that a sellout?"

The man's face was blank. "A what?"

"First you articulate some grand vision of the future," Bromley recounted. "Demanding change and all that. Now you've reduced yourself to demanding payment. In money. Under threat of violence. Is that all your life has become?"

"Have I threatened you?"

"Certainly, you implied it," Bromley said.

The man had a pained expression. "Implied?"

"By the tone of your voice."

"The anger," Winston added.

"The insistence."

"The hostility."

"And all for money," Bromley said.

"Money is merely a device for quantifying value," Winston opined.

"Value in the sense of worth."

"But what is worth?" Winston asked. "What do you value? How much does it cost?"

"I would say," Bromley suggested, "that we value movies over books."

"Sports over learning."

"Persuasion over fact."

"Celebrity over substance."

"Action over contemplation."

"Right now," the man interjected, "the only thing I value is the money in your pockets."

"That's not true," Winston responded.

The man struck a defiant pose. "You calling me a liar?"

"No. I'm saying the thing you value isn't the money."

"Well if you're so clever," the man sniped. "Tell me what it is I do value?"

"Strawberry wine," Bromley answered.

"Don't get cute with me."

"I'm not cute."

"He's asking for money," Winston noted.

"Then why didn't he just say so?"

"I did," the man snapped.

"No." Bromley shook his head. "You asked if I had any change."

"Give me a dollar," the man demanded.

"No, thanks."

The man scowled. "What? You just said why didn't I ask. And now I'm—"

"He means, not today," Winston explained.

The man turned to him. "Then you give me a dollar."

Winston smiled. "No, thanks."

The man pressed. "I said, give me your money."

"No." Winston corrected, refusing to budge. "You said, give me a dollar."

The man's face turned red. "I don't—"

From somewhere behind them, a park policeman appeared. "Gentlemen. Are we having a problem?" The man who accosted them took a few steps back. Bromley gestured to him. "This fellow seems to be down on his luck."

The policeman turned to the man. "Asking for money again, Angus?"

Winston's eyes opened wider. "Angus? Is that really your name?"

"It is this week," the policeman said.

Bromley seemed intrigued. "A new name each week?"

The policeman smirked. "A new name each day, sometimes."

"I should like a new name. But every week would do." Bromley glanced at Winston. "That might solve our troubles."

"No need for Wackenhut."

"No need for Walter."

The policeman turned to Angus. "Have you been hitting up these good people for money?"

Angus had a sheepish expression. "Asking," he said. He put his hands in his pockets, glanced down at the ground, and dug his toe in the dirt. "Just asking."

"Insisting," Bromley offered.

"Demanding," Winston added.

"Angus," the policeman said sternly. "I've told you before not to be harassing park visitors."

"I'm hungry," Angus responded. "And they're on their way out."

"Thirsty," Winston corrected.

"Parched," Bromley noted.

"The shelter will feed you," the policeman said.

Angus shook his head. "I don't like the shelter."

"Why not?"

Angus wrinkled his nose. "It stinks in there."

The policeman raised an eyebrow. "How about the jail?"

Angus looked indignant. "What about it?"

"Do you like the smell down there?"

Winston was curious. "You two know each other?"

"We're well acquainted," the policeman said.

"Go back a long way, do you?" Bromley said.

"You might say that." The policeman offered. "Why do you ask?"

"I didn't." Bromley gestured to Winston. "He did."

Winston smiled. "Just curious."

The policeman turned his attention to Winston. "And what are you two doing in here?"

"Just passing through," Winston answered.

The policeman seemed skeptical. "Lot of people come in here for a lot of things. Two men wandering through the woods, together, looks…suspicious."

"Suspicious of what?" Bromley asked.

Winston had a knowing look. "He thinks we might be a couple."

"We are a couple."

The policeman had a satisfied smile. "I thought so."

"Not that kind of couple," Winston retorted.

"Then what kind are you?"

"Two," Bromley replied.

"Two?"

"A couple," Winston explained. "That's two. One is a single. Two a couple. Three or more, several. We are two. Together. A couple. As in, just a couple of men passing through here on their way to somewhere else."

Angus looked askance. "You two are on your way to see Wackenhut."

Bromley appeared surprised. "You know Wackenhut?"

"I know you look like the type." Angus had a snide tone.

Winston was defensive. "And what type is that?"

"The type that thinks they know everything."

"Not us. Wackenhut."

Angus shrugged. "Same difference."

Winston cut his eyes at Bromley. "Have you been here before?"

"Never seen him in my life."

"He talks like you."

"We're all the same. Remember?"

The policeman spoke up. "I don't know about Wackenhut. Never heard of such a thing. Or such a person. But I know we get a lot of men coming in here for untoward purposes."

"And teenagers, too," Angus said.

"Right you are," the policeman noted. "Just yesterday I had to chase some out of here. Come in here with their foul-smelling drugs. Leave litter all about."

"And condoms," Angus offered.

"I wasn't going to mention that."

Bromley gave them a look. "You'll just leave it to our imagination?"

"At least they're being safe about it," Winston commented.

"Better they be safe somewhere else." The policeman hooked his thumbs in his gun belt. "Or be safe by avoiding the activity all together."

"They come in here at night, too." Angus seemed emboldened by the policeman's comments. "Making all kinds of noise. Can't hardly sleep with all the racket they make."

"I wouldn't know about that," the policeman replied. "I go off duty around sunset."

Bromley frowned. "Even in summer?"

The policeman seemed puzzled. "Do what?"

"It gets dark later in the summer," Winston explained.

"And earlier in the winter," Bromley elaborated.

The policeman still seemed not to understand. Winston asked the straightforward question. "Does the length of your workday vary with the daylight hours?"

The policeman had a look of realization. "Never mind about that." He turned to Angus. "Get a move on." Then to Winston and Bromley. "And you two—whoever you are, whatever you are, whatever you're doing, wherever you're going—hustle on through if you're going through. Stop this loitering about."

Bromley nodded to Winston. "Stop. Loitering."

"Yes." Winston understood the pun. "Stop stopping."

"I think he means, 'Stop being stopped.'"

The policeman placed a hand on his nightstick. "Are you two trying to be difficult?"

Bromley frowned. "We weren't—"

Winston took Bromley by the arm. "Thank you, officer." He had a courteous tone. "We'll be on our way right now."

Winston guided Bromley up the trail, hustling him away while Angus went in the opposite direction. The policeman lingered, watching both directions suspiciously. But after a moment, he departed as well.

Bromley seemed afraid to look back. "How did that vagrant know we were going to see Wackenhut?"

"He's rather well-known among some."

"The vagrant?"

"Wackenhut."

"Among some?"

"Yes."

"But not all."

"No."

Bromley seemed to think a moment, considering, then asked, "Some who?"

"Those who concern themselves with such things," Winston answered.

"Those who concern themselves with knowing everything."

"Yes. I suppose. And those who concern themselves with those who know everything."

"Do you think that vagrant knows everything?"

"I very much doubt that."

"I very much doubt he knows anything at all."

"He knows more than you might think."

"How much do you think I think?"

"About what?" Winston asked.

"About anything."

"I think you think a lot," Winston said. "But not much about the vagrant."

"What about him?"

"I think you think he knew more than you thought he would know and that aggravates you."

"Nah," Bromley scoffed. "Why should I care how much he knows or doesn't?"

"You shouldn't at all, and that's the part that makes you angry."

"Which part?"

"The part about him knowing more than you thought he'd know and being angry with yourself that it matters at all to you."

"But he doesn't know everything."

"No," Winston said. "Not everything."

"If he knew everything, he would be Wackenhut."

"They would have a lot in common."

"And if he were Wackenhut," Bromley continued, "we would have no need to go through this wood or take the bus."

"We could just ask him right here."

"Right now."

"I suppose."

Bromley abruptly halted. "Shall we?"

Winston was startled by his sudden move. "Shall we what?"

"Ask him."

"Ask who?"

"The vagrant."

Winston was incredulous. "Ask him what?"

"The questions we were going to ask Wackenhut."

"Don't be ridiculous. And besides, he's not here anymore."

"Wackenhut's not here anymore?"

"No," Winston said. "The vagrant. Angus."

"Angus the vagrant."

"He's not here anymore. And anyway, he's not Wackenhut."

"But he could be, if he knew everything."

"But he doesn't, so he isn't." Winston gestured. "Let's keep moving. We need to get there soon."

"And even if Angus knew everything, he wouldn't be Wackenhut. He'd still be a vagrant."

"But a vagrant who knew everything."

"And that might turn him into something other than a vagrant."

"If knowing something could do that," Winston conceded.

"If knowing everything could do that."

Winston smiled. "Only Wackenhut can be Wackenhut."

Bromley seemed to note the look on his face. "You find comfort in that?"

"As much for him as I do for myself."

"How so?"

"Only I can be me."

"Only you can be you?" Bromley glanced at him quizzically. "I can't be you?"

"No one can," Winston said. "Only me."

"And only I can be me?"

Winston grinned. "Now you're catching on."

"I don't catch on easily."

"I noticed."

"You noticed?"

"It's unavoidable."

"I didn't like that man."

"The policeman?"

"No," Bromley said. "Angus. The vagrant."

"He seemed like an agreeable fellow."

"Except for the tone of his voice."

"Yes." Winston nodded. "Rather belligerent at one point. Nothing more belligerent than a belligerent vagrant."

"And demanding," Bromley added. "The homeless are sometimes very demanding and it always upsets me."

"Not all are, though."

"This one was."

"I'm not sure he was homeless."

"You think he has a home?"

"Yes."

"Where do you think he lives?"

"Here," Winston said, gesturing to their surroundings.

"Here?"

"Yes."

"In the woods?"

"Right here in the woods."

"I thought you said he wasn't homeless."

"I did."

Bromley looked stricken. "You think he built a house in here?"

"I think this is his house."

Bromley looked confused. "What is his house? There are no houses here."

"The woods," Winston said. "The woods are his home."

"You think the wood is his house?"

"Yes."

Bromley gestured. "And this is his home?"

"A rather majestic home at that."

"The roof leaks."

"Only when it rains."

"It rains often," Bromley said. "Especially this time of year."

"Not too often."

"And when it does? What then?"

"There's always the tunnel."

Bromley's eyes opened wide. "The tunnel?"

"The one that goes under the boulevard," Winston said.

"Which boulevard?"

"Parkside."

"We're headed toward Parkside."

"I know."

Bromley looked worried. "I hate tunnels."

"More than the woods?"

"More than the dark."

"They are rather confining."

"And you're proposing we use the tunnel?"

"It's not raining," Winston noted.

"It's getting dark."

Winston gestured. "We're almost there."

CHAPTER 4

At last, the path through the woods opened to a grassy area along Parkside Boulevard. A sidewalk followed the boulevard and next to the sidewalk was a bench. Signs posted nearby indicated the spot was a bus stop. Winston led Bromley toward the bench. "We can take a rest over there," he said, pointing.

"Over where?" Bromley asked.

"On that bench. We can wait there until the bus arrives."

Bromley glanced around nervously. "I hope it doesn't rain."

"Not a cloud in the sky," Winston observed.

"I hate tunnels."

"Wouldn't do us any good now."

Bromley seemed to understand. "Too far?"

"We'd be soaked before we got there."

"Unless we went now."

"You don't like tunnels."

"I don't like getting wet even more."

"The bus will be here soon."

"Will it be crowded?"

"We'll find out."

"Buses are like tunnels."

Winston nodded. "Tunnels on wheels."

"With lights."

"They're smaller."

"But less confining," Bromley noted.

"It's the windows."

"You can see out."

Winston nodded again. "You're inside and outside, at the same time."

"Convergent."

"Co-extensive."

"Space and non-space."

"Bounded and unbounded."

"It's a contradiction."

"It's the windows."

"The view."

"The illusion of space beyond the space," Winston said.

They reached the bench and took a seat. "How long until the bus arrives?" Bromley asked.

"It comes every half hour."

"It's scheduled to arrive every thirty minutes."

"Yes."

"Thirty minutes from when?"

"On the half hour would be more accurate."

"Sometimes," Bromley noted, "I see two buses parked together at the same stop."

"Sometimes their schedules get confused."

"Don't the drivers have watches?"

"I suppose."

"Do their watches work better than yours?"

"Only at telling the time."

"And can't the drivers tell time?"

"I should rather think so," Winston said. "It would seem a requirement of the job."

"And don't they know the place where they're supposed to be, at any particular time during the day?"

"I'm sure they do."

"Well, isn't that the reason they have schedules? To get them to a particular spot at a particular time?"

"That's what schedules are for," Winston agreed.

"And yet, two buses still arrive at the same place, at the same time."

"Occasionally."

"Not infrequently."

"Things don't always happen according to schedule."

"That's just an excuse."

"Do they need more?"

"More than what?"

"More than an excuse. They aren't on trial."

"A reason would be better."

"Every reason is an excuse," Winston said. "Every excuse is a reason."

"If two buses are in the same place," Bromley said, "at the same time, then one of them is in the wrong place."

"You mean one of them is there at the wrong time."

"They're not supposed to be in the same place there together."

"But two buses running the same route are supposed to be at each place on the route."

"But not at any of them together."

"So," Winston said. "Correct place."

"Incorrect time."

"Exactly," Winston noted.

"They're supposed to be there at different times."

"Unless."

Bromley frowned. "Unless what?"

"Unless it's a heavy time of day."

"Some times of the day are heavier than others?"

"And some are lighter."

Bromley had a questioning look. He held out his hands, palms up, as if testing the weight in one hand versus that in the other. Winston looked at him. "What are you doing?"

"I'm trying to feel which one is heavier."

"Which one what?"

"This hand is for now," Bromley said, gesturing with the right hand. "And this one is now." He stopped moving the right hand and began checking the left. "I think I feel a difference. What causes them to weigh more?"

"Not that kind of heavier," Winston said. He had an exasperated tone.

"There are different kinds of heavy?"

"Traffic. Some times have more traffic than others."

"Oh." Bromley seemed to understand. "Some hours of the day are heavier with traffic than others."

"Yes."

"And what times are heavier?"

"Rush hour."

"Ah." Bromley had a look of realization. "In the morning."

"Yes." Winston nodded. "And in the afternoon."

"And then it would be okay to be in the right place at the wrong time."

"Might be scheduled that way."

Bromley raised an eyebrow. "Might be?"

"Which would put them in the right place at the right time."

Bromley frowned. "But together? At the same time. In the same place. On purpose?"

"If they have more people."

"More people?"

"More riders."

"Ah." Bromley nodded. "More riders than could fit in a single bus?"

"Sometimes they do."

"It could happen," Bromley said.

"And sometimes, one bus makes the trip more quickly than the other."

"You mean, one driver drives faster than the other?"

"No…well…maybe."

"But not necessarily?"

"No. Not necessarily."

"If the drivers drive the buses at the correct speed, and they both drive the same route, and it's not rush hour, how does one bus make the trip quicker than the other?"

"It stops less times."

Bromley seemed concerned. "They don't make every stop? What about all those passengers who've been waiting. Some of them have to get to work. To the doctor's office. To school. Some just want to get home. To rest. To take a bath. To eat. Why would the bus not make every stop? And how do they decide to stop here and pass there?"

"If there aren't any passengers waiting."

"They zip right by?"

"Yes."

"Without a pause?"

"Without slowing one bit."

Bromley leaned forward and strained to see down the street, as if checking. "Do they know we are waiting? Now. Will they stop for us now?"

"They will stop."

"How can you be so sure?"

"They can see us."

Bromley craned his neck to look again. "They have cameras on us?"

"The driver looks for us."

"Will they notice us? They won't miss us?"

"We're on the bench," Winston said. "At the stop. At the correct time. It's the driver's job to see us."

"But what if he isn't paying attention?"

"We'll make sure he is."

"How will we do that?"

"Stand up," Winston said.

Bromley, still seated, looked up at him with a confused expression. "Stand up?"

"Yes," Winston said. "We'll stand up."

"That's all it takes? Stand up and they will see us?"

"Most of the time."

Bromley glanced down the street, then abruptly stood. Winston was perplexed. "Why are you standing?"

Bromley pointed. "The bus is here."

Winston looked in that direction, then shook his head. "That's not our bus."

"How do you know?"

"That's the seventy-seven."

"Yes," Bromley said. "So it is. I can see the number on the front."

"That's not our bus."

"We own a bus?"

"That's not the bus that will take us to where we want to go."

"The driver doesn't know Wackenhut?"

"I don't know who the driver knows, but even if the driver knew Wackenhut, that bus wouldn't take us to him."

"How do you know?"

"I know the route for the seventy-seven."

"That's not our route?"

"We need the ninety-nine."

"Really?"

"Yes."

"You're sure?"

"I've taken it before."

"I've never been to Wackenhut."

"I have." Winston patted the space beside him on the bench. "Have a seat. The bus will be along shortly."

Bromley took a seat. "All this sitting and standing. Makes me think of church."

"Without the collection plate."

Bromley was suddenly alert. "They take a collection here?"

"No."

"But we have to pay to ride the bus."

"Yes."

"Drop the coins in the machine by the door."

"Or slide a bill in the slot on the reader."

"And there's your collection plate," Bromley said, with a matter-of-fact gesture.

"It's a meter."

"And the plate in church isn't?"

"It's not a toll."

Bromley seemed skeptical. "What church do you attend?"

"Same one as always."

"Then you know. Put the offering in the plate and God will bless you great."

Winston chuckled. "They don't say that."

"In so many words. Offering in the plate, God will let you in the gate."

"They don't say that, either."

"I hear it all the time."

Do you believe it?"

"Do I believe they say that?"

"That God blesses you greatly because you give greatly?"

Bromley looked worried. "I hope that's not how it happens."

"Why?"

"Because I don't have the ability to give greatly."

"You do proportionally."

"Proportionally to me," Bromley said. "Not to them. And if that's how it works, then those who have more would just get more and soon there'd be nothing left for anyone else."

"That's not how it works."

"How do you know that?"

"Wackenhut told me."

"What did he tell you?"

"That receiving isn't determined by giving."

"No?"

"Receiving is unlimited. We create wealth and value."

Bromley had a pleased smile. "Oh, I'm liking this Wackenhut more and more."

"Others like him less and less."

"Because he doesn't tell them what they want to hear?"

"And, because he tells them what they're saying. Even if it doesn't match with what they said."

"Ahh," Bromley replied. "I get that."

"Knew you would."

"I'm not always slow."

"You're never slow."

"No one ever thinks of what they're saying. Only of what they said."

"Words never get in the way of what they mean."

"The message always comes through."

"They are the message."

"That has become a cliché."

"It's still true."

"In spite of themselves."

"Yes," Winston said. "In spite of themselves."

"Then Wackenhut is the message?"

"Yes. I suppose he is."

"Seeing him is the same as knowing him?"

"Experiencing him is the same as hearing him."

"I'm tired of waiting."

"We could walk, I suppose."

"I'm tired of walking, too."

"Then what would you have us do?"

"Why must we go see Wackenhut at all? Why must we see anyone?"

"What do you mean?"

"Can't we just sit here and think of Wackenhut and be imbued with the same knowledge he has? Just sit here and soak it up." Bromley closed his eyes and smiled. Let the knowledge come to us instead of us to it?"

"That's not the way it works with us mere mortals."

Bromley's eyes popped open. "Wackenhut is immortal?"

"Wackenhut is Wackenhut."

"Why should he be the only one who knows everything? Why can't we know it, too?"

"We're learning."

"But why must we learn?"

"It is our lot in life to learn and be learners," Winston said. "That is all we can do."

"But we learn and learn and learn and then we die and even though we've spent all our lives learning we never move the learning forward."

"How so?"

"We learn and learn," Bromley said, "but the poor fellow who comes after us has to start all over for himself. All over again from the beginning, no less. Learning the same things we learned."

"Not quite."

"Very quite."

"My father plowed the fields with a mule when he was a boy."

"And?" Bromley asked.

"I've never plowed a field at all, with a mule or without. Have you ever plowed a field with a mule?"

"Of course not. But I don't know what my father knew, either."

"But you get the benefit of it."

"I'm benefiting from the things he learned, even though I don't know what those things were?"

Winston had a satisfied expression. "Now you're going deep."

"But how does that work?"

"Knowledge is cumulative, and it has an equitable effect."

"A lasting value."

"A cumulative lasting value."

"So, I didn't start at the same place he started?"

"You weren't born in a rural shack."

"You've seen where I live."

"And you're a long way from where he lived."

"But it's not a mansion. It's not even elegant."

"Can you see the sky through the cracks in the ceiling?"

"Mrs. Langley lives above me. I would see her first."

"My point."

"But I've still spent a lifetime learning."

"That's the way it is."

"But why?"

"How else could it be?"

"We learned two plus two equals four," Bromley said. "Can't the next guy at least start with that in hand? Come down the birth canal knowing it and begin at…three plus three?"

"It could have been that way, I suppose."

"But it's not," Bromley said, with a hint of resignation.

"No," Winston acknowledged. "It's not."

"Can't we change it?"

"How?"

"I don't know. We've changed everything else." Bromley pointed. "That boulevard used to be a two-lane road. They once grazed cows where those buildings stand. The telephone used to only ring at home, now it's in my pocket. Nothing is the same as it was."

"We could ask Wackenhut," Winston suggested.

Bromley nodded. "Maybe he knows."

"If anyone knows, he does."

"Then we'll ask him."

Winston stood. "The bus is here."

"It hasn't been thirty minutes."

"We didn't get here at the beginning."

"He's not early?"

"No." Winston pointed. "She's right on time."

"They have women drivers?"

"Of course."

"You say that like they're supposed to do the job."

"They're not supposed to not do the job."

"Too many nots."

"I'm sure they would agree with you."

"You think women wanted to be drivers all along, but were prevented from it?"

"I think they have wanted to do a great many things they've been prevented from doing. Perhaps even still."

"But you don't know what those things are."

"I am not a woman. I have no way of knowing what it's like to be one."

"But did they always want to do those things? Or just since someone told them they should?"

"Until someone told them they could."

"Same difference."

"I'll let you ask the driver if that's true."

"Maybe they never wanted to do more than they always had done."

"Maybe they just got tired," Winston said.

"Tired of what?"

"Tired of being told no."

A city bus came to a stop at the curb opposite the bench and the doors opened. Winston started toward it. Bromley hurried to keep up. "Maybe we should ask her," he said.

"The driver?"

"Yes."

Winston shook his head. "Maybe we should wait and ask Wackenhut."

"Do you think he will know?"

"Wackenhut knows everything."